D0839002

In a fishbone church

Catherine Chidgey

Victoria
University Press

VICTORIA UNIVERSITY PRESS
Victoria University of Wellington
PO Box 600 Wellington

© Catherine Chidgey 1998

ISBN 0 86473 335 6

First published 1998
Reprinted 1998 (twice), 1999

Earlier drafts of chapters of this novel
were published in *Sport* and *Takahe*

Published with the assistance of a grant from

ARTS COUNCIL OF NEW ZEALAND *TOI AOTEAROA*

Printed by Publishing Press Ltd, Auckland

Contents

Acknowledgements

I am indebted to Pat, Helen and Les Chidgey, who all provided me with invaluable inform- ation and support while I was writing this book. Bill Manhire and Damien Wilkins offered the guidance and encouragement necessary both to finish and start it. I am grateful to Fergus Barrowman and Rachel Lawson at Victoria University Press, to Kate Camp, to Joe Chidgey for his advice on fossils, and to Sydney Chidgey, whose diaries were such a wonderful resource. Special thanks to Virginia Fenton for her patient suggestions, and for letting me steal her magpies.

For Dad.

The
distribution
of stones

Gene copes well; everyone says so.

'He's being very brave,' says Carnelian. 'He hasn't shed a tear.'

Beryl says, 'He was the same when Mum died.'

At the funeral Gene delivers a eulogy which can only be described as thorough.

'My father used to joke that he never got any older,' he says, 'because whenever anyone asked him his age he could always give the same answer.' *The bowels have been acting up something shocking, Gene. Old age is a terrible thing.* '"I'm as old as the century," he always said.' A few of the mourners laugh.

Gene is pleased. 'Only a few days ago, at the age of 85, he was out doing one of the things he enjoyed most: hunting for fossils. He had an incredible energy.' *Can't a man listen to the cricket in peace?* 'My father was a hard worker. I remember he would arrive at the shop early so he could get the window display perfect.' Chops all overlapping the same amount, sausages evenly looped, parsley sprigs in straight rows. 'And he was never home before seven o'clock at night.' The virgin newspaper unfolded and presented, *run and get him his slippers, Gene,* the chilled bottle of beer, *pour it down the side of the glass, boy, tilt it, tilt it.* 'He was a serious man, honest. A strong social conscience.' *You're going to be a builder like the Palmer boy. The country needs houses, not bludging university students.* Gene looks out at the silent faces lining the pews, all waiting for him to make them feel better. 'When Beryl and Rob took over the shop, and Dad retired,' *promise me you won't let that idiot ruin the shop,* 'he was delighted. He'd always hoped the family business would continue to thrive,' *he's done away with the sawdust floors, the fool,* 'even though Etta and I had by that time shifted to the North Island.' *Your father won't come with me. He says he's never left the South Island and he's not going to start now.*

Beryl's husband Rob is preserving the occasion on video. He was at school with Gene, although they were never friends. Rob has, in Gene's opinion, more money than brains, and he can't help feeling tremendously satisfied when his brother-in-law stumbles over the corner of the altar step.

'Dad was a doting husband,' says Gene, 'always looking out for Mum and buying her treats.' The birthday disappointments. The anniversary thank-yous. *A wringer. Super. Thanks, love.* 'My father was a generous man, and during the Depression and the war he often helped out his customers and his friends. A few chops here, some mincemeat there. I know many of you present today will remember his favours.' *Sylvia Liddle was in again today when you were at lunch. Asking for you. Just tell him I called in, Mrs Stilton, she said.*

Rob moves in for a close-up. Gene watches him for a moment.

'Dad made a lot of friends through his rockhunting, and more than a few significant discoveries.' *Dad, look at this, look what I found!* 'Over the years he gained a reputation as something of an expert on local Canterbury fossils, and several articles about his finds appeared in the papers.' *It's nothing, Gene. Probably a dud. Leave it.* 'We were all very proud of him.' *But I found that one. It's mine.*

There is a general clearing of throats and shifting in seats as Gene steps down. He acknowledges a few people he recognises, and some he does not.

His sisters nod at him, wiping their eyes.

'Lovely,' Beryl whispers.

'Christ,' mutters Gene. Rob is crouching and scuttling round the coffin. 'If he gets any closer he'll be in there with him.'

'Yea though, I-hi walk, i-hin death's, dark vale,' Etta sings. She nudges Gene, and holds the words in front of him.

'And i-hin God's house, for e-hevermore, my dwe-helling place, shall be.'

Rob hovers over the flowers on the casket – red carnations and roses.

'He always liked red,' sniffs Carnelian.

'I'll say he was generous,' says Cyril Palmer at the reception, nudging Gene's forearm. Beer slops on to the carpet. 'He provided free sausages for more than one cash-strapped housewife, didn't he? The old devil. Ha!'

Beryl eyes them coldly as she pushes past with a tray of club sandwiches. Rob noses in like a giant insect, video camera still attached to his face.

'Chickadee,' he says to Beryl – he always calls her that in public and, some fear, in private – 'you offer Gene a sandwich. Gene, you take a couple.'

'For God's sake put that thing away,' says Carnelian. 'Nobody will want to watch it.'

'Now Gene,' says Beryl, after the guests have gone and the glasses have been rinsed and the leftover food packed away, 'you'll be taking the diaries of course. Dad did want you to have them.'

Gene remembers his assurances to Clifford that he would look after them.

'Perhaps Carnelian would like them,' he suggests.

She would not.

Nobody knows what to do with them. Clifford's clothes have been sorted into boxes and rubbish bags for the Salvation Army and for the tip, his lawnmower has been given away, his car advertised, his kitchen things divided among the flatting grandchildren. Even his collection of fossils and rocks and shells, and of jewellery made from his own polished stones, has been distributed. The diaries, however, have been piled on to the window seat in his lounge. Every afternoon the sun warps their covers, makes them swell.

'Take them,' says Beryl. 'I've got enough to look after. I have to sell the house, remember.'

Gene does remember; he doubts he'll be allowed to forget.

'I could stay a bit longer, perhaps,' he murmurs. 'Show people the car.'

Beryl snorts. 'Just take the diaries. Carnelian and I'll do the rest.'

'Yes,' says Gene, rubbing a cool agate pebble between his thumb and finger. 'The thing is, I don't know that they'll fit in the suitcase. We've already got so much –'

'Gene. I now have a house full of rocks. So does Carnelian. I don't care if you take them back to Wellington or not, just get them out of the way. I have to sell the house, remember.'

❖

Gene keeps the agate pebble in his pocket for the rest of the time in Christchurch. He hasn't taken many pieces from his father's collection; his wife Etta says they have enough at home already, and that she's the one who has to dust them, after all. The girls are not interested either. Dad, says Christina, if we want stones and shells we can go to the beach. And Bridget says all those petrified crabs and bones and things give her the creeps. So Gene takes a chunk of Brazilian crystal, a shoebox full of polished stones, and two pairs of cufflinks made of greenstone and obsidian, which he will never wear. He also takes a fossilised groper's head, because it has been labelled with his own name in Clifford's gaunt handwriting, and cannot be disregarded. And he agrees – says Beryl – to take the diaries. She reminds him of this on his last day in Christchurch.

'Here,' she says, thrusting some supermarket bags at him and watching while he squeezes the diaries into the flimsy plastic.

'If you ever want to have a look at them, let me know,' says Gene as he and Etta and the girls are leaving to catch their flight.

'Ha!' says Beryl. 'Pulse rates and cricket scores and bowel motions?'

At the airport Gene carries the bags on as hand luggage. The plastic handles cut into his fingers as he climbs the metal steps to the plane.

'Don't look down, girls,' Etta is saying, her collar pulled out of shape by a bulging amethyst brooch. Gene glances at the bags of diaries banging against his shin and sees below his feet, through the grid spaces, the shimmering tarmac. He wants to drop the bags then, watch the diaries slip through the slot at the back of the step and fall, pages fluttering, the bags puffed out in the breeze and rising translucent white. Floating away from his fingers like escaped balloons. But then he is showing his boarding pass to the smiling combed hostess who smells of makeup and has a silk scarf knotted smoothly around her shoulders, and she is saying, 'Towards the back, on the right, sir,' and he and Etta and Bridget and Christina are squeezing down the aisle to their seats.

'Here,' says Etta, motioning for the bags after she and the girls have stuffed their own things into the storage compartments. She folds and rearranges, trying to make room for the diaries, which, being hand luggage (as Christina points out), have to be stored under the seat in front of you, or in the overhead compartments.

'Let's just put them under the seat,' says Gene, but Etta says no, no, and with one almighty shove manages to shut the flap.

Gene feels uneasy all the way home. The plane keeps hitting small pockets of turbulence, and, each time, Etta glances over at his pallid face and pats his hand and says we're nearly there, not much further now. But it isn't the flight, as Etta suspects, nor is it suppressed grief (Bridget), nor is it the plastic-wrapped cracker with cheese which Gene mechanically consumes (Christina). What is troubling him is the thought that the overhead compartment, so tightly packed, might at any moment spring open, showering on his head pages and pages riddled with his father's black ink.

When they are back in Wellington, Gene puts the diaries away in the hall cupboard, which everyone still calls the toy cupboard, though it is a long time since any toys have been kept in it. As he opens the door a can of baked beans falls out and lands on his foot, causing him to drop the diaries and hop the entire length of the fake Persian rug.

✧

Bridget has made several important discoveries recently. For instance, she knows – through careful Bible study and regular Youth Group attendance – that the Antichrist will soon gain political power, and may in fact already be in office. She knows that most television programmes are evil, and she also knows that Armageddon will be conducted in the form of a nuclear war which will end the world, destroying most of the earth's population. She has started removing non-perishable grocery items from the pantry and storing them away in the toy cupboard. The rest of the family appear to be ignoring her preparations, and it is obvious to Bridget that, even despite Etta's regular church attendance, they do not belong to the chosen few who will be saved.

'We are living in the Endtimes,' her Youth Group leader Craig says at the Saturday meeting. 'It is not enough to simply surrender your whole being to Jesus. You must show others your commitment, through your actions.' He looks down at his hands, then begins to speak so quietly the Group all have to lean forward in their wooden chairs to hear him. Craig waits for the collective squeaking to settle, then continues. 'Last year, when I decided that Jesus was the one constant in my life and that I wanted to rid myself of all the evils that were standing between me and him, I realised I had to give up most of my record collection. I listened to them all, one by one, and none of the songs, none of them, fitted into a Christian way of thinking. So I took them to school the next day and began giving them away.'

A murmur moves through the Group. Bridget grips the splintered edges of her chair.

'But then,' says Craig, 'I realised I wasn't solving anything. I was just passing that harmful material on to other people. Like a disease. So I took back all the records I had given away, and took them all out of their covers, and smashed them. I broke them over my knees, jumped on them, whacked them against the wall, in front of everyone else in the courtyard. They all just stared at me like I'd gone insane. Some of them, guys I'd given records to at first, got quite angry. They thought I was doing it to make them look stupid. So I told them. I said I was breaking records for Jesus.'

The Group laughs; a few people clap. Craig grins and gazes at each one of them in turn. When his pale eyes rest on Bridget, she can imagine how he must have looked that day in the Saint Bernard's courtyard, shards of broken music flying around him.

'It's a true story,' he says, 'and you can do it too. God's love is real; it's there for you if you want it.' He stands up and moves to the centre of the circle. 'Now,' he says, extending his arms, 'I want you to experience the power of God's love for yourselves. Some of you, I know, are going through a lot at the moment. Rosemary, your Dad's left home. Bridget's grandfather has just passed away. Michael's failed his driving test.' Craig's voice rises. 'But I want you to realise that you're not alone, even during the bad times. Especially then.' He extends his arms to the Group. 'I want you to find a space on the carpet, and lie down. I want you to shut your eyes and be very calm within yourselves. And then,' he says, lying down himself, 'I want you to imagine a wooden cross.'

The room is very still; even Jeremy Ward cooperates. Bridget opens her eyes for a fraction of a second. Craig is right beside her, so close she can see the tiny balls of fluff which have formed on his jersey.

'Now,' he says, 'imagine a friend, someone you are very close to, being dragged on to the cross.'

This is where Bridget starts having a bit of trouble. She can't come up with anyone she is close to. Not even a relative. Especially not a relative.

'Nails are being driven through your friend's hands and feet,' says Craig. 'The pain is extreme.'

Someone – probably Jeremy Ward – lets out a fart. A giggle ripples round the bodies stretched out on the carpet.

'The cross,' Craig says quickly, 'is now being raised up. Your friend is in agony, but does not complain. He – or she – is doing this for you.'

Bridget opens her eyes again and looks around the church meeting room. Jeremy is on his side, doing his best to press up against Rosemary Stokes, who doesn't seem to mind.

'That is how much God loves you,' says Craig. 'That is how much Jesus loves you. He suffered that pain so that you can live forever.'

Bridget gazes at him. She observes the rise and fall of his chest, the way his eyelashes rest against his cheeks. When she closes her eyes again, there is Craig hanging on her cross, fully clothed but beautiful.

'Okay,' he says after a few minutes, 'let's get back into our circle.'

The members of the Group stand up and stretch. Jeremy Ward rearranges himself.

'Bridget,' says Craig, nudging her with his toe, 'Bridget. Time to get up.'

✧

Gene is sitting on the toilet when he first hears the voice. Although it isn't a voice, strictly, but a cough – hollow-sounding, regular, polite. And persistent. He can't make out any words.

The houses are built very close here, he thinks, and drops a wad of paper down the toilet.

That night in bed, the coughing starts again, louder this time. Gene gets up to check whether the window is open, but it's not. He thinks he spots something moving in the garden, but when he snaps the bedroom light on all he can see is his own reflection in the glass.

'What's the matter?' mumbles Etta, raising herself up on one elbow.

Gene says, 'Nothing, go back to sleep,' and climbs into bed again himself.

He hardly has the blankets pulled up to his chin and his eyes closed, though, before a violent cough right beside his ear jolts him wide awake. It goes on for a few seconds: five, maybe six short loud blasts like bullets.

This time he doesn't turn the light on. He just lies very still and stares at the ceiling. As he slowly exhales, the voice starts.

Across the low flat river   coming up from my boots   clever and will go a long   neck and six hankies and still   his own business in time   pall bearer for the flu boy

Gene has to strain to hear what the voice is saying, and even then he appears to be missing a lot. It seems familiar, though. Not the voice itself, but the words, or perhaps just the inflection, contains something he recognises. He waits for it to continue, but all he hears is Etta's even breathing and the slow contracting of the house.

The next morning Gene can no longer remember exactly what he heard, but an uneasiness remains with him all day, like the residue of an anxious dream. He doesn't mention it to Etta, although she remarks that he seemed restless during the night. He doesn't want her to worry, although why there might be anything to worry about he cannot say. It's just the tiredness after the funeral, he decides, and all the accompanying duties: fielding sympathetic phone-callers and visitors, refilling the vases of flowers with water (it's amazing how much they drink, Etta says almost every day), remembering to remember who sent which bouquet or baked which fruit cake.

The freezer is bulging with baking.

'I think we'll have to get rid of some of these ducks and things,' says Etta, rummaging round the very bottom. She produces a frost-encrusted bundle about the size of a rugby ball and tries to read the label on it.

'Muttonbird 27.5.83,' she says. 'Are you ever going to eat that?'

'It's a vintage specimen,' says Gene, clutching the cold hard package to his chest.

That night he listens for the voice, but everything is quiet. He catches his breath when he hears a single hard cough, but it's just Etta beside him, and he drops off to sleep.

❖

When he looks out the bedroom window the next morning, the front lawn is strewn with colour. The rubbish bag, which Etta had propped against the lamppost the previous evening, is lying slashed and leaky in the middle of the road.

'Hell,' he mutters, pulling on his thick green dressing gown that Etta gave him for his twenty-first. It's still as good as new – a fact that is remarked upon every winter when it is brought down from the high storage cupboards – and against his wrists and neck, where the pyjamas don't quite reach, it scratches like a blanket that has slipped away from a restless sheet. He grabs a new rubbish bag from the laundry. The girls' white underwear has been soaking there overnight, and in the tub there are glimpses of narrow lace trim; small bras puffing above the suds. The water smells of NapiSan. Etta swears by it.

Gene glances up and down the street to see if other bags have been attacked. They have not. He begins picking up the spilled egg cartons, toilet paper tubes, orange peel, sticky tins.

'Oh, bad luck,' calls Peter Fitzroy from his letterbox, tucking the paper under his arm and patting back up his drive in his slippers.

Gene's toe nudges a cracked lipstick case, sending it rattling along the footpath. He bends to pick it up and the transparent cover, smeared with Hot Fuchsia, stains his hand. It is not a shade he recognises, nor does the plastic casing seem to have anything in common with the cool metal tubes lined up like fingers in Etta's makeup drawer. A bottle of curdled nail polish – Sizzling Coral – lies in the rose bed, next to an empty pot of Maximum Hold hair gel. They clink against baked bean tins as Gene drops them into the bag, holding them between his thumb and forefinger and wondering whether the scattered rubbish might not have been mixed up with someone else's after all. Beside the heady daphne bush he picks up an empty tampon box, two worn emery boards, a makeup sponge stained the colour of someone's skin.

He chases the last few wisps of plastic bags that are blowing around the lawn, snatching at them as they press themselves against the hedge, the foundations of the house, the smooth trunk of the silver birch. The labels on the bags have all been fairly well chewed, but Gene is still able to recognise his own writing, denoting dates, locations, identities. *Paradise duck, Wairarapa, 4.6.85. Canada goose, Cambridge, 27.5.85. Swan, Wairarapa, 12.7.84. Rainbow trout, Otamangakau, 25.12.84 (8lb). Muttonbird, Bob's, 2.5.85.*

Gene has a sudden image of a pack of dogs snarling open the items he has so carefully plucked, cleaned, filleted, smoked. Yellow teeth tearing raw thawed skin, carcasses picked and gnawed and discarded under the white glow of the street light. He looks around the lawn, but there are no bones, no fragments of transparent fin. Just the plastic, clinging to his ankles now, almost tripping him.

What the Stiltons need, he decides, is an extra freezer. One that can be reserved just for his things. He will talk to Etta about it.

Gene stretches out in his armchair, a glass of whisky resting on his stomach. Saturday afternoons are his favourite time of the week. Etta usually does some gardening, Bridget goes off to her church group, and nowadays Christina spends her time either on the phone or down at the shops with her friends. Gene likes to have a snooze in the patch of late sun his chair is positioned to catch.

He shuts his eyes and tunes the radio to the rugby. Just as he is drifting off to sleep, however, and the excited voice of the radio commentator is blurring with the memory of the frozen birds, there is a crash that seems to come from the hall. Gene levers his footstool down.

The door to the toy cupboard is ajar, and the diaries are lying spilled on the carpet. Gene sighs and scoops them back into the bags, jamming the corners into the tight plastic. He shuts the cupboard door with a push of his shoulder and is on his way back to the lounge when the phone rings.

'Gene Stilton speaking.'

There is silence at the other end.

'Hello? Are you there?'

Not a breath.

'Hello? Hello?'

An abrupt cough is followed by a very faint voice.

The police don't put things like that over the air unless they have good reasons

There is a pause, during which Gene can think of no appropriate response, and then the voice begins again, a little clearer this time. Certainly clearer than when he heard it in bed.

It did not arrive   but the sea is still acting very strange   more earthquakes in Chile

'Listen,' says Gene, 'I know who you are, and what you are doing is not in the least bit funny. If you don't stop bothering my family, I'm going to call the police.' And he hangs up.

He refuses to let his hand shake as he pours himself another whisky. It wouldn't be so bad if he did know who the voice belonged to, he thinks. He flops back into his armchair and tries to concentrate on the rugby game.

You know when a fellow dies he loses fear of even Atom bombs   but I think if he really is as brave as all that he should insist on no funeral   nobody likes them anyway

The voice drowns out the rugby commentary. Gene reaches an unsteady hand over to the radio and turns it off. For a moment there is silence, and then it starts again.

I did not rise early   around the Gorges   a little cemetery on the estate   even a monument to the horses killed in the War   such a peaceful place, even the deer from the hills spend time there   I noted droppings all over the grounds   built of river boulders   no telephone no wireless no lighting except the moon no motor cars no roads   nothing except strong hearts and a will to live   I wonder how far away the nearest doctor was

Gene switches the radio back on and turns it up as loud as it will go. He jumps as the sliding door opens and the drawn curtain billows.

'Hey Dad,' says Christina, heading for the kitchen with two other girls Gene doesn't recognise. Their plastic earrings jangle as they walk.

Bridget strolls home humming. The meeting was so vitalising she feels like singing out loud. She manages not to; Drummond Crescent is a quiet street.

'Come to the water, you who are thirsty,' she sings in her head. 'Though you have nothing, I bid you come –'

She glides through the front door, beaming at the hall stand, the tui print on the wall, the lightswitch.

'Call me your father and know I am near,' she hums, 'I will be father to you.'

'God, you're not in love are you?'

Bridget smiles at her sister. 'You could say that.'

'Well don't bring him round here. You're more than enough geek for one household.'

Her friends snigger from the kitchen.

'All right,' says Bridget, still smiling.

'Is she on drugs?' she hears one of the friends say as she goes to the lounge.

Gene is sitting at the table with a screwdriver, poking around inside the radio. Various wires and pieces of metal are scattered across the tablecloth. He glances up at Bridget, then goes back to dismantling the radio. Bridget smiles at him anyway. She takes her Bible out of her bag and opens it at the passages the Group had been discussing that afternoon.

There was a violent earthquake, and the sun became black like coarse black cloth, and the moon turned completely red like blood. The stars fell down to earth, like unripe figs falling from the tree when a strong wind shakes it. The sky disappeared like a scroll being rolled up, and every mountain and island was moved from its place. Then the kings of the earth, the rulers and the military chiefs, the rich and the powerful, and all other men, slave and free, hid themselves in caves and under rocks on the mountains.

'Nuclear winter,' she grins.

'Where are you?' mutters Gene.

Whoever worships the beast and its image and receives the mark on his forehead or on his hand will himself drink God's wine, the wine of his fury, which he has poured at full strength into the cup of his anger! All who do this will be tormented in fire and sulphur before the holy angels and the Lamb.

'The Bomb,' nods Bridget, smiling hugely.

Gene throws the screwdriver aside and stands up from the table.

'Bridget!' he almost shouts, as if he has just remembered her name. He grabs her arm. Bridget presses back into the chair in surprise, as if she is in a rapidly ascending aeroplane.

'You know about religion, don't you,' says Gene, so close she can feel his breath. She eyes him for a moment, then smiles. Perhaps it is not too late for him to be saved. Although the Jim Reeves records would have to go.

'What do you know about spirits?' he demands. 'Hauntings.'

'Dad,' she says, as if she is talking to a very young child. 'Evil is real. It's everywhere. *Evil*,' she says, taking his hand, 'is the opposite of *live*.' And she turns back to her Bible.

The foundation-stones of the city wall were adorned with all kinds of precious stones. The first foundation-stone was jasper, the second sapphire, the third agate, the fourth emerald, the fifth onyx, the sixth carnelian, the seventh yellow quartz, the eighth beryl . . .

Gene twists his head to see what she is reading. Bridget looks up again, watches her father frown and twitch his mouth. She waits for him to speak. He keeps twitching.

'Can I help you with something?'

'Is there . . . is there anything in there about . . .' He gulps. 'Ghosts?'

'Ghosts.' Bridget stops smiling, puts a hand on his forehead, the way Etta sometimes still does to see if either she or Christina has a temperature. 'Possession by demons, you mean? Dad. Have you been possessed by a demon?' As if he has done something very naughty.

'I don't know. I heard . . . a voice.'

'Did it tell you to perform evil deeds and to make Satan your king?'

'Ah . . . is that what they normally say?'

'Prayer time!' Bridget announces, and kneels down on the swirled mustard carpet, motioning for Gene to do the same.

'Our Father, who art in heaven,' she begins.

Gene doesn't know the Our Father by heart, or any prayers, for that matter, so he just closes his eyes and concentrates on Bridget's voice.

No doors between rooms   paintings of birds on the walls   on the walls themselves   a tui a bellbird a fan-tail   strangely there were two native pigeons outside   quite tame and the colours in them very beautiful

Gene opens his eyes and looks at Bridget, and it's as if he is watching a dubbed film. Her lips are moving, but they don't match the words he hears.

'Bridget,' he says, very quietly. 'Bridget.'

She opens her eyes.

'Thank you. I feel much better now.'

Bridget opens the hall door and listens. She can hear shrieking and laughter coming from Christina's room.

'Don't you want me baby?' someone – possibly Christina – is singing. 'Don't you want me, oh, ohohoh.'

Bridget tiptoes into the kitchen and opens the pantry. Tins are lined up on the shelves, labels facing outwards. Beetroot, sweetcorn, spaghetti, beans. They shine at her. Pineapple, tomatoes, fruit salad. She grasps a large tin of baked beans just as Christina appears at the door.

'Stocking up for the End of the World again, are we?' Christina grabs a bag of chippies.

'What's that supposed to mean?'

'Your stash,' says Christina. 'In the toy cupboard.'

Bridget flushes.

'Everyone knows about it. Half my class know about it. Just leave the beers for me, okay?' Christina drops her voice to a whisper. 'I'm going to sneak a couple of cans for tonight.'

Bridget nods vigorously, too stunned to tell her sister that those who would be saved would have no need for liquor.

'Actually,' says Christina, 'you do have your uses. Dad'll just think you stashed them away for Armageddon.' And she pinches Bridget's cheek.

'Wait a minute! Does Dad know too?'

'Everyone knows. Mum, Dad, Dr Kerr, the guidance counsellor. Everyone. You're the weird Stilton girl.'

Several whiskies later, Gene decides that the voice can only belong to one person. Clifford.

'Dad,' he mutters, and Etta, who is just coming in from the garden to put dinner on, peers at him and says, 'Anything the matter?'

Gene clears his throat. 'We lost the rugby,' he says.

At the office there are murmured sympathies, apologies. Little is expected of Gene for the first few days back; people are unnaturally cheerful and shield him from anxiety. He is not told, for instance, that all the linoleum in the new science wing has had to be lifted and replaced because the contractors used the wrong glue, or that five of the pine doors have warped and will no longer lock. Statements are, nonetheless, loaded; ordinary words are given strange emphasis.

'I made your coffee with *full* cream,' says the receptionist. 'I *know* how you like it.'

'Perhaps you could sign *these*.'

'Do you really *want* to look at that today? It can *wait* until you're *ready*.'

Gene plays along for a little while, accepts the extra biscuits, allows his phonecalls to be screened. Until about the fourth day.

'Michelle,' he says, 'I think I'd like to be on my own for a bit. Sort through some things.'

And Michelle freezes for a moment, then scuttles away saying of course, Mr Stilton, of course, and his door is gently shut and he is alone.

And then the man walks through the office.

He looks about forty and is dressed in a musty pair of corduroy trousers and a Swandri.

'Can I help you there?' says Gene, very much hoping this isn't one of the unfortunates Shirley Davis keeps asking them to take on. The last one couldn't even hammer a nail in straight. 'Are you looking for someone? Is it about the labouring job, did Mrs Davis send you?'

'I walked out in the paddocks for two hours,' says the man. 'They had quite a pub there. I drank five rums and lemonade and was I sick.'

'Oh great,' sighs Gene. He'll have to have a word to Etta about Shirley's good deeds. He puts out a hand to take the man's arm and says in his most soothing voice, 'Come on, now,' but the man shakes him off.

'Come morning I hadn't died. Up before dinner, singing loudly to allay suspicion.'

'Yes,' says Gene.

'Went for a drive and we took our guns just in case.' The man's voice is rising. 'It rained like hell. The lake is very high and he put his maimai in such deep water, I would say dangerous. Went sour at him.'

'I can ring the police and they'll be here in five minutes flat. Probably less, probably more like two.'

'Mum and the girls mushrooming in the afternoon. A treble

of swans in one go. I don't like the water too deep when the waves commence.'

'I'm dialling, do you see?'

'Talk about a gale, the poor bloody birds couldn't fly,' shouts the man. 'My advice is,' he walks over to Gene and places a finger on the disconnect button, his voice suddenly dropping as if to tell a secret, 'take up indoor bowls. Don't stand up to your arse in water.'

Very slowly, Gene puts down the receiver.

'The lake is very high. He put his maimai in such deep water. After the gale we shot till seven with the help of the moon.'

Gene reaches his hand out and touches the prickly Swandri. 'This –' He looks into the man's face. There was a gale, he remembers. And he'd put his maimai in too deep and his father was angry with him, and Gene thought it was because he wanted the best spot for himself. It must have been thirty years ago, just after he and Etta married. They were building their first house, and she hadn't wanted Gene to waste the whole weekend, she said, but really she couldn't bear him arriving home with dead things to be plucked and cleaned and cooked and consumed. And then Gene was busy with night school and working for Conway's, and Clifford was diagnosed with an erratic heart, and they didn't go hunting much any more – or not with one another. But that day, in the gale, they shot one hundred swans between them, just him and Clifford. The air around them was filled with the dark shapes of the birds, and often they hit two or three with one shot. They piled them all on to the trailer, and driving home over the hills they could feel the weight of the birds pulling at the car. They had to give most of them away; only so many could be stored in the coolroom at Clifford's shop. They donated a lot of the swans to an orphanage, and Gene remembers Etta tried to roast one for a family dinner and burnt it beyond recognition, and Clifford patted her hand and said, 'Never mind, love, you'll soon get the hang of it.'

Gene swallows. 'Dad?'

The man is silent.

Gene sits down at his desk. 'You think I've forgotten all that, but I haven't. I haven't.' He arranges his pens and pencils and highlighters in a row beside his blotter, brushes lead-coloured specks of eraser to the floor. The man still says nothing. 'I was too busy after that. I had the house to finish, and night school, and work on top of that. I had no time.' The man folds his arms. 'I would have had more time. If you'd have let me go to university, I would have had more time.' Gene's voice is rising. 'I would have had a degree by then, and a job with the paper. They wanted me, they said I had talent. Age sixteen, and they told me I was journalist material. And you said houses are what we need, not stories about houses. You're going to be a builder like the Palmer boy.'

'Mr Stilton?' Michelle is standing in the doorway. 'Sorry. I did knock.'

Gene looks around his office. The man is gone. He crouches down and checks under the desk, behind the filing cabinet.

'Have you lost something?'

'Did you see a man leaving just now? About forty?'

Michelle frowns. 'Nobody came past reception. Perhaps you'd like a cup of tea, does that sound nice?'

Gene wanders to the dinner table that evening still wearing his reading glasses.

'Bye Dad,' says Christina, on her way past in a mist of fake Poison. 'I'm going to Janine's for tea.'

'Mmhmm,' nods Gene.

'Are you hoping for a menu to browse through?' says Etta when he sits down. He stares at her blankly. She reaches across and removes his glasses.

During dinner she chats about how well the garden is doing, and how there should be new potatoes for Christmas dinner. Bridget appears at one stage and serves herself some bean salad and beetroot.

'There's corned beef too,' says Etta, lifting a couple of slices towards her daughter's plate.

'Yes, for the moment, there is corned beef,' says Bridget. 'There will not always be corned beef.' She takes her plate to her room.

Etta sighs. 'I think we should have a talk with her. I mean, it's great she's getting involved with the Youth Group and making some friends, but this food business is definitely not normal.'

Gene contemplates a boiled potato.

'Gene? It's not normal, is it?'

'No, no,' says Gene. 'Very strange indeed. Quite worrying.'

'All right then,' says Etta.

After dinner Gene retrieves the diaries from the toy cupboard and sorts them into order. There are more than he expects, and only one year is missing: 1955. He knows why, too. His mother had thrust that one at him when she and Clifford were shifting to a smaller house.

✧

Gene was helping his mother Violet pack some of her more fragile things. They'd worked their way through the house and were finishing the last room, her bedroom. And Clifford's. Violet was wrapping ornaments in handkerchiefs and scarves and nylon slips and placing them in fruit crates. She took her wedding photo from the dressing table and looked at herself, twenty-eight years younger, peering out from the shadow of a low hat.

'You're a good boy, Gene,' she said, wrapping the photo in a woollen singlet. 'I know you're busy enough with your own place.'

'It's hardly a place yet. We're still clearing the section.'

Violet lifted a drawer from the dressing table and began sorting through hairclips and curved combs which had become meshed. 'You haven't taken on too much, have you love? I don't know when you find the time to even see Etta, and the two of you just three months married.'

Gene crumpled newspaper and packed it into a lidded crystal dish. 'I have to go to night school. I can't be a builder all my life.'

'You're a very good builder. Fred Conway wouldn't know what to do without you, he said. His wife told me so, when she was in the shop.'

'Are there any more crates in the garage?' said Gene. 'These are all full.' And he tucked some extra sheets of newspaper around the parcelled ornaments.

'A husband should spend time with his wife. Take her out. Do you still go out?'

'Mum. Please.'

Violet opened Clifford's bedside cabinet and took from it a book bound in red. She handed it to Gene. 'I don't care what you do with it,' she said. 'I don't want it in the new place.'

Gene ran a finger over the date stamped in gold on the front of the book: 1955. 'I gave Dad this. Last Christmas. Mum –'

But Violet had turned away and was holding one of Clifford's singlets up to the light. 'This'll do for a duster now,' she said.

When Gene and Etta had cleared the last of the gorse and broom from their section, they piled the branches on to the trailer to take to the tip.

'All that work for an empty piece of land,' said Etta, and slouched against the car.

'You don't need to come to the tip,' said Gene. 'Have a rest, I'll go.'

But Etta said no, she wanted to come, the tip was one of her favourite places. You never knew what you'd find there.

Gene slipped the diary on to the back of the trailer with the prickly mass of broom and gorse. It wasn't difficult to dispose of it when they arrived; Etta was too distracted by what other people had thrown away to notice him dropping it underneath the trailer.

'A couch!' she called. 'Gene, it's perfectly good!' She prodded a squat fridge with her toe, causing the door to fall open. She examined a gutted radiogram. Gulls were everywhere, circling, screeching.

There were scratches on Etta's arms after she and Gene had raked all the branches off the trailer. She rubbed at them in the car on the way back to their flat. As he was falling asleep that night Gene recalled the paleness of her skin in the stark sunlight, the whiteness of the gulls' bellies, the red scratches, the red diary against the mud, and how yellow the gorse flowers glowed.

Two weeks later, when Clifford discovered that 1955 was missing, he turned the new house upside down. This happened on a Sunday, when everyone was there for lunch.

'It'll show up,' said Carnelian. 'You haven't even finished unpacking yet.'

Violet set the carving knife down at Clifford's place at the table, next to a roast swan. 'Are you coming now, love?' she called.

Clifford could be heard moving things around up in the ceiling.

'I'll carve,' said Gene.

For the next half hour they sat at the table eating while above them were sounds of dragging and crashing. Violet chatted away, asking Etta if she would like any old kitchen things that they really didn't have room for in the new place. She could have a mincer if she liked, good as new. At one point it sounded as if Clifford was going to crash through the ceiling, and land in the middle of the glistening swan. Eventually he appeared, dusty and red in the face.

'No luck, Dad?' asked Beryl. 'Colin, sit up straight.'

'I don't like this,' said Colin, spitting out a mouthful of half-chewed meat. 'Mummy, I want some cake.'

Clifford took his seat at the table. 'I'll find it.'

'Colin!' Beryl caught a piece of pumpkin before it fell to the floor. 'Rob, do something.'

Gene pushed swan bones to the side of his plate through a puddle of dark gravy and was silent. Violet helped Clifford to mashed potatoes and peas and roast pumpkin, saying, 'There now.'

'A diary, how interesting,' said Etta. 'I'd never have the patience. Do you write in it every day, Cliff, or only when something interesting happens?'

'Every day, don't you, Dad?' said Carnelian. 'Even if absolutely nothing's happened.'

Clifford stopped looking for the diary eventually, although he did still mention it from time to time, for years afterwards. 'Make sure you keep track of everything you pack,' he said to Etta when she and Gene finally shifted into their new house. 'Things can go missing very easily. I lost a diary that way.' And again, when they moved to Wellington, 'Do all your own packing,' he insisted. 'I recommend making a list.' The diary was even mentioned when Beryl's cat was run over. 'You have to keep an eye on things all the time,' Clifford told her, 'otherwise you lose them. I have never located my 1955 diary.'

Gene thinks of it now, decomposing in the mud, slowly covered over by thirty years of refuse. He doubts that any part of it remains; paper and cloth, he imagines, would be broken down fairly rapidly, like the soft flesh of creatures without bones. They would have dissolved, Clifford's comments and observations, his 1955 secrets, leaving behind just an imprint of themselves, a shadow in layers of mud.

A swan
story

1954

Jun 15 Tue
Had a rotten day   woke up with a stiff neck & the trots & a
cough that is coming up from my boots   reckon I have used
six Hankies

Jul 7 Wed
Gene & Etta to marry September next year but not the full
church show as Gene is not a Catholic   Etta's mother is
refusing to come   fine by me   A message to young couples

remember this, money is a blasted pest   if you have good
health don't worry about money. Its hard to get, its hard to
keep, its hard to hide, & its hard to stop the Government
knowing you've got it. When you are young you are inclined to
think that if you could climb up a rainbow you would find a
pot of gold. Take my advice don't try to climb at all, you have
better than gold you have your health & you have one another.
Love & be loved & go on loving & some day that pot of gold
will slide down the rainbow & save you that climb   beer, yes,
in moderation, smoking no, a dirty stinking expensive habit,
never start, a car, yes, by all means after you have your own
home. A job you must have & always be a worker but don't be
bossed around by no boss if you are doing your job well, the
boss should not worry you if he does get another boss. I say to
Hell with the boss with the big stick if nobody will work for
him what will he be boss of   well   over to Cyril's to hear the
rugby

Jul 16 Fri
I am worried about my health and have been for a while   from
time to time my heart misfires it is most unsettling   of course
I have not mentioned it to Mum she would only worry

Jul 21 Wed
Gave Mum £5 today for helping me in the shop. A bit of Pocket
Money for her. Beryl & Rob round for tea, with little Colin.
He is walking now & into everything he tried to eat some of
the stones I have been polishing on the emery wheel

Jul 24 Sat
Carnelian is missing & has been for 2 hours   she is supposed
to be having a bath but I reckon she might be swimming Cook
Strait
Health Good

Jul 25 Sun

I did not rise early, when I did we decided to go for a 100 mile trip around the Gorges. We went through Rangiora & Loburn, across the low flat river on the road to Oxford & after 38 miles we arrived at Birch Hill. My daughter Beryl I think I have mentioned it previously is acting Matron at the Ford Milton Childrens Home there. I took a couple of good stones from the river for my Collection & Beryl took us to see the little Cemetery on the estate, where old Colonel Milton is buried   there is even a monument for the horses killed in the 1914-18 War. It is such a peaceful place that the Deer from the near hills spend a lot of time there   I noted droppings all over the grounds. We left the Cemetery with a feeling that here lay some real pioneers. Our next visit proved this, we had a look at the original home of these famous people. It was built of boulders evidently carried from the river. Rough but homely & very strong, a tribute to the days when men were tough   I wonder how far away the nearest Doctor was. No telephone, no wireless, no lighting except the Moon, no motor cars & no roads, nothing except strong hearts & a will to live   nearby was a wooden house it was very old but quite sound it was probably regarded as a very fine building in those days sometime in the late 1800's   it amused us, there was only 1 door to each room; no doors between rooms. On the walls were some good paintings, that is on the walls themselves. A Native Pigeon was the best one, there were also paintings of a Tui a Bellbird a Fantail   strangely enough just outside, there were two live Native Pidgeons & they were quite tame & the colours in them very beautiful. What a contrast this wooden house from the old Boulder house. Gene you could have learnt a thing or two about building if you'd come with us   supplies were evidently arriving in the country the pioneers had won their greatest battle. We went a little further & there stood the last home of these great folk. It is situated on a rise, surrounded by well laid out gardens   contains something like 25 Rooms. What a difference. What a home   a Dream Come

True   I stood outside on the spacious lawn & I looked at the Mansion   here was everything that a man required. Telephone, wireless, electric light in every room (& doors), 2 pumps electrically driven for the water, no carrying it from the river, an electric stove, an electric washing machine. In the yard were several motor cars capable of 80 Miles an hour & more & perfect roads leading to all parts of the Island   even as I looked an aeroplane flew overhead, it could be in Wellington in 1 hour.

But what the Bloody Hell is the good of it when you lie in that quiet little Cemetery. The Old Colonel must have been a wise old man & he did not want anybody to come & live there in comfort in a home already built   he had built that Boulder Home with his blistered hands he must of wished nobody to just step in after he was gone. So what did he do he left all his property to unhappy children it is a home for them. Two other farms go with this one to support the home. What a great gesture & it means that no lazy cocky can step in & reap the profits of that great Family.

His name was Colonel Milton
And his wife's Maiden name was Ford
Hence the name of the childrens Home   "Ford Milton"

If you ever get the chance, go & see it for yourself

Jul 29 Thur
Gene at home for once this evening he is kept busy with his night school & his girl. Mum will miss him round the house when they are married they are to get a flat until their house is finished. It seems he does not want to stay on with us though perhaps it is Etta who is against it or her folks. He gave me a hand fixing a rod for a while, he is quite clever & will go a long way. He will have his own business in time.
Pulse 87

Aug 6 Fri
Took Mum shopping in the car this afternoon   I hope I am
not spoiling her. Left Rob in charge of the shop & no real
disasters. He fetched Beryl & Colin round for tea Colin likes
the stones today he was playing with the giant fossilised crabs a
good kid.
Pulse 88

Aug 22 Sun
I went round to Cyril's to see his new stones. He has some real
beauties but wouldn't say where he found them. We swopped a
few I reckon I came out of it better off. He doesn't have much of
an idea of value that's why he ended up with Vera. God help
the whitebait this season, I don't have to ask any boss if I can go
to the river like Gene has to. He doesn't have much free time
these days they keep him at it.

Sep 6 Mon
No visitors tonight. Mum is asleep in her chair by the fire, she
never seems to stop work I don't know how she keeps it up
Pulse 85

Sep 26 Sun
A very low tide at the Avon this morning   I thought it would
be a big one with the Full Moon. No luck with the whitebait,
Gene either. Home by 8 a.m. & I did some gardening I planted
Peas (Greenfeast) Carrots (Taranaki Strong Top) Parsnips
(Student) Onions (Pukekohe) Beetroot (Derwent Globes).
Took Mum Gene & Carnelian whitebaiting in the afternoon.
Etta came too but just watched from the bank. I caught ¾lb.
Mum made us a nice whitebait supper.

Dec 2 Thur
Gene fetched Etta round for supper tonight she stayed for a
while when he went off to his night school & she dropped a big

bomb. She told us that her & Gene were going to the Coast for Xmas with her folks & would arrive at Kai Koura later. So with Beryl & Rob at Nelson & Carnelian working on Xmas Eve it looks as though Mum & I will sit down to Xmas Dinner on our own. I could write a lot on this Subject but someday somebody might read this & get hurt.
Pulse 93

Dec 4 Sat
Cyril & Vera Palmer came for the evening we listened to the cricket. After they had gone I was surprised as Mum broke down & had a good howl. It was over Xmas I think she is upset because nobody will be with us & also she was afraid I might say some unkind words to the family. As much as it hurts one to think of Xmas without any of the family   I will bear it & keep it to myself

Dec 18 Sat
Tonight I rang up Cyril & Vera to invite them to Kai Koura for Xmas & Boxing Day. They accepted.
I would like to mention here the fact that I offered Gene 6/- per hour for any overtime he cared to do for me in the shop the last 6 weeks before Xmas. Tax free, but he never showed up I only hope he will always be so well-off in the future. Perhaps 6/- per hour was not enough for him. I could have done with a hand & he could have learnt a few things. A lot more independent than I ever was. Health Fair.

Dec 19 Sun
Did up my fishing gear ready for the attack at Xmas

<u>Xmas holidays at Kai Koura</u>
We had a grand drive up, called in at Mr Quinns Caravan at Goose Bay & he shouted good whisky. We arrived at our nice little house about 8 p.m. The only thing about it was it was very

popular & Mum & I only slept in our bed twice in 3 weeks. The Palmers stayed with us for four nights. Cyril caught some fish for a change & was very pleased with himself. We both found some good stones I let him keep a couple of mine he doesn't have as good an eye as me. The day they left Myra & Len Booth & 2 daughters came. Gene & Etta also arrived, & Beryl & Rob the following day. I took them all fishing & they were thrilled. We caught 60 sharks in one day. Gene & I shot nine deer & 1 pig but the most exciting thing that happened during the 3 weeks was me getting a green pea stuck in my windpipe & believe me I nearly crossed the border. Yes the house was good but boy we had some callers. It was no holiday for Mum one day she made 100 cups of tea.

1955

Jan 28 Fri
Today Cyril asked me to make a couple of bamboo fishing rods for his boss Mr Drury 7 shillings a go with the possibility of further orders. I am kept busy with the shop but hell am I doing all right I always make my £30 per week & there are a lot of General Managers that don't get that much & I'll bet they have a lot more worry. I will get all the Family on the job   things are going very well for us   well tonight I go fishing for the weekend but of all the winds there are it is a South West & that will make the sea rough   anyway   I cannot order the wind to suit me
Sylvia 5.30 p.m.

Feb 19 Sat
Cyril & Gene & I went to the Heathcote at 10 p.m. to get some eels for bait. I slipped on my bum in a drain, Cyril nearly went into the river he was suspended in mid-air for a while but Gene made no bones about it he fell in properly & got everything

wet except his hat. Cyril & I had a great laugh, in fact we nearly had hysterics.

Pulse 86

Sylvia 7.30 p.m.

Apr 3 Sat

Entertained the Treasurer and Sec (Lady) of the Christchurch Lapidary Society for 3 hours   looking at stones

May 1 Sun

Gene & I put the Mai Mais in position but I don't think we will be able to use them as the lake is very high in fact I went sour at Gene because he put his in very deep water   I would say dangerous   Beryl Mum & Carnelian made quite a bit of progress on the rods they are good little workers

May 8 Sun

Mothers Day   I gave Violet a pair of Stockings she has done all right lately. Fridge, Carpet, Hoover etc so I didn't spend much. Left for the lake at 10 a.m. A good South Wester. Gene had to vacate the deep water. I shot 38 swans Gene got 26 swans 1 goose 2 ducks making our total for the weekend 116 birds. I did not go out to the deep water as I considered I would get all the shooting I wanted closer in & with more comfort I don't like the water too deep when the waves commence   as it was I used up every cartridge I had

Marsha 5.30 p.m.

Sylvia 7 p.m.

May 11 Wed

Mum looked after the shop so I got out to the Lake at 2 p.m. Talk about a gale   the poor bloody Birds couldn't fly. I made for an Island 300 yards out in the Lake but after 1 hour my Island sank so I beat a retreat back to shore. Got 2 ducks & 5 swans & missed the goose I so badly wanted. Unable to retrieve

3 of the swans as I never had a submarine with me. Gene wants to come out tomorrow. My advice is take up Indoor Bowls, don't stand up to your arse in water in a storm
Health Fair

May 13 Fri
Did no work today. Away I went to the Lake for a days shooting on my own. A Mr McBride of Greenpark walked across his property & drove the Swans off. A lot flew over me & I shot 10 in a few minutes. Finished up with 35 Swans & 1 big Grey Duck. A great bit of fun it is different in a paddock to the open Lake, when you see the Swans in the air you know they are coming right to you getting lower & lower until they are only 20 or 30 yards away. More comfortable in a paddock too, the water was only about a foot deep & plenty of big rushes to sit on, hide in, & great shelter from the wind. The car is left only 100 yards away so you tow the birds through the water to it. I used swan & duck decoys & some of the birds landed right in amongst them. It was a grand sight to see the Swans in the air they showed up plainly against the mountains. After my shooting I drove to Mr McBrides & he is a fine chap & invited me & all my friends to go out anytime & shoot & he offered to take the tractor down to bring the swans back. A Gentleman. Bought more cartridges for tomorrow. What a great sport to see those big birds crash alongside you. It is not cruel there are thousands & thousands of them.
Marsha 7 p.m.

May 14 Sat
I hope you will believe this Swan Story as it is rather fantastic. Gene & I arrived at the Greenpark Paddock at 7 a.m. it was a mild morning & sunny. As we entered the pond we put up a few hundred Swans & some Canadian Geese but we never had a shot until we got into position. We both put decoys out. It was good to be alive on a morning like this & having my son

with me. Once again the dark shapes of the Swans could be seen against the mountains. Closer, closer, 100yds   80yds 60yds   40yds hell let loose   range zero. Bang – Swan Bang – Swan   Bang Bang – Swans more Swans   our stockpile grew high. Around 8 a.m. the wind picked up without warning & soon it was blowing a gale but do you think we packed up, no fear. By Mid-day we had 80 Swans. When we got a chance we would have a cup of Mum's hot soup or some tea & a bite to eat. The way the birds were coming in we could have had a table & chairs & kept the guns beside our plates. Luckily Gene had brought his trailer with him. When we got to 90 we decided we would stop at 100 as the wind was not letting up at times we could hardly stand & that's tough work. We were back at the car by 4 p.m. Goodness knows how many we would have got had we stayed but 100 had more than satisfied us & we could not carry any more on the trailer, as it was we had ½ ton of Swans.

May 27 Fri
Etta had a Birthday today so we had a high tea. Mum did a goose that Gene shot on the weekend it had been kept in the coolroom at the shop. It made a beautiful meal, on that we were all agreed. Gene & I appreciated it most as we had seen it fall. Mum & I gave Etta a roasting tin so now she can cook her own birds.
Marsha 5.30 p.m.

Jun 29 Wed
I am turning some agates on the emery wheel. I am nervy while waiting for this visit to the heart specialist, any little chest pains seem very big.
Sylvia 7.30 p.m.

Jul 22 Fri
I went to Mr Green the Specialist tonight about my pulse I prefer to say pulse instead of heart. He took my pulse for a full minute and it was 117   it is now 93 (11 p.m.)   the Dr is putting me on Digitalis and I have to go back in 2 weeks   he named my complaint (about 1ft long). I don't like it   you know when a fellow dies he loses fear of even Atom bombs, but I think if he is really as brave as all that he should insist on no funeral, nobody likes them anyway, no flowers either, they are beautiful but be truthful who can afford them. All that is wanted is a driver for the hearse & somebody to lift him in. Instead of going to the funeral everybody should go to the house & take along some eats & drinks particularly the drinks a good party has to have the plonk I hereby give 10 gallons of beer.
   – Feb 25 '59   still beating but only 88 (10 p.m.)

Jul 30 Sat
Mrs Chalmer of the Christchurch Lapidary Society called today regarding our exhibition   she has notified the papers & they are very interested in it   Mum made us a lovely afternoon tea she quite outdid herself   Mrs Chalmer complimented her several times on her pikelets
Pulse 93

Aug 6 Sat
Tonight my mother's brother Norman Black called for the evening he is 80 next birthday & does not use glasses to read with. Had a great yarn. He went to the First World War about 1915 was wounded & shellshocked in France & when he returned his wife had left him so Norm got full of booze & has been on it ever since so don't tell me booze is unhealthy. His second wife Christina is 20 years younger than him he fetched 4 bottles of beer & is never objectionable.
Rae 4 p.m.
Pulse 90

Unique Collection of Nature's Beauty in Stone

Aug 8 Mon
I had the second appointment with Mr Green (Hearts Repaired) this afternoon. He said my blood pressure was up slightly, but I could fix that if I would get my weight down. I am to go on a Diet for 1 month & then go back to him. Eat everything as usual but about ¼ less. Hell, the Whitebait is only 3 weeks away. Instead of having 12 Patties I can only have nine, well that will be all right, I will get Mum to make them bigger. Its no good getting old unless you get cunning
Marsha 7 p.m.

Aug 17 Wed
Pulse better, & I am sticking to my diet   I weighed myself today & had lost 6lbs in about 9 days. I want to lose a stone yet.
Marsha 6 p.m.

Sep 9 Fri
M was in the shop this morning. Mum refused to serve her   enough said. She only wanted 2 chops. The time is now 11 p.m. & I will soon be asleep in the car at the river. Would you leave a nice warm bed to catch whitebait? It's hard to explain but those little buggers I just can't resist pitting my wits against theirs. Gene & Etta getting all geared up for their big day they are not allowed flower girls etc or any guests except the witnesses we all have to wait in the church while they get hitched out the back   I wonder how Etta is so agreeable belonging to a church like that hell they won't even let me & Mum in to the service. They have found a flat in Lyttelton a bit further away than I would like however I have no say in these matters. Gene you could save yourself a few bob if you'd stay on at home. Beryl has made a beautiful lace horseshoe for Colin to give to Etta at the wedding breakfast. Mother Moynihan still refusing to come   let's hope it lasts
Sylvia 9 p.m.

Oct 6 Thur
Went down to the Floodgate at Midnight but I was not early enough Cyril was there so at least if I am mad what the hell is he   Gene & Etta back from their honeymoon they went to Lake Wakatipu. Wonder if he got any fishing in   I expect he will be visiting us less often now he is a married man & not living under our roof. We have sold the house & will move before Xmas. Mum very upset I am surprised   the new place is smaller so she won't have so much to clean
Sylvia 7 p.m.
Rae 8 p.m.
S very stroppy & keeps asking me. Hell that's the last thing I'd do, I've got it too good at home. If there's one thing I dislike in a woman it's stroppiness.

Nov 3 Thur
Went to the river at 11.30 p.m. & had a good sleep in the car.
Raining like hell. A Police car came at 4 a.m. & put the spotlight
on me it is a wonder they didn't put me into the mental hospital
Pulse 86
Marsha 6.30 p.m.
(S still stroppy)

Nov 6 Sun
I was on the beach at 6 a.m. & saw the sun rise caught a small
school shark on the first cast. Dolly Randall fished for herring
alongside me & we had a lot of fun she is a grand girl. What a
difference not stroppy at all when things don't go her way. Just
like dear old Mum. At 12.30 p.m. I landed a 28lb groper & was
the hero of the beach there was an earthquake recorded at 1
p.m. perhaps I started it. On the way home at Norwood I saw
a soldier lying on the road & another standing beside him it
gave me quite a turn.
Pulse 94

Nov 7 Mon
In the paper tonight it says the soldier was killed instantly when
struck by a car. Bad luck for him but they were walking on the
wrong side of the road   some day that will be a very serious
offence.

Nov 9 Wed
This book is my property so don't be so bloody nosey. I have a
feeling it is not the first time that you have had a peep in here.
If the year is 1955 these few lines are for you. However if it is
after 1970 read as much as you like & take what advice you can
Dolly 6 p.m.

An
impression
of flowers

Etta is running through a field. To the left and right of her are flowers. Tulips, irises, daphne, beds of lavender, all blooming at once. She does not find this odd. Her feet vibrate the ground. Pollen falls.

There are drawers and drawers in Etta's room. They are crammed with white pillowcases, made a long time ago by her mother Maggie, before she became engaged to Etta's father. Maggie never went to school; she was raised to be a lady. At home she was taught needlepoint, and crochet, and the art of conversation. She began making her trousseau at age thirteen, and by the

time she met Owen she had a dozen hem-stitched supper cloths
with matching napkins (linen); twenty-six embroidered tray
cloths; eighteen nightdresses (smocked, pure cotton); four dozen
fine lace handkerchiefs; twelve pairs of double sheets (lace-edged,
linen); ten crocheted milk-jug and sugar-bowl covers (beaded);
two dozen pairs of cotton bloomers trimmed with lace; and
forty embroidered pillowcases (crewelled).

Fortunately, Owen's house had a lot of space where things
could be tucked away.

Etta does not know how many pillowcases there are in her room,
exactly. She knows there are enough for her to use a different
one every day for a month, and still not have used them all. She
has tried this.

They are all embroidered with flowers. A discreet bunch in
a corner, usually, or slim garlands, or a ring around a butterfly.
More occasionally, an initial. They smell of mothballs.

Etta thinks they are very beautiful. She can't imagine how
her mother had the patience; Maggie is not a patient woman,
on the whole. Etta sleeps with her cheek on the stitching, and
when she wakes there is an impression of flowers on her skin.
In the mirror the patterns are the right way around, the same as
on the pillowcases. This is all as it should be.

They fade in the bath, and by the time the steam has cleared
from the mirror they have gone. Etta can go down to breakfast
then, and nobody will say a thing.

She would not call herself a secretive person, but there are
some things one simply does not discuss. This is not lying,
exactly, but it can lead to a certain awkwardness. Etta reads
a lot. She also creeps out at night, sometimes, and goes for a
walk.

She walks down the sharp drive in bare feet, the house growing
smaller behind her. It is a relief to reach the road. She avoids the
edges, with their dark macrocarpas, choosing instead to walk

right down the middle. It is the safest place.

Mr Hoffmann, their German neighbour, sits at the piano in his front room. Sometimes Etta thinks she can hear him playing, but she's not sure. Sometimes he just sits there staring at it, his hands folded in his lap.

She strolls past the swings, which are always deserted after about five o'clock. She supposes it is the sort of place odd people might go, but she has never seen any. At the other side of the field is the stream. It is the same one that flows through their farm, but it is wider and deeper here. Sometimes it floods. A boy was swept away once, and all his mother could do was watch, but Etta does not remember this very well. She crosses the field. It belongs to nobody. A couple of years ago there was talk of planting it with potatoes for the War Effort, but nothing was done about it.

Etta is not afraid of the stream (she should be). She paddles in it during her walks. There are no sharp stones. Then she goes back through the field, and past the swings, and home. She creeps in the back door, which is never locked, and up the back stairs. She knows to start with her left foot, otherwise the ninth stair creaks. Then she sleeps.

It is almost spring. Already some lambs have been born, and there have been the usual tragedies. Up until now, Etta's father has always given her one of the motherless lambs to look after – she's good with them, like Saint Francis, he says – and it has always been called Topsy. Nobody has mentioned that there is a new Topsy every year, and that it never gets any older. Etta is a sickly child; often ill. She has a blood type which, she is told, is strange and thin. Owen likes to give her the occasional treat. He tells her that she can choose her own lamb this year.

She goes to the sweet-smelling shed and offers a finger to a moist bundle. It stands up, sucking, fluttering its tail.

'I'll call her Dandelion,' says Etta. She inserts the teat of a bottle into the pink space. One of the farm cats curls around her legs, then springs off to a corner, where it has spotted a mouse.

'Not Topsy?' says Owen.

'Dandelion.'

Owen lights his pipe. 'Well, don't go getting too attached, love, will you. She'll have to go out with the rest of them next year, when she's bigger.'

Etta is aware of her clothes tightening. The stitches in her jersey are pulling sideways, opening almond-shaped slits. Behind them is her skin. She will have to mention this soon. They let the air through, especially at night, when she goes walking.

Owen puffs a cloud into the rafters. 'Your mother thinks it would be better if you didn't spend so much time outside.'

Etta stiffens.

'She could do with your help inside, now that Bernadette and Theresa are out so often with their young men. I've got men out here to help me. They're around here most of the time. We both think it would be for the best.'

Etta breathes again. 'All right.'

'There's a good girl,' says Owen, but he doesn't touch her.

Etta tucks Dandelion into a blanket and takes the empty bottle.

'Nip in to the meat safe on your way back, would you Eileen?' says Owen as Etta is going out the door. When Maggie isn't around, he sometimes calls her Eileen, which is her middle name. 'Your mother wants that roast for tonight.'

Etta passes rows of hanging ducks and rabbits, their necks at strange angles. Their eyes are open. There are a few chickens; a turkey. One wild swan. A string of fat white sausages, untouched. Weißwurst, from the Hoffmanns.

'I doubt even the cat would eat those,' said Maggie after Mrs Hoffmann brought them over.

Mrs Hoffmann spoke with a strong accent although she had lived in New Zealand for years. She wore her hair in fat white plaits crossed over the top of her head. From time to time she brought the Moynihans small gifts.

'She means well,' said Owen.

Etta's jersey brushes hanging carcasses, ribs splayed like wings. She prefers these to the smaller ones that are still feathered or furred. There are no eyes. She unhooks the beef for her mother.

'How now, brown cow,' she says. Sister Michael has told her to practise her elocution regularly. Maggie doesn't want her ending up with an accent from hearing so much Irish. Maggie was born in New Zealand, but she ended up with one.

'The leaves on the trees leaped in the breeze,' says Etta. 'Father started for the dark park.'

'Good Lord, girl, you're filthy. Into the bath with you,' says Maggie. She sips her sherry, and does not get up from her chair.

'I brought the roast for tonight.'

'Just leave it on the bench.'

The Moynihans have a deep, deep bath made of Royal Doulton china. It is dark green on the outside, and paler on the inside. A person could drown in there, says Maggie. Owen's Uncle Henry brought it out with him from Ireland. Owen says when they got off the boat they couldn't walk properly for a fortnight. Three months on water will do that to a man, he says. So will three months on whisky, says Maggie, but Owen just smiles at this. He doesn't drink. When Uncle Henry died, Owen got the bath and the house around it.

While the water runs, Etta undresses in front of the mirror. The glass clouds, until all she can see is a luminous after-image of herself; a ghost. The mirror came out on the boat too.

The bathroom smells of Three Flowers face powder, and Lily of the Valley. Bernadette and Theresa, Etta's sisters, have been getting ready for a dance. Bernadette must be feeling better; she's had the flu for the past couple of days, and has stayed in bed. She often gets the flu, and creeps around the place holding a hot water bottle to her stomach. There is a smudge of lipstick on the mirror, as if someone has tried to kiss it. The hand basin is streaked brown. Bernadette and Theresa have been painting their legs; stockings are still scarce.

Just as Etta is stepping into the bath, Maggie pushes open the door.

'You brought the wrong one,' she says. 'I wanted the mutton.'

Etta has one foot in the water and one on the floor. 'I'm sorry.'

'The cat was in there. You let it in, didn't you?'

'I don't know.'

'Idiot. All that meat, ruined.'

'I'm sorry.'

Maggie is raw in the face. Her breath is stale, acidic, the way Bernadette's and Theresa's floating dresses smell after a dance.

'I'll teach you sorry.' Maggie's hands are raised. She has beautiful hands, white as linen. Flowers have spilled from them, pastel petals, the initials of someone cherished. Etta concentrates on these. She thinks: satin stitch, loveknots, lazy-daisy, chain stitch, crewelling. Her mother's hands, her needle fingers. Idiot. Wicked. I'll teach you.

Etta is giddy. She feels as if the bath is moving away from her, like a ship leaving dock, with only half of her in it. She will be pulled in two, starting at her thighs, straight down the middle. She is giddy. She is falling.

'Be good,' says Bernadette, stroking a gloved finger over Etta's cheek. Then she and Theresa float out the door in their butterfly dresses, leaving the scent of flowers behind them.

Etta is good. She has been good all afternoon. She cleaned up the mess in the meat safe; the cat was nowhere to be seen. The cool air was soothing on her bruises. She picked up the feathers from the ducks and the swan. They shone. Precious things, kept safe. She sat on the floor and waited for Maggie to come and let her out. She could be very patient when she had to be, like Saint Elizabeth waiting for a child. There was no sign of the cat for the rest of the day.

'A bit of face powder would cover those for church tomorrow,' said Theresa when she saw the purple marks on Etta's face.

'She is thirteen years old,' said Maggie. 'I will not have my daughter looking like a hussy.'

Etta slipped over when she was getting out of the bath. She's at a clumsy age. She'll be all right.

It is night. Etta has tiptoed over the cold cattle stop. She has wondered how it would feel for a foot, a leg, to slip through those bars, to have to wait there all night. The air is cool on her bruises. The flag on the letterbox is up, and she can hear the stream. She pauses at the Hoffmanns' house. Mr Hoffmann is sitting at the piano; the lid is down. She passes the swings, which are still. She is in the field. A button pops off her blouse and is lost in the grass; she does not stop to find it. She goes to the stream. She stands on the bank and dips one foot into the water. The stream has swollen, she thinks. Under the water her foot is luminous. She steps from the bank, pulls off her skirt. She stands thigh-deep in water. Her legs are made of moon. The water flows between them. She smiles. Another button pops from her blouse, and another. They sink and become stones. She has no need for stones. Her blouse crumbles from her shoulders and dissolves. She inches down into the water, into the bed of the stream. Until she is kneeling. The water creeps up her body, parting to let her in. She glows. She is silver from the neck down.

Maggie cannot sleep. She throws back the hot eiderdown and places a foot on the cool floor. It is a high bed. She can just reach. Her hand hurts. She hit her knuckles too hard. She didn't mean to hit so hard. She wonders how these things happen so quickly. She thinks, I am unravelling. She will try to be more understanding, less irritable, more generous, less impatient. More gracious. More serene. More Christian. She will have a little brandy and fall asleep.

Owen is sailing in the green bath. It is the colour of leaves. It turns the water the colour of leaves. The mirror is foggy. Owen looks through the fog and thinks he can see land. A misty green island. His Uncle Henry plays the violin. One of Owen's feet is placed level on land. He ripples. His other foot is removed from the water and placed on land. He shivers like a view through old glass. People think he is drunk. He is not. For two weeks he cannot walk without falling over. His Uncle Henry plays the violin, and gives him a job cleaning the silver, so he can sit down.

Maggie's glass – finest Waterford – drops from her fingers. Her face sinks into white linen.
'Violin,' says Owen.

Mrs Hoffmann is back in Dresden. Buildings are cracking like bone china. She must run to avoid the falling shards. A library smashes to the ground; pages flutter around her, shuffling themselves to form stories nobody would ever believe. She looks again, and people are cracking. Life-size, bone-china people. A man on a bicycle shatters. A girl with a dog smashes to dust. A woman in a floral dress explodes, showering Mrs Hoffmann with sharp flowers.

Mr Hoffmann watches the shut piano. He thinks, ivory, ivory. Such a strange language.

At the dance, Theresa swallows another vodka.

'That's the end of Bernadette's,' she says. She produces a hip flask from the folds of her dress, and leans back against George Morton's best suit.

'It's lucky you girls have such long frocks,' says George, slipping his hand under a layer of voile. 'What else have you got under here?'

'Dirty bugger,' says Theresa, laughing.

'Where did a good Catholic girl like you learn that sort of language?'

'Some of the men on the farm will teach you anything you want to know. Isn't that right, Bernadette?'

George snorts.

Bernadette arranges the powder blue layers of her dress around her, smoothing them over her knees, folding them along her body like wings.

'She's a quiet one, your sister,' says George. 'You girls still thirsty?' He reaches inside his coat and slides a bottle out.

'Gin!'

'Nothing like a drop of mother's ruin.'

'Shame we haven't got any proper glasses.'

'The first champagne glass,' says Bernadette, 'was formed around Marie Antoinette's bosom.'

'Pity it wasn't round Theresa's,' says George, gripping the neck of the bottle. 'Lean in front of me while I open this, would you love?'

Etta stays in the water until she cannot feel her bruises. She does not think she is cold. She can smell flowers. Under the water she gleams bone-clean. She stands up, slowly. Being careful not to slip. She is so clumsy. She curves her feet over round rocks, gripping with her toes. There is a shadow in the water where she was kneeling. It washed out of her; it spreads in the water. It is possibly red. It is possibly the colour of wine. It is dark.

It is dark. Etta can't find her clothes. Something brushes her thigh, and when she looks down she sees that her skin is still glowing. As if she has become a ghost of herself. A velvety moth has landed on her thigh and is beating its wings, slowly as a heart. Another one is on her foot, fanning her toes with cool breaths. She can feel them settling on her back, her arms. They are clouding around her, making the air whisper. They are covering her shoulders, her chest, her small breasts.

Her mother hates moths, especially the fat ones that beat against the windows at night. When they get inside, she hits them with the back of her shoe.

'They're just night-time butterflies,' says Owen. 'They're a hundred times smaller than yourself.'

'Dirty creatures,' says Maggie.

Etta holds up her fingers. They are covered with moths. She is not afraid (she should be). She feels warm. They do not fly away when she walks.

She crosses the field, passes the swings. She comes to her road. She wonders if anyone will see her. Macrocarpas arch across her. The light is still on in the Hoffmanns' front window, and a few moths are drumming on the glass. Etta stops and looks in from the road. Mr Hoffmann is still sitting at the piano; the lid is down. The moths on his window come and sit in Etta's hair. Mr Hoffmann looks up and frowns. He walks to the window and cups his hands round his eyes. Etta stands in the middle of the road (it is the safest place) and stares back. Mr Hoffmann pushes up the sash and leans out.

'It is Etta.'

'Yes.'

'Hello.'

'Hello.'

'Etta is your full name?'

'Henrietta.'

'I have daughter called Ete. Margarete.'

'Oh, I've never met her. Where does she live?'

'She is in Germany with her man. She is died.'
'I'm sorry.'
'In bomb.'
'I'm so sorry.'
'Yes.'
'Thank you for the sausages.'
'Ah, please, please.'
'They were lovely.'
'You enjoy Weißwurst.'
'Yes.'
'My wife give you more. You come tomorrow.'
'Thank you.'
'Please.'
'Goodnight.'
'Goodnight.'

When she places her foot on the cattle stop, Etta hears a sigh. Or rather, hundreds of tiny sighs. The air around her is moving; the moths are leaving. They arc away from the house, growing smaller. Etta looks at her body. It is not glowing any more.

She creeps up the stairs, starting with her left foot so the ninth stair won't creak. She is very tired, and she buries her face in her pillow. The pillowcase smells of mothballs.

Maggie comes into Etta's room at seven in the morning.
'Up you get, I want to get the washing done before church. And you have to feed that lamb of yours, it's driving me mad with its noise.' She pulls back the blankets. 'Your face is all marked. Looks awful.'

Etta gets up to look in the mirror. 'Oh, that,' she says. 'That's just from the pillowcase.'

Maggie is looking at her sheets. There is a stain on them. Etta doesn't know where it's come from. She didn't think she'd been cut when she fell over in the bathroom, just bruised. She's hardly ever been actually cut; with her strange and thin blood, this is a complication to be avoided. She hopes she won't slip over in surprise. She's so clumsy.

But Maggie just strips the sheets off the bed and bundles them up. Then she sets her jaw, pulls off the pillowcase and tears it down the seams. She folds the pieces into squares and hands them to Etta.

'Here. You'll need these.' She sighs, picks up the sheets, and leaves.

In the bathroom, Bernadette's and Theresa's dresses are hanging to air. They look like shrivelled skins, and are stained under the arms. Etta looks in the mirror. There is an impression of flowers on her cheek, circling a butterfly. At least, she thinks it's a butterfly. She turns the pieces of pillowcase over and over. They are still warm. She wonders what on earth she is supposed to do with them.

It is
wiser to be
modest

During the lunch hours at Sacred Heart College, when the classrooms are locked and the girls must get some fresh air, which is good for the teenage complexion, Bridget listens to the Beautiful Girls. They talk about various members of the Saint Bernard's First Fifteen or the Saint Pat's debating team. They assign identities. A honey, a sweetie, a spunk, a user, a stud. Available, taken. Experienced, romantic, desperate, a good kisser. When the Beautiful Girls roll their white ankle socks down over their feet and rub baby oil into their skin, Bridget sits in the shade.

'I don't tan,' she says, watching the Beautiful Girls compare white wristwatch marks and the slimness of ankles. Her legs grow hair, which she does not remove. God made this hair, she thinks, therefore it is both beautiful and good.

At night she reads the Bible in bed. Her aim is to memorise passages of it, so she will have relevant quotes for every occasion.

Beautiful Girls, she says to herself between her soft flannelette sheets, people who are proud will soon be disgraced. It is wiser to be modest.

She takes to the translucent pages of her Bible with a pen, underlining and circling and starring and ticking, sometimes even writing short comments in the margin, such as 'JODIE D', 'DANCE COMMITTEE' and 'NETBALLERS'.

At school, however, the right quote never occurs to her, and she finds herself saying entirely inappropriate things which at first make the Beautiful Girls say 'Excuse me?' or 'Sorry?' and then just make them laugh. Sometimes they ignore her completely.

Bridget has been praying for stigmata to appear on her body, so that they will know she is holy. She stares at her palms, her white feet, her soft right side, and wills wounds to appear. They do not.

Angela Gill is not a Beautiful Girl, although for the fortnight or so leading up to her arrival at Sacred Heart, she is the New Girl. She has just emigrated to New Zealand from Ireland with her mother and two brothers, and there is much speculation at the school as to what sort of accent she will have, if she will be arrested for protesting against abortion, how pale she will be, if she will have red hair. There is talk that her father and one brother were accidentally shot by IRA terrorists, and that she saw it happen. There is also much discussion about the two remaining brothers, who will be going to Saint Bernard's. Everyone wants to meet her, even the Beautiful Girls, and especially Bridget. She and Angela will start a lunchtime prayer group, Bridget decides. They will be praised for their holiness, and the Beautiful Girls, with their turned-back socks and their oiled legs, will look on in envy. Bridget will take Angela to the Youth Group. They will do the Forty Hour Famine together, ration each other's barley sugars. She will come and stay at the Stiltons' house on weekends, sleep in Bridget's room. They will build a bomb shelter together, fill the shelves with tins of food and bottled water, line the walls with lead.

When Angela Gill is finally introduced to the fifth-form assembly, however, she is not what anyone was expecting. The hall falls silent and everyone simply stares. One girl's pencil case slides to the floor, and the contents – pens, coins, cough drops, a plastic protractor – go spinning across the polished wooden boards. Angela's face and arms, and what can be seen of her legs below her too-long uniform, are covered with raised patches of red. She looks as if she has suffered severe burns. Sister Juliana clears her throat.

'Girls,' she says, 'I'd like to introduce the newest member of our community. I hope you will make her feel welcome.'

Then the music teacher bangs out a hearty few bars on the piano, and the fifth form lurches through the school song while Angela Gill stands at the front of the hall for all three verses, as if she has been accused of something.

They begin to call her Scaly Angela. Not to her face, of course – they are far too well brought-up to do that – but after the novelty of her Irish accent has worn off she is not paid much attention. In fact, most try to look at her as little as possible, including teachers, and including Bridget.

'So the Forty Hour Famine is a very real way of helping,' says Craig. 'We've got permission to stay in the meeting room overnight, so we can get some videos, bring along guitars, games, whatever. Just no food!'

Bridget gets her family to sponsor her.

'I think it's a very noble cause,' says Etta. 'It wouldn't hurt any of us to find out what it feels like.'

'I hardly think going without your Weetbix and chops for a day and a half quite compares,' says Gene, 'but put me down for fifty cents an hour.'

'It's a very real way of helping,' says Bridget.

'Cool,' says Christina. 'You get to help the starving millions, and maybe lose a few pounds yourself.' And she pats Bridget's stomach. 'But hey, no sharing sleeping bags with the other Christians, right?'

Bridget sighs. 'It's not that kind of party, okay? In fact, it's not a party at all.'

'I'll bet it's not,' says Christina, and begins singing. 'Nearer my Craig to thee, nearer to thee,' she croons.

The famine starts well. Craig supplies the Group with regular speeches, which stop Bridget thinking about food.

'I want to tell you more about the Endtimes,' he says. 'About the signs we will witness – the signs we're already witnessing – that signal the beginning of Armageddon. Look around you,' he says, so Bridget scans the room. 'How many new churches have sprung up recently, how many splinter groups of long-established religions? On American television, evangelists are appearing like weeds – new ones every week.'

Bridget nods. So does Rosemary Stokes, who is wearing a very low-cut blouse.

'It can be upsetting,' says Craig, 'to see so many frauds claiming to be working for God. But we in the true church recognise this as a sign that the Endtimes are here, and that salvation is at hand.'

Rosemary leans further forward in her chair, her blouse gaping open. Craig clears his throat.

'There will be an increase in natural disasters – ever wondered why they're called acts of God? Famine and false prophets will abound, people will speak in tongues. A land in the far north will gain international power.'

'Russia!' yells Bridget, leaping to her feet. 'Russia's getting more powerful!'

Craig looks her in the eyes, nods solemn approval. 'That's right, Bridget. The USSR is indeed gaining prominence. Some believe,' and he pauses, 'that it is already the lair of the Antichrist.'

'Gosh, Craig, do you think so?' says Rosemary.

'I wonder,' says Etta, 'how healthy these Youth Group meetings are.'

'Nothing wrong with them,' says Gene. 'And God knows she needs to make a few friends.'

'Who's for a barley sugar? Bridget?'

Bridget shakes her head, not even looking up from her book. Craig offers the box around the rest of the Group. Jeremy Ward takes four, and Craig pretends not to notice.

'Right then, it must be time for another video!' Craig runs his finger down the stack of tapes. '*The Ten Commandments, Lawrence of Arabia, Annie, War Games, West Side Story* – any preferences?'

'*Big 'n' Bouncy*,' says Jeremy Ward.

Craig chooses *Star Wars* from the pile. 'Right then, I'm just going to check on the car. Back in a few minutes.'

'A long time ago in a galaxy far, far away,' begins the video.

Bridget pretends to keep reading, but she sees Rosemary Stokes get up from where she is sprawled on the floor, pull on a jacket and let herself quietly out the door. It's the third time she's done it now. The first time was when Craig had to check that the gate was locked, and the second time was when he thought he heard something outside. This time they're gone for over half an hour. They don't even bother returning separately any more.

'What have I missed?' Rosemary whispers to Bridget, stretching out in front of the TV.

'I've been reading,' says Bridget. She closes her book. 'Just going to the toilet.'

She takes her jacket with her, the pocket heavy with the weight of her purse. There's a service station right around the corner. She buys a king-size bar of chocolate, a bag of potato chips, two packets of Toffee Pops and a can of Fanta. She hides her purchases under her jacket and walks back to the church. At the door of the meeting room she can hear Craig talking quietly over the sound of the video. She continues to the next door, which leads to the church toilets. She locks herself in. She eats.

A severe
blow

1956

Jan 1 Sun
I am keeping my diary locked away as 1955 was mislaid when
we shifted early December. It seems bedside cabinets are not
private. I suspect foul play but will not mention names. Gene
& I had a look at the recently found cave at Kai Koura   the
peep hole was in the roof & it felt deep & dangerous

Jan 15 Sun
At 5 a.m. there were 16 rods on the beach & it was very hot. It
looked as if a storm was coming the sea was flat I couldn't stand

the heat & became afraid of the brewing storm. Went & heard the cricket at Cyrils.
Dolly 6 p.m.
Pulse 89

Feb 26 Sun
Examined crabs today, quite a few reject stones   blank inside   Mum went all weepy on me but wouldn't say why   she does have her spells   dear old Mum I think she worries about my health more than she lets on
Dolly 4 p.m.

Apr 18 Wed
Had a Mr & Mrs Ian Colbourne to see the stones tonight   we saw his collection of clocks last week

Apr 30 Mon
My Brother Ivor rang at 1.10 a.m. to tell me that my Brother Reg was seriously ill in the Sunnyside Mental Hospital (he has been a patient there for about 40 years). I got there just too late. Had a few phone calls today but not many people knew of him. Reg was 2 years 9 months older than me and has always been a pathetic case. He is better off.
Pulse 93

May 19 Sat
The time is 11 p.m. & it is blowing a strong South West wind so I don't know about tomorrow   bugger these Ducks & Swans   when I walked out into the lake today with a Storm threatening I wondered whether I was game or nuts
Dolly 4 p.m.

May 31 Thur
Beryl did some rods for me today she will have more time when Colin starts school. I had to get the emery wheel repaired it has

been playing up & I don't want to spoil my stones. In the evening Mum & I went over to the Palmers & I was coaxed into a game of euchre   we were not playing for love & I won £1-10-0. When I got home at Midnight Mum had just finished varnishing the rods she had come home at 10.30 p.m. & got stuck into the work, she is a hard case. Health Reasonable

Jun 15 Fri
Beryl & Rob announced that Colin is to have a little brother or sister in December. Of course having a baby then will bring problems to the Stilton Family   for instance you can't take a 2 weeks old baby fishing to Kai Koura.

Jun 17 Sun
Mum & I had one visitor to see the collection, he was looking for someone we didn't know but he enjoyed the stones.

Jun 20 Wed
A miserable day. Mum is in Greymouth, fine weather there to meet her. It seems funny that Mum & I should be on different sides of the Island, her in sunshine & us in winter. Caught 7 flounders at Redcliffs. Not feeling so good, a cold in my chest & Mum away. How would you feel. Even the fish I'm catching are flat. Health Rotten

Jun 22 Fri
Worked on an order of rods this evening & Carnelian put the transfers on. I discovered a way of lifting the skins off tins of varnish. Just a wire ring that reaches to the bottom & is soldered to the lid. When the lid is removed the skin comes out too. I wish Mum was back it is going to be a long weekend. Health Fair. Bowels acting up.

Jun 25 Mon
Busy in the shop without Mum. Fred Conway's wife was in she

had only good things to say about Gene again   he is their best
worker. I gave her a couple of extra slices of ham but they do all
right Fred has branches in Dunedin & a new one opening in
Wellington. (He doesn't look any the better for it.) Will meet
Mum's rail car tomorrow at 3.40 p.m. Carnelian has been just
wonderful, looking after me as though I was worth it   I
always try to be fair with them all they are all favourites.
Marsha 9 p.m.

Jul 1 Sun
Gene & Etta excited about Beryl's news. Etta says, nothing to
enter in the diary on her account.

Jul 15 Sun
Every time young Colin comes I have to make sparks for him
on the emery wheel, he demands it. He asked me a mighty
queer question today, we were in the workshop & he said Gran
Gran, who is going to get all this stuff when you die. Hell how
old do I look.
Pulse 92

Jul 19 Thur
We had hail stones as big as marbles & I thought they would
come right through the shop windows. Plenty of lightning &
thunder. After tea we went to Gene & Etta's new place built by
Gene   it is a strong brick home. Etta hates lightning but I'll
bet I hate it more.
Dolly 6 p.m.

Jul 27 Fri
Took the rods into the warehouse & received a cheque from
Mr Drury for £59-4-0. Very sweet. Also fetched home another
76 rods to do at 7/6 each so that is good business. I gave Mum
£5 for her self, she is worth looking after   such a help
to me

Aug 29 Wed
More visitors to see the stones.
Rae 6 p.m.

Sep 27 Thur
At Redcliffs I caught 8 flounders, 3 cod, 5 herrings & a strange
fish which Cyril is taking in to the museum. It barked & Oh
Hell try & pick it up by the tail & in a flash its mouth would be
there instead. Met a fellow from Southland he had some petrified
wood from Mount Somers & it seemed so good it might have
come from another world.
Health Good. Bowels Good.

Oct 1 Mon
Cyril called in to say the museum identified my fish as a catfish.

Nov 10 Sat
Carnelian has gone dancing. Beryl popped in & they think the
baby will be on time but they will not be coming to Kai Koura.
This is a great pity & I told her so however she has Rob now &
doesn't need her old Dad.
Pulse 92

Dec 2 Sun
Gene & I left at 7.15 a.m. for Chertsey. Didn't catch any good
eating fish but Gene got a large Grey Nurse shark with 16 live
young ones in it about 1ft long.

Dec 6 Thur
We are very pleased with the Barometer I bought Mum for last
Xmas it is most interesting & reliable. I don't know how we did
without one.
Pulse 85

Dec 11 Tue
Today I went with Mum to see Beryl & I also saw
    James Clifford
for the first time. Believe me, he is the goods

Dec 18 Tue
Gene has his name in the paper tonight he has passed his 2
exams. <u>Foreman</u> and <u>Supervision</u>   Fred Conway has offered
him a position as Foreman not bad for 25
Well done my lad you will be clever like your Dad
Health Good

Dec 22 Sat
Gave Mum a cheque for £2-10-0 for helping out in the shop
also gave her a fiver for Xmas. She bought a dress with it.

1957

Feb 13 Wed
Mum picked the pears. She got 721 off the one tree. I do enjoy
them preserved & she makes a lovely job of it. Went to see the
1956 model James Clifford who is grand & is really a lovely
baby, none finer.

May 26 Sun
At 9 a.m. my brother Ivor & 2 cobbers arrived to see the stones.
This afternoon a girlfriend of Carnelian's called to ask if she
could bring friends to see them in the evening. The stones are
becoming rather a nuisance.

Jul 15 Mon
Mum fetched me a cup of tea just after 6 a.m.   good old
Mum   this has been going on for nearly 40 years & I like it.
Rain predicted tomorrow you cannot expect cherry blossoms

in July. Health all right my biggest worry is a few missing beats of the heart perhaps 6 a day.

Dolly 8 p.m.

 – Jul 16 '65 Not so many misfires now on new pills. Pulse 85.

Jul 26 Fri

Little Jim is such a good baby but Colin is a hard case & completely bosses Rob, anybody would think Rob was the child & Colin the father. I must admit I would warm his bum for him I do like obedient children & I can honestly say that all mine were very well-behaved. Rob you will regret not being firmer. Win the first battle & you have won the lot. Health Good.

 – Apr 8 '68 I have been proved right Colin is now a stroppy teenager

Sep 11 Wed

Another hell of a day, wet & cold just like winter at its worst with a lie attached: the trees are all in blossom

Oct 29 Tue

Tonight we paid an overdue visit to my brother Ivor's. His hobby is tropical fish.

Marsha 5.45 p.m.

Nov 18 Mon

Gene called for a whisky he was off work today. He did a stupid thing yesterday at home he was up on their roof doing some repairs and he fell off, missed the fence, grabbed a very small tree and finished up at the feet of his neighbour, flat on his back on the concrete path next door. No bones broken but the Doctor has ordered him to bed for a couple of days. Etta saw Gene's dark form flash past the window she was very upset and said how could he climb all that scaffolding at work and then fall off the roof at home. Next time take a ruddy parachute with you Gene. Health all right but this bloody indigestion keeps me awake.

Dec 11 Wed
Oh what a disappointment regarding Gene and Etta going to live in Wellington. We had the whole family nice and handy and now Gene has spoiled it. Mum & I are not fond of travelling so we will not be seeing much more of them I repeat it is a severe blow.

1958

This diary was given to me by Gene & Etta for Xmas & I told them that some day they should have it back. We are many miles apart now that you have left the South Island so I will record all the main events of my life and also little events which will be of interest

Feb 7 Fri
My Birthday. Born 1900 in grocer shop corner Durham St & Bath St Christchurch. Well I am another year older but it took twelve months to happen. Another two years to the pension. The family came round in the evening, except Etta & Gene. They telephoned from Wellington.

Mar 16 Sun
A Day of Worms. Cyril & I went to Redcliffs & dug a lot of sea worms for bait. Then I went out to Moynihans' farm   Etta's father was ploughing & I followed picking up the worms. Had a whisky with them for St Patricks Day I'll take the drink but leave the prayers. Looked like Mother Moynihan had been celebrating for a while on her own   it still hadn't sweetened her up no wonder Owen reads so much. Health Good. Bowels V Good.

Mar 17 Mon
A Day of Work. Finished off the last of the rods. Mr Drury wants to buy my binding machine (my own design) but I'm not even considering his first offer either he thinks I'm an idiot or he's meaner than I thought. He is a queer chap his wife comes into the shop now & then & always buys the cheapest cuts I'll bet he doesn't give her much to come & go on.
Marsha 5 p.m.

Mar 30 Sun
Rain & wind all over NZ   86 miles per hour wind in the NI   snow on Arthurs & Lewis Pass. This will bugger up my fishing the Heathcote is bank to bank. Gene the way it is blowing now you would get all the shooting you wanted. Remember the swans in McBride's paddock, 100 by 4 p.m.
Palm Sunday, have a coconut.

Apr 6 Sun
Mum's birthday I brought her a cup of tea in bed. The family (except Gene & Etta) came round Mum cooked a goose shot by me. Carnelian gave her a Nylon Petticoat & she got a beautiful Maiden Hair Fern in a pot from Beryl & Rob. Young Colin gave her a teatowel & Etta & Gene sent a flash manicure set from Wellington. I gave her a new Eiderdown & took her to Tingeys on Friday to select wallpaper for our bedroom & ordered the tradesman to do it so I reckon she had a pretty good innings.

May 3 Sat
Opening of the duck shooting & I stayed home getting old   no   getting sense. It's different now, there are more regulations than hairs on a cat's back.
Dolly 3.30 p.m.

May 26 Mon
A Black Day. Was not well at all & I think it was my Chest.

Went home at lunchtime & Mum looked after the shop. I wouldn't like very many days like today it is too upsetting & you think a lot of strange things. Went to Beryl's tonight Mum had a good sleep there in the arm chair she can never stay awake. Pulse 95

Jun 11 Wed
What could be sweeter than to have a Blonde
A fishing rod and bait and a nice little pond
    – Original
Health Good.

Jun 12 Thur
The Blonde I referred to on the previous page
Is to bait up my hooks, think of my age
Health Good.

Jun 25 Wed
Beryl & Rob left the boys with us while they went to the Pictures. Jim went up to the barometer & gave it a couple of taps & said Oh Jesus. At least Etta wasn't there but Mum was none too pleased. Wonder where he learnt that. No news from Wellington of any grandchildren on the way. Health Good.

Jun 30 Mon
Went to Beryl's for dinner & all Jim would say was bugger bugger. Beryl not pleased with me. Hope all is well with you Gene it's been half a year now.

Jul 4 Fri
Mr Drury rang at 7.30 p.m. & blasted me for putting coloured binding on the rods. I thought they looked good but he is sending them back to be altered. He was very bloody annoyed & I am too. He can shove his rods. I'll make him pay one way or another he still wants to get his hands on my binding machine

& do the rods using girl labour. I think my price has just gone up another £50 yes £50 per insult. Health Fair.

Jul 14 Mon
I didn't feel much good this afternoon I had a very fast pulse (95). I think the spot welder makes one nervous, on edge all the time. Carnelian always says you won't die till its your turn well that's no bloody comfort is it.

Aug 4 Mon
We had a terrible night with the flu Carnelian Mum & I coughing in unison. Mum went grocery shopping today so she must be the toughest of the 3 of us. Beryl looked after the shop & seemed to cope all right no thanks to Rob. They want to take over the business when I retire well I don't know about that.

Nov 13 Thur
Had a letter from Etta she writes every week a lot more often than Gene does. They are keen for us to spend Xmas in Wellington but I hate being far away from home, don't like travelling   to me it is always a risk. Health Fair.

Nov 22 Sat
Up at 4 a.m. Cyril & I went down the Cam in Cyril's boat but the bloody whitebait had stopped running. Home at dinner time as we had to go to Dawn McKinnons wedding (Baptists). Everybody came away with Christ in their Hearts & no booze in their stomachs.

Nov 30 Sun
Beryl & family went to Hororata where Jim while sitting in the river found his first piece of agate with crystals   well done Jim

Dec 25 Thur
Xmas Day & I can't see the sea, I'm really lost. Cyril & Vera

came over for a spot this morning & I had a cup of tea at Beryl's in the afternoon. How bloody exciting. No Gene no Carnelian & Mum's feeling crook. Beryl & Rob came for the evening. They gave us a clock. Gene & Etta rang from Wellington. Gene sounded homesick.

1959

Jan 7 Wed
When I'm gone what advantages will I have not many   but   I won't be afraid of Lightning my greatest fear I would rather face a maniac with a gun   I won't mind the storms the floods the heat the cold the Atom Bomb   the fishes in the sea will surely declare it a holiday when I pass on

Jan 8 Thur
This will surprise you but I never go past the Sydenham Cemetery without crossing fingers on both hands   one for my Fathers memory and the other for my Mothers. I have done this for years.

Jan 9 Fri
If we had gone to Kai Koura this Xmas it would have been the 40th year but I have lost the urge. The fishing is not as good & the hills are steeper & the rocks harder. And I hate the boats up there & Cyril always takes a boat & I sit on the shore & wonder if it is safe. They tell me there were lots of spear fishermen underwater there this year   that's not fishing
Dolly 8 p.m.

Mar 27 Fri
Up at 1 a.m. this morning not for the fish but for Mum she had a terrible pain in her chest. I didn't know what to think for a while but I'm all right again now.
Pulse 93

May 14 Thur
Had a letter from Etta, Gene got his limit of ducks on opening day & a pheasant & a brace of quail on Sunday.

May 31 Sun
Mucked about today I made 2 keys up one for Carnelian's 21st birthday & the other one I will keep for a pattern. I have made them out of Stainless Steel wire & on each one I have brazed a small cup hook. The idea is (unlike the usual 21st key which is useless) you can hang these up on the wall & keys can be kept thereon, making the 21st key a useful article. I will make enquiries re price & may sell some. A good standby if the rod orders run out.

Jul 1 Wed
Tomorrow Gene & Etta fly to Christchurch. I wonder how they feel, because a plane with 23 people on board has gone missing near Auckland believed crashed in the mountains. Very unsettling. Colin got the strap at school today I reckon his teacher has the right idea

Jul 2 Thur
The plane lost yesterday has been discovered all 23 on board were killed instantly & burned. Mum & I met Gene & Etta at the Airport at 5.15 p.m. Gene fetched some photos of his Wellington job down with him & they show just how good he is as a Forman. Health V Good.
Marsha 6 p.m.

Jul 4 Sat
The big night Carnelian's 21st party. 130 guests were there & she got about £230 worth of presents. We had 22½ galls of beer, 4 doz bottles ale, 12½ bottles of sherry, 2 whisky 2 brandy 2 gin 2½ galls punch as well as soft drinks. Alma, Mum's sister, who made the cake, said it weighed at least 43lbs that is 13lbs short of

½ Cwt. Jimmy amused us all he had a go at rolling one of my cigarettes & he made us laugh when he did the licking part. He doesn't miss a thing, he is sharp like his Grandad. He used 2 swear words tonight   Shitpot & Bugger   he also had a glass of beer he's tough

Jul 12 Sun
We took Gene to the airport. Etta is staying on for a few days with her folks. Gene presented us with a Pheasant he shot, he had it mounted & its wonderful. Gene it will be yours someday. He flew out at 3.40 p.m. Carnelian had a little cry Mum had a big cry.

Jul 18 Sat
Etta telephoned from her parents she is not allowed to see us it is beyond me.
Dolly 4 p.m.
Marsha 7 p.m.

Aug 13 Thur
No Beryl, she rang, had Colin to the Doctor, he will live. In the meantime I have no staff.

Sep 5 Sat
Carnelian had Neville round for tea   Carnelian & her fancy chipped potatoes, the house full of stinking smells & blue smoke. I told Neville that when I see him now I associate him with crook smells. Carnelian not pleased. I heard Colin got a hiding from his Father. Ha Bloody Ha.

Sep 22 Tue
Mum finishing a cardigan for me. Gene out Deer Stalking in the Taupo district.
Later – Mum has finished my cardigan it is lovely. I have it on. Heard tonight Gene wounded a pig & his mate got a Deer.

Oct 3 Sat
Bad luck in my garden today I put so much chicken manure on my main row of raspberries that I killed them

Oct 25 Sun
How does a champion feel to run second. I went out to the Waimak at Midnight to get one particular whitebait spot & Rob was to bring the family out this morning. Alas, champion that I was to get there before 1 a.m., I only came second. Blast the enemy. I came straight home & slept in bed instead. Drove over a hare on the way. Neville & Carnelian were apparently asleep on the couch (Oh Dear) & Mum got up & let me in.

Nov 20 Fri
Out this morning at 5 a.m. but these bloody whitebait don't run to suit me, only themselves. I got 2ozs & was in the shop by 9 a.m. Beryl & Jim came for tea Beryl talked about her & Rob taking over the shop. I am considering it but Rob will have to get a bit of sense. Jim aged not quite 3 called me an awkward mongrel

Dec 6 Sun
Carnelian Violet, who at the moment has the place smelling like a Chinese shit house with whatever she is cooking in special oil, is expecting <u>Arnold</u> over for tea. When he was introduced to Beryl & Rob I remarked take a good look its his third visit here. Afterwards Carnelian was very sour about it I got a shock she would be so sour

Dec 7 Mon
I have not said much to Carnelian today

Dec 19 Sat
Went to Beryl's for a Xmas Party tonight Carnelian dressed as Father Xmas & Jimmy didn't know her. We gave him a gun

with caps for Xmas & it was really to his liking, bang, bang all night. We ate the skate caught by me at Birdlings Flat & it was as good a fish as I have ever eaten.

Expenses for Carnelian's 21st:	£-s-d
Ale 22½ galls	12-10-0
Parking	10-0
Poultry	5-0-9
Hire of glasses	1-6-6
Hall	8-8-0
Orchestra	11-10-0
Caterer	38-5-0
Spirits	19-11-6
Invitations	2-10-0
Potato Chips	1-2-6
Chocolates	1-5-0
Cigs	1-0-0
	102-19-3

A short
survival
guide

'I've decided to write a book,' says Gene one morning. 'Now that both the girls are away, and I'm not working, I've decided to do something productive with my time.' He folds the newspaper and pushes his chair away from the table.

Etta looks up from her toast. 'A book? What sort of book?'

Gene converts Christina's room into a study. He brings her old desk in from the garage and dusts it, and he shifts her dressing table out. The hinged mirror wobbles as he carries it, so he presses his cheek against it to hold it steady. He's puffing by the time he reaches the garage. His breath creates clouds on the mirror.

When Christina comes home at Easter she has to sleep in Bridget's room.

'What have you done with my dressing table?' she says. 'And my toys? Where's Blue Doggie?'

Gene laughs. 'How old are you?'

Christina ignores him.

'Now, then,' says Etta. 'All your things are just out in the garage, safely packed away. Dad needed the room. He's writing a book.'

'Why can't he use Bridget's room? Since she's off flatting with the Antonychrist.'

'Well we don't know how long that'll last,' whispers Etta. 'Antony is a very unusual boy.'

'I can't believe you let her move in with him. There was such a huge stink when I wanted to go out with Donald Musgrove, just because he had a motorbike, and now Bridget's shacked up with the Prince of Darkness himself.'

'They're just flatting together. Aren't they, Gene.'

'Don't you believe it,' says Christina.

'He wears makeup,' says Gene. 'I don't think he likes girls.'

Etta touches Christina on the arm. 'It's still your home, love. You know there's always a bed here for you.'

'Yeah. In the garage,' says Christina. 'What sort of book?'

When Etta and Gene are out she creeps into her old room.

It smells of new paint; Gene has been redecorating. The walls are a mossy green, which actually isn't too bad, but it looks like he only had the patience to do one coat. The sun is streaming in, and Christina can make out the old dark pattern of her wallpaper through the green.

She opens the wardrobe and finds it filled with other people's clothes: a couple of Gene's old suits that are too good to give away, Etta's best outfits, still like new and covered in filmy plastic which is printed with suffocation warnings. There are a few things she doesn't recognise at all.

She is surprised to see that Gene has positioned the desk under the window. He discouraged her from doing this right through school. It provides too many opportunities for distraction, he said. He had learnt that at night school in the fifties, in his Construction Management classes. When Christina left for med school Gene's one piece of advice was 'Don't put your desk by a window'. Different subject to what I studied, he said, but many of the principles are the same. He's got no idea, Christina said to Etta, and Etta said no, probably not, but he'd not been able to go to university, and she should count herself lucky.

She leafs through the notes that are sitting on the desk, feeling quite justified in doing so; it is her desk, after all. There are biro sketches of shelters made of branches and leaves, and different methods of building a fire, and numerous lists.

To my father, for all his useful advice on
Dedicated to Clifford Stilton, who showed me
This book is dedicated to my late father, in thanks for his wise
To Cliff (1900-1985), without whose advice I would never
For Dad.

Christina scans a neat table showing The Effects of Water Loss on the Body. *Thirst,* it says in the first column. *Vague discomfort. Economy of movement.* It seems accurate; it corresponds with what she has had to learn by heart. *Flushed skin. Impatience. Increased pulse rate.* She moves to the second column. *Dizziness,* she reads, nodding. *Tingling limbs. Blue skin. Slurred speech.* She wonders how he knows this; he left school at fifteen. He must have looked it up somewhere. He could have just asked her. *Cloudy vision. Shrunken skin. Numb skin.*

She is tempted to add some comments of her own – *never administer hot drinks to victims of exposure* or *always remember to remove a tourniquet* – but she places the pages back in their original position and when she leaves the room it is as if she has never been there at all.

That night she tells Gene he should invest in a computer.

'You can't seriously be intending to write the thing out longhand,' she says. 'I know a guy who'd give you a good deal. Possibly a spreadsheet package.'

Gene nods and says yes indeed, he'll certainly think about that.

'It was very thoughtful of her,' he says to Etta. And he is pleased Christina is interested in his project, but it would be cheating, he decides, to write a survival guide using a computer. He would feel like one of those high-tech anglers with their electronic fish-finders, or a hunter who uses radar equipment to find a stag.

'By the way, Dad,' says Christina, 'why did you put the desk under the window?' And Gene clears his throat and says there is a very good reason for that, a *very* good reason. It is so he can look out at the bush and visualise what he would do if he were missing in it.

✧

Gene shuffles his notes, trying to get them into some sort of order. He can't decide whether River Crossing should come before or after Making a Fire, and whether he should include anything on medicinal plants at all. *Poisonous Plants,* he writes at the top of a page, and underlines it in red. Then he doodles a skull and crossbones in the margin. And another underneath his heading. He looks at his moss-green walls, then out the window at the hills, then back at the walls. He's done a pretty good paint job, if he does say so himself. Not too bad at all. Maybe he'll do his chair as well; there should be enough paint left.

There are twenty-five bricks per row in the fence across the street, and twelve rows, which makes a total of 300 bricks. Gene has always been good at maths. The Fitzroy family back out of their drive at 11.25 a.m., return home three minutes later, and drive off again at 11.32 a.m. Peter Fitzroy drives with one hand, and runs the other through his thinning hair. Etta has said she will divorce Gene if he goes bald. Ten cars pass, of which three are white, two red, one brown, three blue and one green. This includes the Fitzroys' car (blue), which is counted once only. Don Crandell takes seventeen minutes to mow his front lawn, and does not do the strip by the footpath in front of his house.

Perhaps, Gene thinks, it wouldn't be such a bad idea to ask Christina about that computer deal. One has to move with the times. He thinks back to his days as an apprentice, when he did all his calculations on paper. Everyone did. He covered reams with figures determining the correct angle for a mitred corner, or the amount of cladding needed for a three-bedroomed bungalow. But now even he uses a calculator, and it does have a Space Invaders game on it.

✧

'Best thing I ever bought,' he says, a number of times. 'The typing still needs a bit of practice, but you can't fight technology.' Every night he places the dust cover over his computer, and every morning he removes it again, and begins work.

Bridget won't go near the thing when she visits. She says computers emit harmful levels of radiation, and are probably evil. Etta says she hopes this doesn't mean Bridget is going odd again, and Gene says he's sure she's all right, if she's not interested she's not interested. Because now that he's become accustomed to using the computer, he doesn't want anyone else touching it.

There are many sources of nutrition in the New Zealand wilderness, and there is no need to fear starvation should you find yourself lost. Statistically speaking, you have a much greater chance of being killed by a wild animal such as a boar or a stag than you do of starving; the only fine print is that YOU MUST ARM YOURSELF

WITH KNOWLEDGE. This means learning in advance and by heart the skills that may save your life.

Most of us think of meat when we think of food, and New Zealand is certainly one of the best places to be stranded. Indeed, when we consider that, in a survival situation, protected or endangered species become fair game, I am sure many sportsmen would choose to go missing for a few days! But even if you have never hunted before, animals should always be your first avenue of nutrition. And who knows, you may wish to pursue this hobby once you are safely back in the civilised world.

You may be unable to take advantage of the surrounding wildlife, however, if you are suffering from exhaustion or injury. If this is the case, you must not despair; in the wilderness such an emotion can be far worse an enemy than any physical impairment. While many hunters may scorn a vegetarian diet in their day to day life, plants do represent a viable food source when survival is at stake.

The following list, with accompanying photographs, is a selection of some of the edible plants in the New Zealand bush. They have been chosen on the grounds of availability, ease of gathering and preparation, and nutritional value.

Pieces of information begin to materialise in Gene's head; things he has read over the years, or learned from experience, or been told by Clifford: that pollen has a very high energy value; that the purple-black berries of the tutu plant cause paralysis if eaten; that the nectar of flax may be sucked from the flowers. And then there is other information he cannot remember learning, but seems always to have known: that bracken roots can be as thick as a man's finger; that the heart-shaped leaves of the kawakawa will reduce inflammation if applied to the skin; that in some parts of the country the weather can change without warning.

While I would consider it wise to adhere to the above list, there are of course other possibilities I have not included because of their scarcity, their low nutritional value, or the difficulty involved in either obtaining or preparing them. If you are unsure about the edibility of any plant, the following test should be performed.

'Put this on your tongue,' said Clifford, picking a bright orange berry from a tree and handing it to Gene. 'Hold it there until I tell you.'

They continued along the steep track, Gene kicking up leaves with the toes of his blunt boots.

After a couple of minutes, his tongue started to tingle. He rolled the berry around inside his mouth and kept walking, trying to step exactly where Clifford did. The tingling intensified; it felt like a spot of very potent sherbet was fizzing on his tongue. Then it started burning.

'Dad,' he said around the berry, but it came out like, 'Thath.'

'Well? Anything yet?' said Clifford.

Gene nodded vigorously.

'Here.' Clifford held out his hand and Gene spat into it, then grabbed his water canteen and gulped down several mouthfuls.

'Karaka berries,' said Clifford. 'The burning tells you it's poisonous.'

There are several plants in the New Zealand bush that should never be ingested.

'Ssh!' said Clifford, and held up his hand. Gene heard movements in the bush ahead. He stood very still, his palm cupped around the butt of his rifle. Then, slowly, Clifford crouched down, and motioned for Gene to do the same. A few yards ahead of them, a fully grown wild boar emerged from the cover of the bush. It snuffled around in the leaves, unaware that it was being watched, and that Clifford was edging forward, easing his rifle into line with its heart.

If you have a rifle with you, it can be used to
a) alert help
b) light a fire
c) obtain food.
When attempting to shoot any sort of animal, always aim at a vital
spot. The chest or the shoulder are the best targets with larger game.

A frond tickled Gene's cheek, but he didn't dare brush it away.
In front of him, Clifford had stopped. Gene could smell the
damp forest floor, gun oil, wool, his own sweat. He glanced
into the dark centre of the fern, where the new fronds lay curled
like small, hairy fists. Then he looked back at the boar.

Conserve ammunition as much as possible. Get as close as you can
to your target before firing; do not be tempted to shoot too soon
from too far away. Remain calm. Excitement or nerves will cause
the barrel to tremble and the shots will probably be wild. Fire from
a prone position if at all possible; otherwise kneel or sit rather than
stand. If one is available, use a rock or a log to steady the rifle.

Gene was just thinking how yellow the tusks were, not polished
and white like the ones on Clifford's mounted trophies, and
then there was a single shot, and the pig was heaving and
screaming, and then it fell.

'Stay!' hissed Clifford as Gene leapt to his feet and began
running towards the boar.

Reload immediately, even if the animal appears to be dead. Keep
your eye on it at all times.

They hadn't brought the whole carcass back with them; it was
far too heavy to carry. Clifford hacked off the head instead, and
had it mounted. He hung it in the shop, above the bacon slicer,
and sometimes hooked his apron over its tusks.

❖

Gene expects the finished book will sell extremely well. He imagines himself posing for his cover photograph: a bush backdrop, perhaps, and a well-polished rifle over his shoulder. A khaki jacket with lots of zips and pockets, a hat with sheepskin earflaps.

'Did you know,' he says to Etta that night as they are getting into bed, 'that should you have no alternative but to cross a glacial stream, it is best to wait until morning?'

'Ah,' says Etta. 'The book.'

'Mountain streams are at their highest during the day, and begin to fall around the middle of the night. *And,*' he says, before Etta can comment, 'you should never attempt a crossing if boulders can be heard bumping along the bottom.'

'I see,' says Etta. 'Well well.' And she closes her eyes.

'You should also avoid looking at the water, as the movement upsets a person's equilibrium.'

'Mmhmm.'

'Never grasp at rocks.'

Etta does not answer, and eventually Gene falls asleep too. He dreams about the time he was hunting rabbits on a farm, and touched an electric fence. And just the way it happened then, he is thrown backwards with the force of the shock, and the only sound he can distinguish is the warbling of the magpies.

Remember, he types in bold the next morning, *if you find yourself on private land, fences may be electrified.*

Emergencies

Bridget is beginning to dread Wednesday mornings. Every week, from nine till midday, she is required to descend to the ground floor of the biology building, which in fact is not on the ground but below it. Very little natural light reaches the lab, and under the fluorescent bars it has an over-exposed feel which remains with Bridget for the rest of the day.

Through the small, high windows, only the feet of those walking to and from lectures are visible. It is amazing, Bridget thinks, how many people do not look after their footwear. More often than not the shoes are scuffed, dirty, the laces frayed and trailing, the toes permanently curled. Even the quality pumps, the modest court shoes – belonging, Bridget suspects, to the Beautiful Girls – show signs of neglect when observed without the distractions of a body, a face, sleek gold earrings, half-moon nails. The heels are worn down at odd angles, indicating incorrect posture, a lazy gait. This pleases Bridget.

She gasses drosophila flies and examines their scaly anatomies under a microscope, measures the fins on long-dead, icy fish, sketches the division of cells. In the interests of science she draws her own blood, which is shown to be neither strange nor thin, but which, the tutor assures her, is common; plentiful in an emergency.

For most of the exercises they have to work in pairs. There is little choice involved; on the first day the tutor simply told everyone to find a partner. When the class continued to sit staring at her she sighed and said that they weren't at school any more, and they had to start doing things for themselves, otherwise how did they think they would ever survive in the real world, where decisions had to be reached all the time, and deadlines met, and sacrifices made.

Bridget's partner is Raymond, who is majoring in biology. Every Wednesday morning as she walks to university she complains about him to Antony.

'He's grotesque,' she says as they cross the Kelburn viaduct. 'Polyester jumpers, white sneakers. Shiny grey trousers.'

'Christian?'

'More than likely.'

In the lab the air smells of chloroform. The tutor looks as if she never sees the sun; her long white fingers and her colourless hair remind Bridget of plants grown in the dark. There is always an irked expression on her face as the students file out. Ominous chains dangle from the ceiling; when pulled, they are said to dowse negligent students in water. Beside them are signs: *For use in emergency only.* Bridget wonders if acute boredom counts. When she looks at the clock and there are still two hours to go, she imagines dreadful accidents happening to Raymond and the other students she dislikes: an eye splashed with acid, a Bunsen burner catching a greasy strand of hair.

'You mustn't be so critical,' Etta says when Bridget tells her about her classes. 'They might think you look a bit odd too, you know.'

Bridget does look odd; she's cultivating it. She's grown her nails and her hair; she colours her lips dark berry. On a leather string around her neck she wears a crucifix that belonged to Etta's father, part of his old rosary beads. Etta doesn't mind her borrowing it, as long as she's careful. In fact, Etta says she's delighted that the faith still has a place in Bridget's life. She thought that had all gone out the window.

Raymond smiles at Bridget when she slides on to her stool.

'Hearts!' he says, flicking open his text book.

Bridget imagines a nasty slip with the scalpel; Raymond's hand accidentally gashed.

'We're dissecting sheep hearts today. It's going to be in the exam, I know it.' Raymond bounds up to the front desk and returns with the plump, glistening organ.

'One between two, I'm afraid,' he says. 'Bridget, will you share my heart?'

This is definitely an emergency. Bridget feels her hand begin to reach for the water chain; already she can picture Raymond standing there drenched, his white sneakers squelching, the wet heart drooping through his fingers.

'Excuse me,' she says, her hand over her mouth. 'I don't feel very well.' And she runs out of the lab and up the stairs to daylight.

✧

At the party Bridget moves from room to room, talking to people she does not know. Antony does not join in their conversations, but Bridget is conscious of him watching her, keeping her in his sight. She drinks gin from a black hip flask which many admire.

'It belongs to my father,' she says to one boy, who tells her he is called Philip, and who presses his hand, cold from a clutched beer can, into hers. 'He takes it with him when he goes hunting.'

She doubts Gene will notice it missing from his things in the garage; it is summer, after all, and the season doesn't open until May.

The lamps in the room have been covered with red paper, and in the altered light faces appear pale.

'Deer, geese, pheasant, wild pigs. Sometimes swans,' Bridget is saying. 'He's even had some of them mounted.'

'Hey,' says Antony, touching Bridget on the shoulder. 'Have you got a cigarette for me?'

'Philip, Antony, Antony, Philip,' says Bridget. 'Here you go.'

'It's some accessory.' Philip rubs his hand over the taut leather flask, balancing it on his open palm as if assessing its value.

'She brings it with her whenever we go out,' says Antony.

Philip raises it to his lips and tilts his head quickly back and forth. 'Exquisite,' he says, looking at Bridget.

'So you flat here with Sarah?' says Antony.

'Right. She's in the kitchen, if you're looking for her.' Philip takes another sip of Bridget's gin and slowly twists the silver lid back on the flask. 'Have you seen the gravestone in the garden?' he says, already taking her hand.

'Yeah, Sarah told me –' begins Antony.

'It was here when we moved in. Come on.' Philip leads Bridget towards the back door, weaving between pale figures balancing drinks and cigarettes. Antony sits down on the arm of an occupied chair and watches them leave.

✧

'Henrietta Louise Grayson,' reads Bridget, '1848 to 1885. Henrietta's my mother's name.'

'Sarah swears she's seen her moving through the garden,' says Philip. 'Henrietta I mean, not your mother.'

'She's a bit weird, isn't she?'

'Sarah's okay. Smokes too much. She wants to try growing it out here.'

Bridget frowns. 'Oh,' she says.

'She's got a spot all picked out. Over there, where the ground dips down. The neighbours can't see it.' Philip gestures with one hand to the far dark corner of the garden, taking Bridget's arm at the same time. They walk through the long, dry grass together then, away from the noise of the party and the house with its red-lit windows, and away from Henrietta's stone. The tall stems flatten in their wake, indicating their path. Bridget is glad of this; she can find her way back, should she need to. The house recedes.

'So is she your girlfriend?' The boy sitting in the chair looks up at Antony through a cloud of smoke.

'Bridget? No, we're both from Lower Hutt.'

The boy seems to find this hilarious, and doubles over in the chair, his head almost between his knees, laughing. On a small television wedged against the opposite wall music videos are playing. Four young men dressed in black slouch around a bright white background, avoiding the camera.

'Listen to the girl, as she takes on half the world, moving up and so alive, in her honey dripping, beehive . . .'

'We're flatting in town now, though,' says Antony. 'Together.'

The boy wipes his fingers under his eyes, smearing black eyeliner.

'Lower Hutt, pride of the south of the North,' he says. 'So where's your Ford Escort parked, mate?' He screams with laughter again.

Bridget shifts under Philip's weight. There is a tree root, or possibly a stone digging into her back, but she decides it would be rude to interrupt. She shifts once more, and notices when she does so that Philip grunts more loudly, so she does it again, and keeps doing it until he emits a strangled 'Oh God', and collapses on top of her. Now the stone or whatever it is really hurts; Bridget imagines a permanent hollow in her back. She is just about to say something – although she's not sure what – when Philip rolls off her, tugging at his trousers. She brushes the ground with her hand until her fingers close over a stone. She slips it into her pocket.

'Great party,' says Antony, 'but I have to get up early tomorrow. Got my last exam on Monday.'

The boy in the chair says, 'Ah,' and continues to stare at the television. The tiny figures stumble along a tiny railway line.

'Sometimes, I walk sideways, to avoid you, even though I love you,' the singer is pouting.

Antony takes his jacket from the dark heap in someone's bedroom – Philip's, he suspects. He observes the stereo dominating one wall, the pyramid of beer cans, the vast record collection. The bed – a rumpled double – he avoids. He doesn't bother to retrieve his beers from the kitchen, although he's hardly touched them.

Bridget also leaves alone. Philip has passed out on the couch, so she can't ask him where she put her coat. Antony has gone; everyone has gone. She wanders around the silent flat for a while, trying to find the door, which she cannot remember coming through, and then, when she has found her way to the street, heads towards where she thinks her own flat is. She smells rocks and moss, sharp berries, a tar-sealed path cold from the moon. She grasps the handrail at the side of the path and pulls herself up the incline. It cuts right through the bush; tree roots have cracked and warped the tar sealing. There is no lighting. Every so often the handrail bends back under her weight and she leans towards the steep, leafy drop. When she falls, it comes as no surprise. She sees the handrail giving way, uprooting itself, her knuckles sharp against the dark bush. She sees her feet moving from under her, first one, then the other. She sees her bag landing in a patch of ferns and the hip flask spilling out, and she feels the air rushing past her, forcing itself out of her.

People ask for her good arm every so often and pump blood pressure cuffs around it. She thinks it might explode, and laughs to herself at the image of shredded muscle slapping against the thin cubicle curtains, fingers plopping on to the lino. Lights are shone in her eyes. Blank people wander corridors, wait for news. White uniforms swish curtains open, shut, open, and ask her what the date is, who the Prime Minister is. Don't they know, Bridget whispers to Gene and Etta, aren't they in charge? Don't cut my hair, she insists as a doctor approaches. You are not cutting my hair. This took ten years to grow and you are not cutting it.

It is light outside by the time they put the cast on her arm.

At home – at her parents' home – Bridget is helped into the deep bath. There is a lot of blood; it turns the water to rust.

'Bridget, Bridget,' says Etta. 'It's just like having a baby in the house again.'

Bridget whimpers as she feels her mother's skin, and the water trickling over her blackberry scratches. She sits very still in the bath, her face as pale and strange as a daylight moon.

They go to see the place a few days later, when Bridget is feeling steadier on her feet. It is steeper and sharper than she told Gene and Etta, than she herself remembers. The crushed ferns and blackberry and onion weed still betray the shape of her falling.

'Thank God you finished your exams,' says Gene.

'Stay with us for a while, at home,' says Etta. 'We'll soon have you feeling as good as new.'

So Bridget spends the summer at home, being looked after, watching the firebreaks snaking up the hills.

'You can't see those from the flat,' she tells Gene.

Etta washes her hair for her every second day, and brushes it, and plaits it at night. She makes macaroni cheese sprinkled with breadcrumbs, and stuffed pumpkin, and cheese and Vegemite sandwiches, all of which Bridget eats.

At the start of the academic year, she returns to her flat. The cast has come off and her arm feels like it's floating. She has performed a range of stretches to the satisfaction of two doctors and a physiotherapist. When they clip her x-ray to the illumin- ated panel they seem pleased. The physiotherapist – who believes in involving the client as much as possible in the rehabilitation – points to the ghost bone and says, 'Look, you can see where it's healed.'

Serious
historical
problems

Etta Stilton has always been big on saints. In times of crisis she calls on them, automatically. Some people even call her one, though not to her face. When she loses things – car keys, borrowed books, a child at the supermarket – she prays to Saint Anthony. When she can't get her cheque book to balance, she prays to Saint Matthew. She frequently asks Saint Joseph to stop her husband from falling off scaffolding. Gene is tolerant of this.

She prayed to Saint Gerard – patron saint of mothers and babies – when she and Gene were trying to have children.

'You have to do a bit more than pray,' said Gene.

The doctors said Etta must not blame herself. With her blood type, which, as she knew, was strange and thin, miscarriage would always be more of a danger.

She received letters of comfort from Gene's sister Beryl. Beryl knew that, some day, Etta would be blessed with children as wonderful as Colin and Jimmy. Beryl could feel it.

Fourteen years later, Etta and Gene adopted, and only then – another year later, in fact – did they have a child of their own.

'You see, he did answer me,' said Etta.

Today is July 24th, 1979: one day after Gene has returned from a fishing trip, the feast of Saint Christina the Astonishing, the day the Stiltons' cat is due for another worm tablet (which everyone has forgotten). The freezer is full of trout; Etta plans to stuff one of them for dinner.

It's early in the morning – not even light – and she can't get back to sleep. She has the flu. She opens her bedside cabinet, feels for her fat volume of *Butler's Lives of the Saints* which is now two weeks overdue at the library, and turns to today's date. She places her lamp on the floor before switching it on, so she won't wake Gene.

When she was twenty-two, Christina had a seizure, was assumed to be dead, and in due course was carried in an open coffin to the church. During her Mass of Requiem, after the Agnus Dei, Christina sat up, soared to the beams of the roof, and there perched herself. Everyone fled from the church except her elder sister, who, though thoroughly frightened, gave a good example to the others by stopping to the end of Mass.

Etta does not think she's heard of Christina the Astonishing, Virgin, AD 1224. This is surprising, because when she named her daughter Christina, she consulted several anthologies of saints.

'It has to be a saint's name,' she told Gene at the time.

They were sitting on their new vinyl couch, eating dinner from their new tray tables. Etta had cooked a duck Gene shot on the opening day of the season.

'Mum will never forgive me if it's not a saint's name.'

Gene removed a lead pellet from his mouth and dropped it on to his tray table. You always got some in the meat; that was how you could tell it was real wild game.

'I don't think she has anyway,' he said.

'What's that supposed to mean?'

'She calls me John.' Gene spat out another pellet. 'She did when I first met her, and she does now.'

'She is in her seventies,' said Etta. 'She forgets things.'

'She's remembered I'm not a Catholic all right.'

'I was thinking about Christina,' said Etta. 'What do you think? Or Josephine. I thought that would be nice, you know, from Joseph, patron saint of builders –'

Gene sighed. 'It's been a long day,' he said. 'I really don't want to hear about any more saints.'

Etta pushed a duck leg around her plate. A few fine hairs still clung to it. 'Mum thinks I've been taking the Pill. She asked Theresa if that's why I was so nervy these days. She still thinks that's why Bernadette died at thirty-five.'

'God knows how you turned out so normal,' said Gene, wiping his fingers and putting an arm around Etta. 'I hate to think what she was like when she was young and fit.'

'She's still fit enough.' Etta tried to saw through a piece of tough meat.

Gene looked at his plate. 'What was she like, really?'

'Ouch!' Etta crunched a lead pellet between her teeth. She felt with her tongue for any damage, then spat the gritty fragments into a serviette. 'Can we stop talking about my mother now?' she said. 'Do you think?' She clasped the serviette into a tight ball. 'It has to be a saint's name. So I know there's someone looking after her.'

Gene stood up to turn on the news. As he moved his tray table away, the pellets rolled around and around on the metal surface. 'And who's looking after me?' he said.

Etta eventually chose the more famous Saint Christina as protector for their new daughter; the one who lived in Italy, and who was pierced through with arrows for refusing to renounce Christianity. *Anointed with chrism*, the anthology said. *She had the oil of devotion in her mind and benediction in her speech*. Etta thought this all sounded rather suitable. (Gene's Great Aunt Christina, who was no blood relation, and whom Etta had met twice, found the decision very touching. To avoid any awkwardness, Etta decided to let her think they'd named the baby after her, which led to a small inheritance the rest of the family would resent for years to come.)

The entry for Christina the Astonishing is short – half a page – but Etta reads the words over and over to herself in bed while she's waiting for it to get light. She wishes there was more, and traces a finger along each line, not wanting to miss anything. Her lips begin to move, air escapes between her teeth, she whispers the story to herself. Finally, she is reading out loud. When the alarm goes off at half past six she stops, suddenly aware of the level of her own voice. She sees the blankets that have slipped over to Gene's side of the bed, the lines of light framing the curtains, the room around her, and she feels strange inside it, the way people do when they wake themselves with their own sleep-talk. Gene rolls over and looks at her.

'I was dreaming about the new building,' he says, 'except it wasn't the new building, it was huge, it had all these floors that aren't on the plan.'

When Gene has left for work and the girls have left for school and the house is quiet, Etta goes to the kitchen. She wants to get dinner ready early, so she can have a lie down in the afternoon.

'It's the best thing for flu,' Gene had told her at breakfast.

'I just hate going to bed during the day,' said Etta. 'I can never get to sleep. Everything's round the wrong way.'

'You don't have to sleep, just rest. You have to look after yourself.'

This is true. Etta swallows the first dose of antibiotics the doctor has given her and then prepares a herbal inhalation for herself, to clear her head. Her own mother swore by inhalations, but Gene and the girls laugh at Etta's home remedies. Christina and Bridget want their bright orange Vitamin C pills in the bottle with Mickey Mouse and Goofy on it. They don't have the patience to sit with their heads under towels for quarter of an hour, inhaling bitter fumes.

'Look at Mummy,' they say, giggling. 'She looks like a ghost.' And they lift up the edges of the towel.

'Careful,' whispers Gene, 'or she'll have your fingers off.'

Now, though, Etta is alone, and free to indulge in whatever remedies she chooses. Perhaps she will take some garlic later on, or draw herself a lavender bath. She pours boiling water over the herbs – rosemary, thyme, some eucalyptus oil – and holds her face above the bowl. She pulls the towel over her head and breathes.

The priest then made Christina come down; it was said that she had taken refuge up there because she could not bear the smell of sinful human bodies. She averred that she had actually been dead; that she had gone down to Hell and there recognised many friends, and to Purgatory, where she had seen more friends, and then to Heaven. There she saw her parents, who had been dead for seven years.

Etta wonders if Christina the Astonishing is still allowed. The edition of *Butler's* she has borrowed from the library is old, published before the church made several alterations to its list of saints. Saint Christopher was one of the first to go.

It was like finding out Father Christmas did not exist, Etta thought at the time. She had always kept a Saint Christopher medal in the cream Viva; she'd got Gene to drill a hole just above Christopher's head so she could hang him from the rear vision mirror. She'd never had an accident in her life. Then, in 1969, the year they adopted Christina, the Sacred Congregation of Rights announced that Christopher was no longer to be regarded as patron saint of travellers. It was forbidden to pray to him when, say, crossing the Atlantic, or on a bumpy car ride. And he was not the only one to be demoted. Exhaustive academic studies concluded that Saint Philomena, Saint George and Saint Catherine of Alexandria all posed 'serious historical problems'.

'That means they probably never existed,' said Gene.

As the Stiltons drove to the Home of Compassion to collect their new daughter, whom they would call Christina, Saint Christopher swung back and forth between them like a lucky penny. Etta wondered what had kept her safe all these years.

When her head feels clearer, Etta will lift the towel away and go to the fridge. She will remove the trout (caught by Gene) and she will try to avoid looking at its eyes. It will be placed on the bench while she makes a stuffing from herbs, onions, lemon juice, butter and breadcrumbs. This dish is always an enormous success, and Etta receives many requests for the recipe.

'Oh, it's very simple,' she says. 'Even Gene could make it, if he tried.'

If anyone examined the Stiltons' weekly menu, they might notice how often bread appears in one form or another. It is Etta's favourite food; she has been known to eat entire loaves in one sitting. Gene thinks this is because she was deprived of it when she was a child, growing up on a farm where there was a steady supply of meat and vegetables even through the Depression. He, on the other hand, was fed on bread and dripping for dinner and it hasn't done him any harm; Gene can take or leave bread. He would no doubt be amazed if he saw the way Etta sometimes demolishes a fresh white loaf, discarding the end crusts and reaching inside, clawing out great puffs of white. She entertains the fantasy of reassembling the hollow loaf and placing it in the bread bin, just to see how long it would take before anyone noticed. She has never actually done this, but she is cunning in her own way. She incorporates bread and butter pudding into the menu with surprising frequency; Gene eats it very fast, licking his lips between each mouthful, and says his mother used to make it as a treat. Chicken is crumbed, soup croutonned, trout stuffed. If she had to, Etta could survive on bread alone.

Etta's head is not clearing. In fact, she feels worse. She opens her eyes under the towel and the fumes sting them. The steam is all around her; she can't see the bowl or the table, or even her own hands. She feels for her face, and touches skin that is hot and moist, like that of a feverish child. When she stands up from the table, with the towel still over her head, she knocks over a stool, sends the telephone spiralling to the floor. She bangs into the bench, trips over a box of toys that are waiting to be collected and donated to the Home of Compassion.

This sort of clumsiness is not unusual for Etta; at times she feels like a disruptive poltergeist in her own house. (Although at forty-six, as many magazine articles have reminded her, she must start to expect certain changes.) It seems she forgets her own dimensions sometimes; she collides with furniture, catches her toes under carpets. When these things happen, she makes herself look at her gold watch lying curled on the dressing table. That is the measure of my wrist, she thinks. She goes to the laundry and looks at the clothes which are waiting to be folded and worn again; filled out by flesh. She holds up her pair of dress trousers, a best skirt. My legs are this length. That is the span of my hips.

Gene's work clothes she keeps completely separate; they are always filthy from the building sites. Before she washes them she gives them a good shake. They are covered in white dust, which floats around her like snow.

'God, Mum,' Christina has been saying lately, 'don't be such a martyr.'

She's only ten; Etta doesn't know where this new sharpness is coming from. When she says those things, Etta feels as if something is growing in her.

Other parents call Etta a saint. Gene has been known to call her his angel. Lately she's been thinking about angels and saints, and martyrs. About what they have in common with one another. Christina's maths class is learning about sets, so Etta has been learning about them too, in case Christina needs some help. She doesn't, usually; she is a fast learner.

Etta finds the New Maths quite different from what she learnt at school. It helps to make diagrams, she finds. She draws around fifty-cent pieces, covering sheets of paper with labelled discs. Martyrs are a subset of angels, and angels intersect with saints. Angels intersect with martyrs. All three sets intersect, forming a shaded area of the most holy. Martyrs are a subset of saints, therefore all martyrs are saints, and all martyrs are angels, but not all saints are martyrs, and some angels are neither martyrs nor saints.

Etta has considered adding virgins to her charts, but decided this would make things far too complicated. Perhaps she should have been a teacher, she thinks.

She grasps the smooth stainless steel edge of the bench and removes the towel from her head. The air rushes cold against her face.

After this, thinks Etta, *Christina fled into remote places, climbed trees and towers and rocks, and crawled into ovens, to escape from the smell of humans. She would handle fire with impunity and, in the coldest weather, dash into the river, or into a mill-race and be carried unharmed under the wheel.*

The box of toys sitting on the floor is to be picked up that afternoon by Shirley Davis, the treasurer of the Catholic Women's League.

'If the girls could just pick out a few things they don't need any more,' she had said. 'Dolls, books, stuffed toys, that sort of thing. Teddy bears are good.'

Shirley is co-ordinating an inter-parish toy donation to the poor orphans at the Home of Compassion. She adopted a baby, Jodie, at the same time as the Stiltons.

Etta got Gene to take a photo of the girls with their toys before they packed them up; she hopes Shirley comes before they arrive home from school so the box will already be gone. She tries to remember the toys she had when she was ten, and can't, and she hopes this means her daughters' sadness will not be lasting. Bridget agreed to part with a yellow bear and a pink dog, while Christina sacrificed two dolls and a brown rabbit. It was only right they should give, said Shirley; if the Stiltons hadn't adopted her, Christina would have been a poor Home of Compassion orphan too.

Etta picks up the yellow bear, which has no eyes. She'll sew on a couple of buttons, she thinks, smarten him up a bit. The fur is worn smooth, like a peach, and the smell reminds her of old paper money; something that has been handled too much. She would like to keep him, really; tuck him away in her bedside cabinet with all her other relics. She keeps everything. She has a pile of cards people sent when Bridget was born. *It's a girl!* they say in pink. *Congratulations!*

When Christina was adopted, Social Welfare advised the

Stiltons to behave as normally as possible. They put a birth notice in the paper, and Etta knitted and crocheted, and there was a baby shower where she was given rattles, stuffed toys, a range of booties. People did send cards, although they were careful to send neutral ones which did not suggest an actual birth.

Etta even tried breastfeeding, using a breast pump the Plunket nurse had given her.

'It's so much better for them,' said Shirley, who expressed milk regularly. 'We like to have an extra supply, in case of emergencies.' She squeezed Etta's dry hand. 'It does take a while to get the hang of it. But even men can produce milk, given the right hormones. You just need to relax.'

Shirley used to be a nurse.

Etta's mother Maggie did not send a card. Each year on Christina's birthday, Etta buys an extra one. *For a special Grand-daughter*, it usually says, and inside Etta writes: *To dear Christina, with all my love for a happy birthday, Nana xxx.* And she inserts a ten-dollar note, which is the amount that always arrives in Bridget's cards.

'She's not stupid, you know,' says Gene. 'One of these days she'll figure it out, and then where will we be?'

Etta knows he's right, but he doesn't offer any better suggestions.

Etta wonders if Shirley has managed to involve Peter Fitzroy in the toy drive. He is always keen to help out with anything she organises. Etta saw the two of them leaving a restaurant together a few weeks ago.

'So Shirley the Magnificent, Treasurer of Treasurers, really is doing her bit, is she?' said Gene. 'No wonder she always manages to sell so many raffle tickets.'

'Don't you dare mention it to anyone!'

'Did they spot you?'

'I hid. I ran into the French bakery.'

Gene laughed. 'Why were you the one hiding?'

Etta puts the bear back in the box. She has to learn to be more ruthless, she knows. Less sentimental. And she does have other mementoes in her bedside cabinet, after all. Locks of soft baby hair; tiny baby teeth; sugar flowers, saved from the girls' christening cakes, which have hardened into bone.

She prayed balancing herself on top of a hurdle, Etta says as she opens the fridge, *or curled up on the ground in such a way that she looked like a ball. Not unnaturally, everyone thought she was mad or full of devils, and attempts were made to confine her, but she always broke loose. She lived by begging, dressed in rags, and behaved in a terrifying manner.*

Etta hadn't liked saying no to Shirley when she asked her to help deliver the toys.

'I'm sorry, but I've come down with the flu,' she said. 'I am sorry.'

It's not that she avoids helping; in fact, she always volunteers to accompany Christina's and Bridget's classes on school trips, despite the fact that she finds zoos unspeakably depressing. Etta does not know that one of Bridget's clearest memories is sitting on the wide warm steps at Wellington Zoo, aged five, eating a sugared doughnut and a bag of chippies for lunch. Not sandwiches.

The trip Etta herself remembers best was a couple of years ago, when Christina's class visited the Home of Compassion. After they had sung for the old women in the geriatric ward, they saw how communion wafers were made; how the nun poured a thin layer of flour and water into a hot iron press and then shut the lid so it looked like a giant toasted sandwich maker. When it was opened and the sheet of wafer was removed there was a big patterned host in the middle for the priest, and smaller ones around it for everyone else, orbiting like moons.

'Don't touch!' Etta had cried, grabbing Christina's sleeve as she leaned forward to get a better look. The other children giggled, and Christina glared at her.

'You must have to be very careful,' Etta said to the nun.

She'd been horrified when the nun had flipped the hot waste bread on to a tray and said to the children, 'You can taste some if you like.'

The nun must have seen Etta's face because she said, 'Oh, it's not been consecrated.'

Etta watched the children pick up the edges of host and drop them back on the tray until they were cool enough to hold, but even then they burned their tongues. They all agreed that it tasted just like icecream cone, and they seemed to have no recollection of the rows of dribbling old women in stale bed jackets. Or at least, it had been no more or less interesting than the chapel, or the gardens with the tree whose branches grew down to the ground like a bell.

Etta does not want to go back there. 'I really should get some rest,' she told Shirley. 'I need to look after myself.'

She removes the trout from the fridge and assembles the ingredients for the stuffing. She likes to have everything ready before she begins. From the wooden spice rack (made by Gene) she takes rosemary and sage and thyme. Above the jars with the green lids that match the green paintwork hangs a verse that Etta knows by heart. Shirley gave it to her when Christina was adopted.

'I thought they'd put it very well,' said Shirley. 'And it might help Christina feel more like she belongs.'

Etta agreed that this was indeed important, and hung the verse where everyone could see it, right at eye level. She usually ends up reading it to herself when she's cooking.

'Not flesh of my flesh,' she says now, sprinkling the herbs into a bowl.

'Nor bone of my bone.'

She melts the butter.

'But still completely mine alone.'
She pours the butter on to the herbs.
'Never forget for a single minute.'
She adds the breadcrumbs and stirs.
'You didn't grow under my heart but in it.'

Christina finds the verse inaccurate. At ten, she has learned
enough about human anatomy to know that the situation
described is impossible. She tolerates nothing but fact; she has
never had any patience for fairy tales, or Father Christmas, or
talking animals.

Bridget doesn't like the verse, and wonders why her mother
keeps it in the kitchen. When she reads it she thinks of a creature
actually growing in someone's heart – fists and feet and a huge
head pushing through muscle, displacing organs; elbows and
knees stretching tissue into points.

It does worry Etta sometimes, how competitive the girls are.
They fight a lot, about anything. They are always coming to
her with pictures they have drawn, or things they have made,
and clutching them up to her face. They ask her which one she
likes best. She likes them both the same, she answers, which
satisfies neither child.

When they brought Christina home and Etta announced her
final choice of name, Gene said, 'But we don't have any relatives
called Christina. Except Great Uncle Norm's second wife, and I
hardly know her.'

'Well we're not calling her Tracey,' said Etta. The birth
mother had called her that, and as far as Etta knew there had
never been any Saint Traceys. 'Anyway, she just looks like a
Christina.'

And Gene said, 'She doesn't look like anyone.'

Etta knows he didn't mean this in a nasty way; Christina really doesn't look like anyone. This, however, has never stopped new or vague acquaintances from spotting resemblances which do not exist.

'Hasn't she got Gene's eyes?' they say. 'Isn't she a real little Stilton?'

'Christina's adopted,' Bridget always informs them.

And Etta tries to soothe Christina's awkwardness and the acquaintance's embarrassment by saying, 'We were very lucky. Not many parents get to choose their babies.'

And Bridget frowns, wrinkling her Stilton forehead.

Sometimes Etta hears Christina pointing out particular family resemblances to Bridget.

'You've got Aunty Theresa's legs,' she says. 'She hasn't got any ankles either. Dad said she's as wide as she is high.'

Etta tells Shirley she's never regretted adopting. 'Not for a moment,' she says.

'And such an attractive child,' says Shirley. 'So many people have said that to me.'

Social Welfare lied, Etta knows. Documents were altered, falsified. She suspected it at the time of the adoption, but, after fourteen years of miscarriage, she chose not to question the information she and Gene were given. Christina's real parents were not university academics; they were not engaged; they did not marry. They were not Catholics who were in their late twenties. It was a time of lies; Etta realises this. Unmarried mothers were kept hidden, as if they were not real people. As if they did not exist. Christina's birth certificate names Henrietta Eileen Stilton (née Moynihan) as her mother and Gene Roland Stilton (Project Supervisor) as her father.

Etta has kept track of the birth mother, in case Christina ever wants to contact her. She dreads to think of her trying to find her one day, and discovering there is no such person. She has kept the Cadbury's chocolate box covered with pink paper that Christina's mother made. The sisters at the Home of Compassion gave it to Etta when she and Gene picked Christina up. In it are a pair of booties and a matching bonnet, also made by Christina's mother, which are in remarkably good condition. As if they have never been worn. Etta keeps everything.

Joanne Susan Fairfield now lives in Sydney. She is twenty-eight years old. She works as a secretary for a legal practice, and is not married. She has had no other children. Etta is old enough to be her mother.

Sometimes Etta does wonder if she made the right choice. When the girls fight, especially, she thinks things would have been easier with just one. The drive to the lake each year is particularly unpleasant, with Bridget and Christina arguing about who will sleep on the top bunk, who will have first go on the trampoline, who will be able to stay in the cold lake longer, who will go in deeper. Saint Christopher swings from the mirror, lurching to the side when the road twists. Gene hangs his best suit for Midnight Mass from the handle above the passenger window – the bar you are supposed to hang on to for support – and the dark sleeves flap at Etta as they drive through the hills. She is not a good traveller. Gene tells her she should take some Sea Legs, but Etta doesn't like to. They're not on a ship, after all.

What puzzles her is why the girls still insist on sharing a room at home, even though there is a spare one. She's told them they can have their own rooms if they want; she thinks it might stop them from fighting so much. But they don't want. When she goes in at night to check they are still alive, they are breathing in time. Once, they were having a conversation in their sleep.
'I'm the Incredible Hulk,' said Christina.
'I'm frightened,' said Bridget.
It's not as if they fight all the time.

Just recently, in a doctor's waiting room, Etta read that keeping your eyes on one spot in the distance is helpful for travel sickness. Mrs Dorothy Bowles of Hamilton got ten dollars for that, so Etta supposed there must be some truth in it, and she tried it on their last trip to the lake. It was such a strange sensation; she hardly heard what was going on in the car, she was concentrating so hard on the horizon. It didn't help much with the travel sickness, unfortunately, but Etta did notice quite a few things about perspective; how points of reference can shift.

She considers this as she finishes mixing the stuffing with her fingers and lifts open the trout's belly.

Eventually, she says to the trout, *she was caught by a man who had to give her a violent blow on the leg to do it, and it was thought her leg was broken. She was therefore taken to the house of a surgeon, who put splints on the limb and chained her to a pillar for safety. She escaped in the night.*

Etta is beginning to feel dizzy. She looks out the window, searching for a point in the distance she can focus on. Perhaps it is just the flu, she thinks, but she's never felt like this with the flu before. She finds a familiar cluster of trees on the hill and stares at them.

Christina went into the forest. For days at a time she fasted and prayed. To sustain herself she drank the oily milk that flowed from her own virgin breasts. Returning home, suffering strange hysterical fits, she spread this liquid on bread and ate it. Its curative powers are recorded, and she performed many miracles using this unguent.

Etta needs to open the window. As she stands on tiptoe to reach for the latch, her foot slips and she falls to the floor, sending the tray with the trout on it flying.

She lies on the floor and looks at the trout. The trout looks at her. Its mouth is wide open. All its insides have been removed – it has been cleaned – and Etta can see right in to where there is nothing. She wishes she could get up. She has to fill the trout with herbs and onions and lemon juice and butter and breadcrumbs. And then she has to have a rest.

'Go on,' says the trout, 'up you get. You haven't got all day, you know.'

Etta smiles. Yes. She will get up and finish getting everything ready. And then she might play a few tricks on Gene and the girls, for a laugh. They'd enjoy that. Nothing too extreme, just some harmless little jokes, like putting salt in the sugar bowl, hiding the bath plug, leaving a hollowed loaf in the bread bin. Nothing dangerous. Then she will go away on holiday, by herself. Just leave the children with Gene for a fortnight. A week, even a weekend would do. She will jump in the light blue Torana and drive, without dark suits flapping in her face, and without Bridget and Christina fighting in the back seat. She will stop when she finds somewhere nice. She will walk into the forest, sit down in the pine needles, pour herself a cup of tea from her thermos, unwrap her sandwiches.

At home, Gene and the girls will be having to fend for themselves. They will find taps turned off too hard, blunted knives, hollowed loaves of bread. They might panic. They might start looking for goodbye notes.

'You're pathetic,' says the trout. 'What will they say about you? *Made a delightful baked cheesecake? Folded dinner napkins with flair?*'

As it speaks, the trout grows bigger and bigger, until it covers the whole floor, and it's still growing as Etta walks into its mouth where pointed fish teeth rise around her like mountains. She can see through the cloudy fish eyes to her kitchen, where things look swollen and silver, the way they do in a curved mirror, or the back of a spoon. Through the gill slits she feels a cool rush of air, and she walks on, touching the pink walls, surprised to find they are warm. Fishbones arch above her, as if she is in a fishbone church, and she wonders where fish hearts are kept; if she is standing where this one used to be.

✧

'You were very lucky,' Gene is saying. He is stroking Etta's hair and looking into her face, right up close.

'It was just lucky Mrs Davis called by when she did,' says a nurse who is standing on the other side of the bed.

'Pleasure,' says Shirley from a chair by the window.

She comes over to the bed too, and takes Etta's hand. 'You passed out,' she says. 'I came by to collect the girls' teddy bears and you were lying on the kitchen floor. I had to get Peter Fitzroy to help lift you into the car.'

'An allergic reaction to your flu antibiotics, Mrs Stilton,' says the nurse. 'The heart slowed down. Nothing serious. You'll soon be right as rain.'

Shirley leans down and whispers into Etta's ear, 'Your skirt was hitched right up around your hips.'

The next day, Gene helps Etta into the car to drive her home.

'This isn't our car,' she says, scanning the light blue Torana. She peers in through the passenger window. 'What have you done with Saint Christopher? Where's the Viva?'

Of course, after she's had a sleep in her own bed, Etta remembers that they sold the old cream Viva last year, just after their trip to the lake. It had become too temperamental, playing dead in cold weather, sometimes sputtering back to life only on the last try. The Torana was a reliable car, the dealer assured them. It ran smoothly. They'd made a good choice. As she lies in bed now, Etta decides they haven't made a good choice at all. The girls had cried for days when they'd sold the Viva.

'It's not a person, chickies,' she'd told them, stroking their damp hair into curls.

But she wants it back herself, she can't help it. She thinks maybe she could track it down, get in touch with the dealers they sold it to and trace the buyer through them. There must be records.

Bridget and Christina come into the bedroom. 'We made some sandwiches and a cup of tea, Mummy,' they say. They climb on her bed, pulling the sheets tight around her with their weight.

'Tell us a story.' They wriggle closer to her.

They always want to hear stories. They grab Etta's arms at night and beg her to tell them one, about when she was little, and she lies down on the edge of one of their beds and makes something up.

Now, she sits up in bed and balances the tray on her lap.

'A girl goes into the forest,' she says. 'She sits down under the trees and cries because her parents have both died, and she and her sister have to look after themselves. She curls up in a ball, and wild animals come and sniff at her, but they don't harm her. And they don't talk to her. The girl suffers from strange fits, where her whole body shakes. People think she is very odd. Then one day she has such a bad fit that she appears to die, and she is taken in an open coffin to the church. During the Mass, though, she comes back to life and flies up to the beams in the roof of the church. Everyone is terribly afraid and runs away, except her sister, who knows that the girl has always been unusual. After this, people are frightened of the girl, and she seems to have miraculous powers. She finds she is able to cure the sick, and she travels the country making people well. Although she doesn't know how to read or write, people listen to her. She lives alone, and is very happy.'

'Does she get on TV?' asks Bridget. 'She could get on TV if she wanted.'

'No,' says Etta. 'This was a long time ago, before they had TV.'

'She couldn't really fly, then,' says Christina. 'She must have jumped or climbed or something.'

'She might have flown,' says Bridget, playing with the bedspread fringe. 'It might have been magic.'

Christina snorts. 'It might have been magic,' she mimics, flapping her arms. Some tea slops on to the sandwiches.

'Careful now,' says Etta.

'It wasn't even me!' says Bridget.

'Anyway,' Christina says, 'if she was so great why did she live on her own? Didn't she have any friends?'

'Just like you,' says Bridget, running for the door, giggling.

Christina just watches her, lets her go. Etta is relieved; for once, Christina's not biting.

'So what happened to the trout?' Etta asks her.

'I think Mrs Davis took it. She said she was having someone round that night, so it wouldn't go to waste.'

'And what about you and Dad, and Bridget?'

Christina rolls her eyes. 'We can cope on our own, Mum,' she says. She sounds just like her father. 'We didn't go to church today. Dad said we wouldn't go to Hell if we missed one Sunday, because you were sick.'

'No,' Etta says, 'you won't go to Hell.' She smiles; she thought Christina had decided that Hell, like Father Christmas, did not exist.

'I saw you,' Christina says quietly. 'When you were lying on the floor. I came in when Mrs Davis was ringing the ambulance.'

'Oh.'

'Bridget was still outside. You were so white. I went and got her and we waited in Mrs Davis' car to go to the hospital. I didn't bring her inside.' She is sobbing now, softly, into the pillow. 'We weren't supposed to tell you. Dad said you'd worry.'

She rolls over and cuddles into Etta's chest. After a while her crying fades, and Etta thinks she must be falling asleep, but she looks up again for a moment.

'Mrs Davis' car,' she says. 'It was full of toys. There was hardly any room for us to squeeze in. Bridget sat on a plastic truck and it broke, and we hid it under the seat.'

Christina closes her eyes and puts her hot face against Etta's chest again. 'She didn't take our toys,' she says sleepily. 'No room anyway. The other ones were all squashed up against the back window. Looking out when we drove away.' Her voice sounds distant; on the verge of sleep. Etta imagines the dreams that might be forming behind her warm forehead: rushing to church in a plastic truck, a view of wild animals from the beams of a roof, trying to breathe in a car full of toys without eyes, twin sisters who swim in a cold lake and turn into fish, dead mothers lying in the forest.

An
erratic
heart

Adelaide, South Australia 5001
November 27, 1984

Mr Clifford Stilton
138 King Street
Christchurch
New Zealand

Dear Mr Stilton,

I have received your letter of November 20 and I accept it as evidence of your interest and 'keenness' in having your finds identified promptly. I can assure you we are taking the utmost care in our preparation of your specimens, and do not wish to compromise this level of attention by rushing. Your technical comments on a preliminary reconstruction will certainly be taken into consideration. When the description of the fossils is published you will appreciate that they have undergone considerable preparation with modern equipment, revealing features which may not be obvious on other specimens in your possession. If on the other hand those other specimens show characters not visible in the material which is on loan to us, we cannot be blamed for resulting discrepancies.

I can assure you that I regret the delay as much as you do. The general situation is that it takes many years to have material examined and described by experts free of cost, i.e. in their spare time, as they have other duties to perform in their paid jobs. In the British Museum (Natural History) in London it might take up to 25 years to have material described, although the officers there have no teaching duties to perform.

Your material has been described by one of my research students, Mr R. M. Andrews, and as soon as I can find time to draw the necessary conclusions and complete the paper I will forward it to the Canterbury Museum, along with the two crab specimens, as promised.

Yours sincerely

P. W. Maple (Professor)

> 138 King Street
> Christchurch
> New Zealand
> 5.12.84

Dear Professor Maple,

I was very pleased to hear that my spider crabs are now receiving your attention. I am a little surprised that a student is playing so vital a part in the process of identification – I was under the impression that you personally would be tending to all stages of the procedure. However, I am no expert in these matters, and am confident my specimens will be handled with the utmost care.

Yours sincerely

Clifford Stilton

Canterbury Museum
Canterbury
15.3.85

Dear Mr Stilton

As you are no doubt aware, Professor Maple of the University of Adelaide has arranged for one of his students, Mr R. M. Andrews, to describe for publication the spider crabs from Glenavrick. It was Mr Andrews who prepared the drawing of the reconstructed animal sent to you earlier this year.

Mr Andrews has decided that the fossils belong to a new genus and species and intends to call it *Atinotocarcinius stiltoni*.

The two specimens which I borrowed from you last year and which were forwarded to the University of Adelaide have been returned to me. They are regarded as of particular importance by Professor Maple and Mr Andrews. Mr Andrews has studied them carefully and worked out that one is a male and one is a female. These appear to be the best specimens available and he is designating them type specimens of the species. The female specimen has been selected as the holotype which is the all important specimen and represents the species. The male specimen has been selected as allotype and is the type representing the males of the species.

Type specimens are of great scientific importance as they are the basis of the naming of plants and animals both living and fossil. It is highly desirable that such specimens be preserved forever so that they can be referred to by scientists studying these animals in the future. For this reason I would be grateful if you would consider either presenting the specimens to the Canterbury Museum or leaving them with the Museum on loan.

Yours sincerely

Roger Park
Keeper of Geology

✧

'The trouble with the Indians,' Clifford tells the local reporter, 'is that they won't help themselves. If they're prepared to starve rather than eat their cows,' he says, 'then I have no sympathy for them.'

Clifford has been expounding his socio-economic theories for more than an hour, despite the fact that the reporter has come to do an interview about fossils.

'And so you found the stones at Glenavrick, is that right Mr Stilton?' she says now, cutting Clifford off in mid-sentence.

'That's correct, yes,' says Clifford. He then begins outlining the reasons why divorce statistics are so high these days.

When the article is printed, Clifford sends four copies to Gene with a note that reads, 'One each!'

Etta tucks hers away, for future generations of Stiltons she says, although it is not sighted again.

Bridget uses hers as a bookmark (Revelations 4:11) until it slips out on the bus and is never missed.

At a party, Christina writes Donald Musgrove's phone number along the white edge of hers and puts it back in her jeans pocket. It does not survive the spin cycle.

Gene sticks his copy to the fridge with a magnet shaped like a pineapple. Every time he goes to get the milk or the cheese, there is Clifford beaming at him beside his cabinets of stones, holding a perfect specimen of *Atinotocarcinius stiltoni* which he found at Glenavrick one Tuesday afternoon.

Most of us know Clifford Stilton as the cheerful local butcher who had the shop on Durham Street for 40 odd years. But not everyone knows that Clifford's lifelong hobby of rockhunting produced not only one of the most extensive rock and fossil collections in the South Island, but also an important scientific discovery.

'He's pretty famous in some circles, you know,' Gene tells his family, who fail to be impressed. 'He has the only five *Atinotocarcinius stiltoni* ever found.'

Even at 85 years old Clifford can spot the minute signs betraying the contents of a rock.

'That's how he found the spider crabs,' Gene says. 'The *Atinotocarcinius stiltoni.*'

Gene wishes he had been there. Perhaps he might have

detected what Clifford had: the tiny tip of a pincer in the smooth surface of stone, as if something were trying to hatch.

In the article, the Canterbury Museum commends Clifford on the way he opened the crabs, the care he had taken to preserve the contents.

Some amateur collectors are so impatient to see what's inside a stone that they ruin the specimen. It doesn't take much: a chip here, a gouge there, and the piece is valueless. Mr Stilton has shown the utmost respect for his discovery. He spent hours tapping away (like a sculptor, imagines Gene), *slowly removing stone, until the rare* (perfectly petrified) *creatures inside were revealed.*

'A very exciting find indeed,' quotes Etta from halfway inside the fridge. 'These are an entirely new genus of crab. The scientific community has Mr Stilton's remarkable eyesight to thank –'

'It is exciting,' says Gene, remembering the hours spent with his father on assorted beaches, gathering empty stones. 'Don't you think it's exciting?'

❖

Clifford had good eyes and a bad heart, which was one of the reasons he became even more keen on his rockhunting during retirement. Ever since 1954, when his doctor had detected his erratic heart (and at the same appointment had congratulated him on his excellent vision), Clifford had been waiting for his Time to Come.

Pulse 84, he would write in his diary, which he kept more as a record for future generations than for his own reference. He knew how facts could be buried over the years, how layers of interpretation could settle and harden. He fully expected the diaries to be published one day, and more than once in recent years he had urged Gene to 'look after them' when he was gone. Gene didn't enjoy these moments at all, and tried to soothe his father by saying, now I'm sure there's no need to talk like that. Which usually made Clifford even more agitated, and he would clutch at Gene's sleeve and say, 'But you will look after them, won't you? There's a lot of valuable information in them that shouldn't be lost. God knows I can't rely on Colin, or even Jim.' And Gene would say yes, yes, of course he'd look after them, there was nothing to worry about.

Clifford did worry, though; it was one of the things he did best.

Pulse 93, he would record. *The exercise helps keep it down, but it is a worry . . .*

His daughters and his grandsons were quite accustomed to finding goodbye notes when they popped round to visit, often scrawled on toilet paper. *Goodbye all,* the notes read, *tried to phone but everyone engaged   no answer at Beryl's   no bloody hymns please   goodbye.*

Gene and Etta didn't pop round, of course, living in Wellington as they did. They'd never been forgiven for leaving the South Island.

'It killed your mother,' Clifford told Gene whenever the subject came up. It came up quite often.

Violet Stilton had died when Gene was thirty-three and had been living in the North Island for seven years. She had been in hospital a few times with chest trouble, but nobody thought she would be dead by the age of sixty.

'It was very sudden,' Gene's sisters told him. 'She just sat down on the couch and lifted her arms in the air and died.'

Gene did not blame himself for her death. He had always visited regularly; after they shifted to Wellington he and Etta were summoned at least annually because Cliff was about to die. Once Christina and Bridget were born, well after Violet's death in 1964, they had to visit him too.

'He has an erratic heart,' the Stiltons kept explaining to neighbours, friends, employers. 'He could go at any time.'

Then when they arrived in Christchurch, Clifford would be sitting up in his armchair sucking peppermints, and the kitchen would be full of baking and casseroles.

Carnelian and Beryl would glare at Gene and say, 'You don't

know what he's like, he's a very sick old man, you don't see him every day.'

Then Clifford would call out, 'Where are my geologists?' and Bridget and Christina would have to go and sit with him and look at shells and stones. He gave them presents: brooches he'd made from cloudy pieces of amethyst; polished discs of paua, in which, he assured them, entire landscapes could be seen; smooth lozenges of petrified wood; translucent slices of forest floor.

'Hold out your hands,' he would say, scraping a chunk of soapstone with a razor blade. As the white dust collected in the creases of the girls' palms, he would look up and announce, 'Talcum powder!' as if he had invented it himself, or conjured it out of air. If Colin and Jim – the older, local grandchildren – were there, they would smirk at one another over their small glasses of beer. Clifford had given up forcing his demonstrations on them.

The home-made artefacts were a bit of a joke between Etta and Gene. The girls joined in too, when they were old enough to have acquired good taste, or at least that of their parents.

Whenever they were visiting Christchurch they stayed with Theresa, Etta's sister, who lent them her car and stayed out of their way.

'The last thing you want is me showing you the Square and the Gardens and everything else you've seen a million times before,' she always said.

When they lay in their tight twin beds with the pink candlewick bedspreads in Aunty Theresa's spare room, Bridget and Christina would wonder to each other why they couldn't be shown those things, which they had never seen. It wasn't fair, they whispered, they'd come all this way and they didn't even get to look at the shops.

On one visit when Clifford was, he assured them, nearing the end, and Gene and Etta and the girls were driving round to see him twice a day, Christina mentioned this to Gene.

'Da-ad,' she said as she was climbing into the car, stretching the word into two syllables the way she always did when she wanted something, 'how come we never get to do any sightseeing?'

'Dad's very sick,' was all Gene said, buckling up his seat-belt, and Christina was so surprised, almost shocked, to hear him call someone *Dad* that she left it at that.

'Wait!' Etta said just as they were pulling out of the drive, and she ran back inside to Theresa, emerging a few moments later with a selection of Clifford's jewellery.

'Here, put these on.' She thrust huge mounted agates at the girls and a greenstone ring the size of a golf ball at Gene, and she hung a chunky obsidian bracelet from her own wrist.

'Hey Dad,' said Bridget, leaning forward from the back seat, 'don't go swimming with that on.'

'I hope there's room in the boot for today's lot,' said Christina, laughing.

'If he keeps giving it to us at this rate we'll be charged excess baggage on the way home,' Etta said. She turned to Gene. 'Are you sure you're all right to drive wearing that?'

✧

Nobody was more surprised than Clifford when he fell to his death at Glenavrick. Simply failing to see the edge of the rocky precipice was rather disappointing for a man whose sharp eyes had spotted the only five *Atinotocarcinius stiltoni* ever found. He was out with fellow rockhound Cyril Palmer when the accident happened, just three weeks after the article had appeared. They were looking for more specimens. There were those who muttered darkly about Cyril's role in the accident, citing ancient disagreements over bits of crystal, dredging up incidents that had either been forgotten by both Clifford and Cyril or had never happened at all. The business of rock collecting was a competitive one, and it was true the two had often argued. What really happened that day at Glenavrick, however, was very simple: Clifford, buoyant with the triumph of his crab discovery, forgot about gravity. Killed instantly, of course. Or rather, as soon as he hit the ground. Gene wonders if, as his father whistled through the air, his erratic heart even fluttered.

Stanley
Graham's
ashtray

Nobody would call Gene Stilton a violent man. Etta cannot recall him ever raising his voice, and his daughters know he never so much as smacked them when they were little. He tells them this quite often.

'Your father never swears,' says Etta.

Gene is concerned about the rising level of violence in New Zealand. He remembers the days, he says, when a murder was big news, when the whole country sat up and took notice. Now there are a couple a week, and nobody blinks an eyelid. He watches the news as many times a day as he can manage, and he talks to the television set, making outrageous demands. Video arcades should be shut down, he says; there should be a greater police presence in certain areas; stiffer penalties for thieves. A return to corporal punishment. The streets are not safe, he says, and nobody cares. It's enough to make you weep.

He is a difficult person to buy for.

Whenever Bridget and Christina don't know what to get him for his birthday, or Christmas, or Fathers' Day, Etta says, 'Well, you can't go wrong with a good war book.'

Gene has shelves of them, and, more recently acquired, several videos, which he has politely viewed. One subscription to a *Reader's Digest* series on the SS spawned a succession of gold envelopes announcing that he may already have won a million dollars, or a car, or a cruise.

When he retired, the company where he had worked for forty years, and not many people can say that, presented him with a fishing reel and a limited edition print of the battle of Chunuk Bair. Since they've moved to their new low-maintenance townhouse, however, Gene and Etta haven't quite managed to hang the print anywhere.

'We must get my Chunuk Bair picture up,' says Gene from time to time, but as yet it's still in the garage with the stag's antlers and the stuffed pheasant and other souvenirs. Etta says it depresses her, and Gene isn't sure if she means the actual picture or the plaque confirming his retirement.

Christina arrives home two weeks before Christmas. She lives in Sydney now, and works at a hospital there. Her new Austrian boyfriend is coming over in a few days too, she announces. He is also a doctor. His name is Thorsten.

Gene wonders whether he should move all the war books out to the garage with the other things.

'I think he'll cope, Dad,' says Christina. 'He has been to see Auschwitz.'

Gene says that's different, this is his home, and he doesn't want Thorsten thinking he's obsessed.

Christina just looks at him.

Odd things happen in war time. People help complete strangers; the most placid men learn to kill; women operate machinery. Gene's father never went to war; he was a butcher and was needed at home. It was Gene's job to tear newspapers in half with a ruler, and stack them on the shop counter for his father – or his mother – to wrap the meat in. He was so jealous the day Robert Dalgleish didn't come to school, and it was announced his father had been killed. A few days later Gene had to tear and stack the papers reporting it. Dalgleish, Gunner Edwin Charles; Dalgleish, Gunner Edwin Charles, over and over, as if Robert had dozens of heroic fathers.

Mrs Dalgleish came into the Stiltons' shop for some chops a few days after the announcement, and Gene's mother Violet quickly checked the top sheet of paper before her husband wrapped them.

'That poor woman,' she said at the table that night. 'I hope you're being kind to Rob at school.'

Gene nodded, his mouth full of mashed potato. Just that lunchtime he'd informed Robert of his decision to let him into their gang, and to seal it had shot him and shoved a grenade down his trousers. Robert had started to cry.

After the dishes had been dried and the table wiped down and Gene's father had settled into his chair to listen to the news, Gene's mother produced the sticky bottle from the cupboard.

'One spoon and then bed,' she said. She was plotting to turn Gene into Johnny the Califig boy, who beamed in black and white from the newspaper advertisement.

Temper? Or is it that Johnny needs a laxative?
'Don't want to play,' says Johnny amid upturned toys.
Father: 'Needs the doctor you say? Needs the stick I reckon.'
Mother: Clasps chest.

'No,' says Doctor. 'What you call temper is the result of constipation. California Syrup of Figs will clear up the trouble.'

Now Johnny is a different boy.

Gene always placed the pages with Johnny on them face up on the counter. He liked the thought of blood soaking his regulated grin.

He held his breath and swallowed.

'Good boy,' said Violet. 'Now go and say goodnight to your father.'

✧

'Night Dad,' says Christina, leaning over the reclined armchair and kissing Gene on the cheek.

'Off to bed already?'

'I've had it. I've been on nights all week. And I want to drive up to the lake on Tuesday.'

'All right then, Dr Stilton.'

'You're probably still a bit jetlagged, too,' calls Etta from the kitchen.

Christina pats Gene's hand. 'You look exhausted. You should get an early night as well.' She picks up the newspaper, which he has let slide to the floor, and puts it back in his lap. 'I'm picking Thorsten up from the airport at nine in the morning.'

'I'm fine,' says Gene.

In the kitchen, Etta is loading the dishwasher.

'So how's Dad coping with retirement?' asks Christina.

Etta smiles. 'Oh, you know, a bit of fly-tying, a bit of gardening. He's been threatening to go shooting. What's this about the lake?'

'Ah,' says Christina. 'I wanted to go up this week. You couldn't entertain Thorsten, could you? Just for a couple of days?'

'But we've never even met him,' says Etta. 'And neither of

us know a word of German. Apart from *Achtung* and *Jawohl* and so on.'

'Mum,' says Christina. 'He does speak English. He's been working in Sydney for three years, remember?'

'Oh,' says Etta. 'Yes, of course he has.' She starts the dishwasher. 'I suppose we'll manage for a couple of days.'

'Great. Just as long as Dad doesn't offer to take Thorsten fishing. He's vegetarian too.'

'Oh Lord, is he?' says Etta. 'And I've gone and bought all this meat.'

✧

Gene swallowed. He couldn't get rid of the taste of the syrup. His mother put the bottle back in the cupboard and handed him a cup of tea.

'Take this through to your father, would you love?'

Clifford had his eyes closed. He could have been asleep. Or dead.

'Dad?' Gene put his hand on the warm radio. The wood vibrated under his fingers.

'The time is eight o'clock. Here is the news. Police are engaged in an extensive manhunt following the shooting of a police sergeant and two constables at Koiterangi today. A third constable, and a fifth man, an Education Board employee, were also injured.'

Gene's father opened his eyes. 'Ssh!'

'Stanley Graham, a farmer in the small town of Koiterangi on the West Coast of the South Island, had apparently had a dispute with a neighbour, whom he accused of poisoning his prize cattle. Mr Graham threatened the man with a rifle, and when this was reported to police, Constable Edward Best was sent to Mr Graham's farm.'

'Get your mother!'

'Reinforcements were called for when Mr Graham threatened Constable Best, and as they arrived at the house shots rang out. Two officers were shot dead when walking up the footpath to the house, and a third on the verandah. Constable Best was also injured. Mr George Ridley apparently went to help the police and was himself wounded by a shot.'

That Stanley Graham case, now that was news. It was the talk of the school, of the whole country. Dalgleish, Gunner Edwin Charles was history. Stanley Graham was hiding in a deer stalker's hut; Stanley Graham was living on tins of peaches which he opened with an axe; Stanley Graham could shoot the ace of spades out at a hundred yards. Gene wonders if Etta remembers it. They must tell Christina about it.

Gene's mother and his sisters were scared. Stanley Graham was possibly heading for Christchurch; his only escape route was through Browning Pass and over the Southern Alps to Canterbury.

'If that bugger shows up here I'll give him the biggest steak in the place,' said Clifford. 'Poor bastard must be starving.'

Gene was not afraid. He had a plan. If he spotted Stanley Graham he'd sneak up on him (he could be very quiet when he had to be) and tackle him from behind. The man was wounded, how hard could it be? Then he'd bind his hands and feet together, tie him to the toilet and make him drink a whole bottle of Califig. And then Stanley Graham would shit until he'd shitted himself to death, and the papers would want to interview Gene Stilton, and photograph him pointing at the toilet.

Gene had been in the paper before, sort of. With Clifford, when they found the fossilised groper's head. They were walking on the beach when Gene first saw it.

'Dad, look at this!' he shouted, and Clifford rushed over to find him pointing at a large stone. 'See the brown lines round the edges?' said Gene, and Clifford nodded and said yes, well done, it might be worth having a glance at. Between them they managed to carry it to the car.

Clifford said they'd put it in the boot, and began shifting the empty thermos and the extra jerseys and the fishing gear he'd packed just in case conditions were perfect, but Gene insisted on sitting next to it on the way home.

'It might be something really special,' he said. 'Do you think, Dad? It might be a dinosaur egg. Maybe it's a dinosaur egg, what do you think? Do you think I'll be famous if it is?'

'What I think is that certain boys shouldn't go getting excited about certain stones that usually turn out to be duds.'

They hauled the rock into the back seat, shifting some of the smaller stones they had found that day. Clifford seemed in a hurry to get home, and Gene bumped about in the back seat as they swung round the twists in the road. Going over the hill, as the rear of the car lunged towards the edges of the road, Gene could see right down the cliffs to the sea. He clutched at the rock.

'Dad?' he said quietly. 'I think it would have been dangerous to put it in the boot.' Another flash of ocean. 'I think it would have been too heavy.'

'Good Lord,' said Violet when they unpacked the car. 'Where are you planning to put all these stones?'

'I hope you realise,' said Clifford, 'what an important discovery this may be. And it's very educational for Gene.'

A fortnight later, the Stiltons were famous, more or less.

'You see?' said Clifford as the doorbell went and another group arrived to see the stone.

'Hmm,' said Violet, putting the jug on for the fifth time that day.

Fossil Believed 5 Million Years Old

The man known to us as Cliff, the friendly Durham Street butcher, has discovered the fossilised head of a groper thought to be around five million years old. Clifford Stilton was exploring a North Canterbury beach with his son Gene when the fossil was found.

'We were strolling along a rocky beach, keeping our eyes open for hidden treasure,' said Mr. Stilton. 'Gene was at my side when I just about tripped over it.'

Mr. Stilton said he noticed the strange brown lines around the stone, but such a heavy fossil had to be good to be carried any distance at all.

'Gene was doubtful whether we would be able to manage, but I assured him we could. We got it back, but it seemed to be more nuisance than it was worth. I worked away on the stone most of the next day, with Gene eagerly watching and helping. I was very careful and only took a fraction of the stone off each time,' said Mr. Stilton. 'At the end of the day I had to admit I thought we had a dud. Nothing of significance had shown up.'

Puzzled

He said he was disappointed and left it for a while. The part that puzzled him was a socket with what looked like an eye, he said.

'But who had ever heard of a fossilised eye: not I,' he joked.

'I concentrated on the eye and the more I did, the more real it became. I kept at it, got off all the surplus stone, and suddenly – there it was. I've caught a few groper in my time, but I never thought I would find a groper's head inside a stone.'

Mr. Stilton said that sometimes in fossil finding the clue in the stone was as small as a pin's head – 'in fact, it needs a strong magnifying glass to prove it is a clue. You never really know just how good your find is until the stone is all chipped away and the fossil is safely exposed. Many good specimens are ruined with the use of a hammer in the wrong hands.'

Mr. Stilton offered this advice to would-be fossil finders: 'Never break a stone just for the sake of breaking it, someone else may get a good fossil from it.'

'I'll tell you what,' said Clifford to Gene, when the last lot of stone-viewers had gone, 'I'll make a label.' He lifted the groper's head from its glass case and placed it carefully on an armchair. It stared out the window at the gate, as if hoping for more company. 'Gene, pencil,' said Clifford. 'And glue.'

Clifford cut a strip of paper from his notebook. 'TO GO TO GENE STILTON,' he wrote, and glued it to the stand.

'There now. It'll be yours one day, when I'm gone.' And he lifted the stone head from its comfortable chair and placed it over Gene's name.

Gene was scared that night in bed, and thought he could see the head of the groper moving towards him, its stone mouth opening and closing, swallowing the dark. Over the next few days he dreaded coming across the article in the piles of newspaper at the shop. He was glad when they were all gone.

The Stanley Graham articles, however, were a different matter. He watched out for those. He slid his ruler inside the newspapers, slit them down the fold and put the pages on top of the growing pile, reading constantly. Then he slit another section, and another. By the time he'd finished his hands were black. He picked up stories.

Ran a trail of blood   A desperately wounded man had paused for breath   A piece of flesh   Women who had been feeding   One of their numbers was 'A Nightingale Sang in Berkeley Square'   Provided refreshments with stark dread   To have nine lives   Not sleep sound in their beds for a twelvemonth to come if evidence of death   A flowering peach tree in the midst

Etta takes the milk out of the fridge and eyes the meat in there. As she is taking a cup of coffee to Gene she hears water being run upstairs. She frowns. Then she remembers Christina is home.

'Thorsten's a vegetarian,' she says. 'I don't know what we'll do with all that meat. I'll have to freeze it. Unless you want steak for breakfast.'

Gene has dropped the newspaper again. He is snoring.

'Reckon I could go into business with Stan Graham,' said Clifford. 'It says here that he slit some calves' throats, and shot a bullock for steak. I reckon he'd be useful round the shop. People are crying out for real meat.'

Violet looked up from her knitting. 'People are dying, Cliff. People are scared.'

'Listen to Mum. Nothing a good roast wouldn't fix, eh Gene?'

He winked at him. Gene didn't know what to do, so he winked back.

Across a page of text Stanley Graham took aim at his victims. They were already dead, and so was he now. Last week's news. Gene piled the papers on the counter. Constable Best was squashed against a recipe for eggless date and nut cake. Mrs Graham lay on top of the prize Ayrshire bullock.

'There it is. Take a good look.'

Clifford stopped the car, and he and Gene got out. The place had been torched.

'Aren't you coming, love?'

'I can see it from here. What there is to see.' Violet poured herself a cup of tea from the thermos.

Only the foundations and chimney were left. A three-dimensional plan of a house yet to be built, marking out a sleeping area, a cooking area, a bathing area. An area for living. The finer details were missing. Pots, china, rugs, beds. People had come and taken souvenirs, to remind themselves of something. There were no blackened springs, no shards of bone.

Look what we found, Mum. A melted beer bottle, belonging to Stanley Graham.   Great. Makes a nine-hour drive seem worthwhile.   The boy can use it as an ashtray when he grows up.   Filthy habit. Don't encourage him.   Fine then. Where's the pub.

Yellowing words. Stories disintegrating into fifty-year folds. Gene is not sure what he remembers. He wishes he knew where that beer bottle was. Perhaps he'll have a good look in the garage. Perhaps he'll take up smoking. Only cigars, though, like Churchill. Christina is picking Thorsten up in the morning. He has some photos of Auschwitz to show them. That'll be nice. Perhaps Gene will show him his genuine World War II German pistol, or offer him a cigar, or both.

'Do you know,' says Gene at dinner, 'that when the Japs heard about Stanley Graham they sent a message to him over their propaganda band saying that if he'd hold the South Island they'd take the North?'

'There you go, Thorsten,' says Christina. 'That's how kiwi blokes go about it. None of this "do you want total war" posturing.'

'Thorsten, perhaps you'd be interested in seeing some of my memorabilia,' says Gene.

'That sounds fascinating, yes.'

'Don't get him started,' mutters Christina.

'I remember that story about the Japanese,' says Etta. 'People did come up with some odd ideas.' She takes Christina's plate and serves her some peas. 'Just help yourself, won't you Thorsten? We want you to feel at home.'

Christina inspects the potatoes.

'Were these cooked in with the meat, Mum?'

'Well they were in the same dish,' says Etta. 'They dry out otherwise.'

Christina pushes them away.

'Do you want some bread then?' says Etta, already standing up from the table. 'I've got some lovely fresh bread. Thorsten, a couple of slices?'

Christina sighs. 'It's fine, Mum, sit down.'

'Thorsten?'

'We're fine, this is wonderful.'

'Any mail for me, Mum?' says Christina.

'Not really. Some more medical journals. But your father

may already have won a yacht.'

'God, they're not still harassing you are they Dad? I don't know, you show a teensy bit of interest in Fascism and they never leave you in peace.'

'We got a letter from Bridget the other day,' says Etta. 'She sounds like she's having a lovely time. She said her German's improved so much.'

'Her wallet was stolen from her room,' says Gene. 'Now she locks her door even if she's just going down the hall to the toilet.'

'I suppose that's a risk you take in a foreign country,' says Etta. 'What do you think of Berlin, Thorsten?'

'It's not like he's lived there, Mum.'

'I've only been there once,' says Thorsten. 'But it seems very interesting, lots of museums and galleries, concerts –'

'We must get my Chunuk Bair picture up,' says Gene. 'Thorsten can give me a hand after dinner.'

'You're not hanging that morbid thing in the house, are you?' says Christina.

'Pass your plate, Gene,' says Etta.

Gene stands up.

'Gene, your plate?'

'We really must get my picture up,' he says. He marches out to the hallway and begins tapping on the wall, listening like a doctor for abnormalities.

'Here,' he calls, stopping between the front door and the dining room. 'We'll hang it here. I've found a stud.'

'If only it were that easy,' sighs Christina. Thorsten laughs.

'I'm going to get my hammer,' Gene calls. 'It's in the garage, with the picture.'

'Well,' says Etta, 'we might as well start while it's still hot. You'll have to excuse Gene, Thorsten. He's always dashing off at inconvenient moments.' She unfolds her serviette.

'What's with Dad?' whispers Christina.

'Oh you know him, he's always getting these ideas into his

head and then things have to be done straight away.'

'Like moving here, you mean.'

Etta pats Christina's hand. 'You know we couldn't have stayed in the old place forever. Anyway, it was my idea to move. I just let him think it was his. He wasn't coping at all with the garden.'

'I think you have a beautiful home, Mrs Stilton,' says Thorsten. 'Hardly anyone can afford a proper house in Austria.'

'He's all right, though, isn't he,' says Christina, looking at her plate.

Etta smooths a crease out of the tablecloth. 'He's had a check-up. The doctor told him he should take up a new hobby, something to take his mind off things. Model building, or paint-by-numbers.'

Christina looks at Thorsten. 'Well,' she says, 'I guess he's all right then.'

There is a lot of thumping coming from the garage.

'Maybe I should go and help him,' says Thorsten.

Gene is trying to drag a bookcase away from a cupboard. His hands are shaking, and some books have fallen open on the smooth concrete floor.

'Let me help you with that,' says Thorsten.

Gene looks up. His face is quite white. 'I'm fine,' he says.

Thorsten picks up the books. 'You certainly have an interesting library,' he says, handing him *Hitler's Final Days*.

'Yes, it's a good collection. They were mostly presents.'

Thorsten grasps the bookcase and edges it away from the cupboard. 'If we just move it this way a bit –'

'That's fine there,' says Gene. 'Thanks, I can get it now. You'd better get back to the table. Etta can get quite agitated if she thinks people don't like her cooking.'

When Thorsten has gone, Gene sits down on a sawhorse. He can't seem to stop his hands from shaking. He closes his eyes and takes a few deep breaths, and when he looks again the garage is still there, the bookcase is still there, the pheasant he shot when he was twenty-seven is still hanging above the window. Its neck is a little skewed from the time it fell off its hook when Christina slammed the door; a fight with Bridget, he seems to recall, or was it the wind when Christina was out in the garden, and left the door open? His fishing reels will need re-oiling; he'll have to do that soon, before Christmas if possible. In the corner, his thigh waders seem to be standing up on their own, holding their shape as if someone is inside them. He must go fishing again; it seems like he hasn't been for a very long time, maybe not even since they moved.

'Gene,' Etta calls. 'Shall I put your dinner in the fridge?'

'I'm coming now.' He shuts the garage door behind him, being careful not to slam it.

'It was a bit harder to get at than I thought,' he says.

'Are you all right, Dad?' asks Christina. 'You don't look well.'

'Yes,' says Gene.

He reaches for the potatoes. His white hands knock the salt and it spills across the white cloth. Gene looks at the others, but they are eating again and seem to have noticed nothing, so he unfolds his white serviette and places it in his lap. Then he takes a pinch of salt, closes his eyes, and throws it over his left shoulder. Into the eyes of the devil, or whoever is behind his back, watching, taking aim.

The
sound of
music

Christina studies the weave in the man's jacket: a black and green tweed that is surprisingly complex up close. Two glistening tomato seeds cling to the left lapel.

'You must understand,' says the man, whose name is Jonathan, 'that you can't just throw money at them and expect them to solve their own problems. Speaking as a GP, I believe they have to be taught how to support themselves.'

'Yes indeed,' says Christina, scanning the garden. She recognises a few faces from the staff room at the hospital, but nobody she can name. The only person she knows is Andrew Martin, the Medical Superintendent whose party it is, and he's deserted her to tend to the barbecue.

'Welcome welcome,' he said when she arrived, and pressed a glass of wine into her hand. Then he tied a blue-and-white-striped apron round his waist and moved away, brandishing a pair of long metal tongs, and Christina stood shading her eyes with her hand. She could smell the sun cream evaporating from her own skin.

Jonathan waves a fly away from Christina's plate. He says, 'I mean, it's all very well for them to get subsidised doctor's visits and free prescriptions and the rest of it, but if they still live on McDonald's and beer what's the point?'

'I'm not sure.'

'I see the same scenario over and over again,' he says, 'as a GP. Tragic.'

'Yes.'

'Call me Jonno,' says Jonathan. 'Shall I get you another wine?'

Christina smiles and hands him her glass. As he walks away she notices a patch of deep sunburn on the back of his neck.

She slaps at her ankle. Her sandals are new; one of the first things she bought in Sydney.

'You should come and visit,' she had said to Etta on the phone. 'You'd love the shops.'

What she meant was: I miss you.

'I'm too old to be going overseas,' Etta had said.

Christina scratches her stomach through her slippery dress – water satin – and promises herself that she will stop drinking for the evening after this glass. She'll be working with a lot of these people.

Over by the barbecue is a woman about the same age as Christina, leaning in very close to Andrew Martin in his blue-and-white-striped apron. The woman keeps waving her hand between their faces in an attempt to brush the smoke away, and is holding a wine glass between two fingers, by its thin stem.

'Here you go,' says Jonno. 'I'm afraid it's a bit warm.'

Christina takes her glass, which is now covered with greasy fingerprints.

The woman by the barbecue skewers a sausage and waves it in the direction of Andrew Martin's crotch. They both screech with laughter. He slops wine on to the barbecue and a hiss of smoke rises.

'I see Claudia is maintaining a consistent level of taste,' says Jonno.

The sausage falls off the woman's fork and lands on the grass. An elderly man, heading for the buffet, steps on it without realising and then begins helping himself to the garlic bread.

'Aaah!' cries Andrew Martin, waving his arms. He crouches in front of the barbecue so that it looks to Christina as if flames are rising from his head. He examines the sausage, then jumps to his feet. 'Is there a doctor in the house?'

'I'm a doctor,' says the garlic bread man, his fingers shiny with melted butter.

'God help us,' mutters Jonno. 'Have you met Claudia?'

'I haven't met anyone,' says Christina. 'I'm new here.'

'Ah! Andrew said he'd invited a couple of the new nurses. The pretty ones.'

'Did he.'

'What department are you in, I'll have to pop in and say hello.'

'O and G.'

'Of course. I'm very fond of babies myself.' He glances at Christina's ring finger. 'Can I get you something more to eat? Some steak perhaps?'

'I'm vegetarian.'

'The shrimps are very good.' Jonno drains his glass. 'It's quite fashionable now, isn't it. A lot of girls come into my practice saying they're vegetarian. Most of them are just anorexic.'

'Actually, Jonno, I think I'll go inside for a bit,' says Christina.

◇

A man is dabbing at a cream linen couch with a teatowel, trying to remove a red wine stain.

'Salt's the answer.'

He looks up. 'Ah. Yes. Look, I'm terribly sorry, I was wanting to have a bit of a rest and I must have closed my eyes for a second and my glass must have tipped –'

'I don't live here,' says Christina.

'Oh.'

'You should sprinkle salt on it.' She steps into the kitchen and opens some cupboards. Olives, dark pickled walnuts, sundried tomatoes. Marinated fetta, small precious jars of pesto. Pine nuts. Salt.

'You're sure about this.'

'It can't hurt.'

They both take pinches of salt and scatter them over the stain, slowly covering it.

'Like snow,' he says.

'I've never seen snow up close.'

He frowns, then says, 'Yes, I forget where I am.'

'Where do you think you are?'

'I'm Austrian.'

'The hills are alive . . .' sings Christina.

He stops sprinkling salt. 'Please. Don't mention *that film*.'

'It's what you're famous for.'

'How would you feel if I sang "Skippy the Bush Kangaroo" every time I saw you?'

'Tell me,' says Christina, 'does it really annoy you when people think you're German?'

'Of course.'

'Must happen all the time, does it?'

'Especially here.'

'I'm not Australian, you know.'

'Oh.'

'I'm a kiwi, mate.'

'Sorry.'

'No worries, mate.'

They cover the last of the stain with the last of the salt. Some of it has embedded itself under Christina's fingernails. It feels like sand.

'There's a queue, is there?'

'Afraid so.' Christina moves away from the door to let Claudia into the bathroom.

She squeezes past, brushing a huge vase of lilies, and bangs on the toilet door. 'What are you doing, bottling it for Africa?' she yells. The lilies shake on their gilt pedestal.

Jonno emerges, wiping his mouth on a crumpled piece of toilet paper. He runs his hands under the cold water tap and splashes his face. 'Hi Chrissie,' he slurs. 'So this is where you've been hiding.'

'Mind if I go next? I'm busting.' Claudia steps into the toilet.

'Hey!'

'Pushy bitch,' says Jonno. 'Always was.'

'I heard that,' calls Claudia. 'Jesus, you could have wiped the seat.'

'Shut up,' Jonathan says to the door, leaning heavily against it. '*Shut, up.*' He runs his wet hands over his hair. 'So Chrissie,' he says, still leaning, his dampened hair the same colour as the wood, 'how about we go see what's happening at the Globe?'

'I don't think so. I . . . haven't tried the steak yet.'

Claudia opens the door and Jonathan falls inside. She steps over him and peers at herself in the mirror, which is framed in gold papier mâché to look like a sun. There are sun motifs on the hand towel and on the shower curtain, too. Cherubs balance soap dishes and pot pourri. Claudia extracts a lipstick from a fringed purse and reapplies colour to her mouth, pouting at herself in the sun mirror. 'Lust,' she says, rubbing her lips together. 'What do you think?'

'Oh . . . yes,' says Christina.

'The shade, stupid. It's called Lust.'

'It suits you.'

'I think so.' Claudia smiles in the mirror at Christina. 'Did you know that the average woman consumes one and a half lipsticks in her lifetime?'

'Shut up you boring cow.' Jonno stumbles into the hall. 'Chrissie, I'll be in the garden.'

Claudia zips her purse shut. 'He and Andrew were at med school together. God knows why, but Andrew feels obliged to invite him to all his parties.'

Christina says, 'Mm,' and shuts herself in the toilet, hitching up her satin dress.

'You're the kiwi, aren't you?' calls Claudia.

'Yes.'

'We're getting quite international at Queen Vic.' Claudia turns on a tap, and raises her voice accordingly. 'We got an English guy last week, a gastro man, and we've got two Pakistanis and an Austrian in Surgery.' There is a sound of water draining away.

'I met the Austrian, I think, just now,' shouts Christina. She emerges to find Claudia doubled over, hair almost brushing the deep carpet.

'Are you okay?'

'What?' says Claudia, straightening, flipping her hair back. She fluffs her fingers through it, adding volume, and Christina recognises the gesture then. She's done it herself, at home and at parties, in the bathrooms of strangers. And sometimes she's caught herself mid-flip in the mirror, hair flung out like seaweed.

'Nothing,' she says. She wonders how Bridget is coping in Germany; if she too misreads familiar gestures.

'So where've they put you?' says Claudia, her fingers an impatient wide-toothed comb, smoothing and teasing.

'O and G.'

'You drew the short straw.'

'I haven't started yet, Andrew's just given me the tour. I start next week.'

'You can forget a social life.'

'Well, I don't know many people yet –'

'I started in O and G. Every third weekend they make you do a 24-hour shift. I had the flu the first one I did. They gave me a pat on the back and some Sudafed. Only the daytime ones, mind you, so I wouldn't fall asleep.'

'Oh.'

'The nurses are pretty good. They make up a bed for you if one of the delivery rooms is free, and you can sleep a few minutes here and there. I never could, though. I was terrified a nurse I didn't know would come in while I was asleep and shave me and put me in stirrups.'

'Oh dear.'

'I'm up in Radiology now. Cruisiest shifts in the place.' Claudia bares her teeth at her reflection. She removes a strand of meat. 'That's where they put you once they've got sick of you everywhere else. Get to work with all the old fossils. The bone people, Andrew calls us. He's a big reader.'

'How did you two meet?'

Claudia frowns. 'Work, of course.'

'Oh. Oh I see. I thought –'

'Me and Andrew?' She laughs, one loud yelp. 'He's a shirtlifter, stupid! God, I mean look at the bathroom!'

Christina feels the heat creeping up her face. She wants to flee this room filled with suns, but she dries her hands slowly, finger by finger, ignoring the motifs on the sun-patterned towel, trying to dampen their smirks.

Monsters
of the
deep

It is eleven o'clock on a Monday morning in 1981. On to twenty-eight pitted wooden desks, twenty-eight papers have been distributed, face down. Pencils have been sharpened, biros held up to the light to check levels of ink. Blouses have been untucked, cardigans hung over the backs of wooden chairs; all bags and papers, including scrap paper, have been placed on the floor. The convent hedge rustles in the breeze outside. A bee, misunderstanding glass, thuds against the high classroom windows. They are so high they have to be opened by long pulley cords, and have not been covered with crêpe paper

Christmas trees and stylised stars and crooked nativities like the others. The looped cords sway back and forth.

Bridget Stilton fingers the Our Lady medal her mother has pinned inside her blouse pocket for luck, and hopes the fact that it has been blessed by the Pope will count for something. That is the thing about her mother, she thinks: she has such faith in her daughters' abilities that she gives them medals before the exam.

Bridget's father is in his office, talking to his foreman on the phone. 'Well what the hell have you guys been doing for the past two months?' he is saying. 'I'm meant to be bringing Burke round for a building inspection tomorrow week, and he will not be a happy man if there's no building to inspect!'

Bridget's mother says a prayer to Saint Gerard, lighting a squat candle which she keeps on her dressing table and which is hollowed from previous tests, school plays, netball competitions, music exams.

At Sacred Heart Girls' College, Bridget's sister Christina folds down her white ankle socks so she won't get a tan line, and stretches her legs in the sun.

Bridget rearranges pens and pencils, a ruler, an eraser.

'All right girls,' says Mrs Fitzroy, 'you can turn your papers over now.'

Who am I? I am an integer between one and 100. I am divisible by four, and —

Bridget reads through all the questions first, the way Gene instructed her to.

Make the necessary corrections (if any) to the following sentence: I am going to Scared Heart.

Around her the other girls are already scribbling away. Bridget reads through to the last question, then begins to write.

At lunch time, the girls compare their answers.

'What did you put for the capital of Switzerland?'

'No, stupid, it was 1939!'

'Did you do the Samoa one?'

'I've failed, I know I've failed.'

Bridget smiles and nods, but she doesn't say much. She found the exam easy, and finished well ahead of time.

'No!' groans Jodie Davis. 'Are you sure? I put Tauranga.'

The other girls scream with laughter.

'Oh, Jodie,' they say.

'I'll *die* if I don't get in to Sacred Heart,' she says, and everyone insists she will have passed easily, and that they only have the exam to make sure no really stupid people apply.

In the afternoon the class goes over to the church to practice some hymns for a funeral the next day. One of the nuns has died.

'All right, girls,' says Father Croft, holding up his hands.

They stop singing.

'I could hardly make out the words of that one,' he says, running his eyes along the rows. 'Bridget Stilton, what should this line be?' He points with his pen at the overhead transparency.

'How great thou art,' says Bridget.

'How *great* thou *art*,' say Father Croft. 'Right. That's what I want to hear. Not "how grey thou are".'

The girls laugh. Father Croft is popular; he was in the Napier earthquake and has been known to burst into classrooms and dance in front of the blackboard. When he strolls around the school grounds in the lunch hours, smoking a cigarette, he is always surrounded by a flock of pupils.

'Father Croft, Father Croft,' they call, holding their cupped hands out to him, and he will smile, and laugh, and maybe let one of them take him by the arm. They follow him over to the presbytery, and if they are lucky he will tap soft cigarette ash into their waiting palms.

'From the beginning,' he says now, and plays the opening chords on the guitar.

Bridget is pleased he asked her; although she has followed

him round the playground with everyone else, she has never been brave enough to seize his arm the way the other girls, like Jodie Davis, do.

'Well?' says her mother when Bridget arrives home from school. 'How was the exam? I said a little prayer for you at eleven o'clock.'

'It was okay.'

'Did you read it all through before you started?' says Gene that evening.

'Yes, Dad.'

'Great,' says Christina. 'I suppose this means you'll be cramping my style next year.'

'I think it's nice for both of you that you'll be at the same school,' says Etta. 'You can keep each other company.'

Bridget and Christina eye one another, but neither comments.

'Make sure you get a good look,' says Christina the next morning. 'I want details.'

'There won't be that much to see.' Bridget pauses. 'Will there?'

'They always have an open coffin, dummy. Don't you know anything?' Christina swings her schoolbag on to her shoulder and rushes out the front door to the bus stop. She only ever carries her bag on one shoulder, although it's very bad for posture. 'Only nerds use both straps,' she tells Bridget. 'You won't last long at Sacred Heart.'

At Sister John's funeral the Form Two class sits at the back of the church. Some of the girls have lacy handkerchiefs tucked in their cuffs – the more daring have tucked theirs in their waistbands – in the hope of sudden, public grief.

Bridget has never seen a dead person before; the closest she's come have been photos of Holocaust victims in Gene's war books. All through the Mass she studies the space between

Sister John and the pews and tries to judge whether or not it is too narrow to let her through without touching the coffin. When she goes up to communion she tries not to look at the body. She stares straight ahead at the golden wheat design on Father Croft's robes, and sings her consonants very clearly. She places the host on her tongue and tries to keep it from sticking to the roof of her mouth – it is bad manners, says Etta, to have to scrape Jesus off with your fingernail – and she bows her head, preparing to scuttle past Sister John as quickly as possible. The girl in front of her, however, is moving very slowly. Bridget looks up, and sees that the people returning to their seats are slowing down as they pass the coffin. Some are even placing a hand on it. Jodie Davis does. There is no way Bridget can rush past without at least a glance.

From what she can see, Sister John appears to be a most unusual colour. Greyish. *How grey thou are*, she thinks, sliding back into her seat, and she giggles. Mrs Fitzroy glances down the row and frowns at her, but Bridget can't stop laughing now that she has started. She laughs so hard she has to be taken outside by Mrs Fitzroy, and even out on the church porch she can't stop. Mrs Fitzroy looks worried.

'Sit down, dear,' she says. 'Are you feeling all right?'

'Ha! Ha! Hahahaha!' cackles Bridget.

'Is everything okay at home? Bridget? Do sit down.'

Mrs Fitzroy presses Bridget into one of the wooden seats.

'I'm sure you'll feel better in a few minutes,' she says. 'Won't you. It's just a nervous reaction, that's all. Sit down.'

But Bridget doesn't feel in the least bit nervous. In fact, she feels like she could do anything in the world. She feels like she could fly.

'That is so cool,' says Christina. 'Janine said her little sister said you just flipped out right in the middle of Mass. You should do that on Sunday, go on.'

Bridget blushes. She's a bit embarrassed now, and some of the other girls have been calling her Weird Bridget.

✧

The Health Nurse pays her annual visit to Bridget's class and shows a film called *Changing*. Rumour has it that she used to be a nun.

'Look at her hair,' the girls whisper. 'See how thin it is? That's from years of wearing a veil. She'll be bald in a few years.'

Everyone calls her the Nit Nurse behind her back. She is so softly spoken it always comes as a surprise to Bridget to hear her say words like 'scabies' and 'lice'. She's already shown the class *Changing* once, the previous year, when she came and spoke very earnestly about Bodies. She wrote it on the board like that, with a capital B, and all Bridget could think of were the photos of mass graves she had seen in Gene's books. *The bodies of thousands were discovered; victims of Hitler's insanity   Initially bodies were cremated in custom-built ovens, but as numbers increased many were disposed of in vast pits   Gold teeth, hair, and sometimes even skin were removed from the bodies   The bodies would be found piled at the entrance to the gas chambers when the doors were opened.*

This year, when the film has finished, the Nit Nurse writes *I am Special* on the board. Several girls snigger.

'Go on, Sima, ask her,' whispers Jodie Davis. Jodie sits in front of Bridget, and likes to flick her very long hair over the back of her chair. Sometimes it brushes Bridget's desk. One of Jodie's biggest drawcards is that her hair is long enough for her to sit on. She demonstrates this regularly.

Sima's hair is also very long, but she never wears it loose. She is new to St Michael's; her family have just moved to New Zealand.

'Go on,' hisses Jodie, so Sima puts up her hand and when the Nit Nurse says, 'Yes?' she says, 'What is vagina?'

A swathe of blonde hair sweeps across Bridget's exercise

book as Jodie tosses her head with laughter. Bridget laughs too.

'That's an excellent question,' says the Nit Nurse, and bustles about with overhead transparencies and coloured markers and a biro which she uses as a pointer.

A week later, letters of acceptance are sent out to parents. Everyone in Bridget's class gets in; Sacred Heart is a very fair school, as the letter points out. It no longer believes in streaming. Five per cent of its roll is reserved for non-Catholics, and another five per cent for Maori and Pacific Island pupils. This way, the girls receive a very balanced education. Bridget is one of the ones recommended for the French and German options; others, including Jodie Davis, are quietly advised to choose typing.

'And is there anything you'd like to tell me about?' says Father Croft.

Bridget quite likes the face-to-face confessions that they have now; the darkened boxes used to scare her, no matter how many times she was told she was just talking to God.

'Ah . . . I was mean to my sister,' she says.

'Mm,' nods Father Croft.

'And I said a swear word.'

'Mmhmm.'

'And I didn't dry the dishes when it was my turn.'

'Yes,' says Father Croft.

'And so Mum had to dry them.'

'Aha.' It is always around this point that Bridget runs out of things to confess. Father Croft sits waiting, eyes closed, a hand at his temple.

'Ah . . . I changed channels when Dad was in the middle of watching the news.' This is untrue.

Father Croft nods. 'Anything else?'

'I wished something bad would happen to Christina.' Also untrue. 'And I pretended I was sick last week so I wouldn't have to go to church.' Another lie.

Father Croft seems satisfied. 'Well Bridget –' he says.

'And I told some lies.'

'Yes. Well Bridget, those are all things you can try to fix, and just telling them to God now is such a good start.'

Bridget smiles, relieved she has managed to come up with a decent lot of sins. She wonders if really bad people, like murderers or kidnappers, commit those crimes just to have something to say.

'So perhaps you can try really hard to be patient with your family, and help out at home even when it's not your turn. And just remember that your Dad works very hard on his buildings all day, and when he comes home he might just want to sit and watch the news.'

'Yes,' says Bridget. 'I will try.'

'All right then. Now, before you go, let's say a prayer for your father.'

'Oh,' says Bridget, wondering what Gene has done. 'Okay.'

'Lord,' says Father Croft, closing his eyes, 'look after Bridget's father Gene, who has helped us so much with the building of the new classrooms. We pray you will reward him for his service to our parish, and guide him towards the church.'

Bridget opens her eyes, about to point out that Gene already knows where the church is, because her mother makes him come to Mass every Easter, but Father Croft continues.

'Open his eyes to your love, Lord, that he may one day join us as a member of your joyful community.' Then he places his hand on Bridget's head. 'Go in peace,' he says.

Bridget switches the television on just as *Arthur C Clarke's Mysterious World* is starting.

'Shh,' she says, glaring at Gene's rustling newspaper.

'Oh, no,' groans Christina, 'do we *have* to watch this?'

'Shh! It's starting!'

'Mum? Do we have to watch this?'

'Now, Christina,' says Etta. 'You know it's Bridget's favourite programme. You get your turn to choose too.'

Bridget flashes a smug grin at her sister, then turns back to the television. A gleaming crystal skull fills the whole screen, rotating against an inky background. The words *Monsters of the Deep* appear along the bottom.

'It better not be frogs raining from the sky again,' says Christina.

'Shh.'

'"I couldn't believe my eyes,"' says Christina in a Yorkshire accent. '"I called out to Bob to come and look, and he saw it too. We put up our umbrellas and went outside and would you believe it? Frogs were plopping down just like very big hail-stones."'

'Shh!'

'What was the sea monster that attacked and mauled this American warship?' says a voiceover.

'A frog.'

'Mum!'

'Did a giant octopus, as big as Piccadilly Circus, come ashore on this beach?'

'Are you on this one, Bridget?'

'*Mum!*'

'Maybe you could do some homework while Bridget watches her programme,' says Etta. 'It is her favourite.'

'Did the legendary serpent of the sea appear to this Cornish fisherman?'

Gene lowers his paper and watches the screen.

'This family is pathetic,' says Christina. 'I'm going to ring Janine.'

'Mysteries from the files of Arthur C Clarke, author of *2001* and inventor of the communication satellite. Now in retreat in Sri Lanka after a lifetime of science, space and writing, he ponders the riddles of this and other worlds.'

Arthur C Clarke appears on screen in a mustard T-shirt and schoolboyish grey shorts.

'Nice bifocals,' says Christina.

'You're in the way!' Bridget peers around her.

Arthur C Clarke is strolling along a beach. 'When one considers the enormous amount of unexplored ocean – there are 6000 miles of empty sea from here to the icy walls of Antarctica – one can believe that out there lurk unknown and perhaps gigantic monsters,' he says.

A black and white photo of a man in uniform is shown, and the voiceover begins again.

'The late Lieutenant Jeremy Cox was returning home to England in 1942 when he encountered one of the Second World War's most nightmarish sea stories. His troop ship was sunk by a German raider in the South Atlantic.'

Gene takes his reading glasses off and places the newspaper on the coffee table.

'Cox found himself on a flimsy raft beset by sharks. After five days came a sinister assault.'

An elderly gentleman sitting with two elderly ladies at a luncheon table appears on the screen.

'Well when I looked at his leg – he pulled up his trousers – I could see scars the size of a penny were dotted at intervals all the way up.'

'Before he died in 1971,' says the voiceover, 'Cox told the story to his sisters as well as to his friend, a biologist, Professor Cloudley-Thompson.'

The sisters sip their tea at the table with Professor Cloudley-Thompson. They are both wearing plain jumpers with pearls and have fuzzy, curly hair permed in the same style.

'All round his buttocks,' one of them is saying.

'He didn't show me that,' says Professor Cloudley-Thompson.

'He did us.'

'Yes, well you're his sisters . . . this was in the Mess.'

Gene laughs.

'An enormous shape appeared beside the raft,' says the

professor, 'and a huge arm came over and snatched one of the men, and presumably he was eaten. And they were still barely recovering from the shock of this when another arm came over the side of the raft.'

Bridget is sitting completely still, staring at the television.

'He saw it silhouetted against the starlit sky and it fastened itself on him, round his leg and round his body. Fortunately by that time people were alert, and so they grabbed on and held him, and instead of him being pulled over the side the suckers pulled lumps of skin off him.'

Etta grimaces. 'I think I might do the dishes.'

'I cannot help but speculate,' says Professor Cloudley-Thompson. 'What we know about giant squid and its attraction to red – I just wonder if the red life jacket might not have contributed to the deaths of those seamen.'

Arthur C Clarke is still walking along the beach in his mustard T-shirt and grey shorts. He is now holding a pair of flippers in one hand. 'I'm making sure my equipment is the appropriate colour,' he says, brandishing a yellow life jacket.

He stops against a backdrop of crashing waves. His arms are flabby in his T-shirt, his shoulders rounded. There are liver spots on his skin. His glasses are blackly prominent against the pale English face.

'The evidence for still unknown sea monsters is over-whelming,' he says. There is a close-up of waves washing over spidery crabs on the sand. 'The solution to this old mystery may come quite soon. At the moment the two greatest powers on earth are trying to develop sonar systems which will make the seas transparent, so they can track each other's nuclear submarines. Those systems will locate the sea serpent, if it exists. Indeed at this moment the evidence for its existence may be somewhere within the Pentagon or the Kremlin.'

'Wow,' says Bridget.

✧

'Hold this,' says Gene, handing Christina the end of some transparent nylon fishing line. 'And this.' A reel of thick green. Then he begins unwinding the nylon, pacing away from Christina, looping it around the trunks of the silver birches. He runs it through his fingers, checking for inconsistencies, weak spots. His cracking shoes ('they'll do for holidays, Etta') leave footprints in the damp motel lawn. When he is back to where he started, he places the empty reel on a plastic bag at Christina's feet.

'Now. Hold them together, very steady.' He overlaps the thick green line with the thin nylon one by a few centimetres and begins painting them with glue. The fumes catch in Christina's nostrils.

'Lovely morning,' calls Mrs van der Wyst, the owner of the motel. Gene does not answer her. He is carefully winding green cotton around the join, leaving no gaps. Then he seals the cotton with clear nail polish and blows softly on it, instructing Christina to turn it, to roll it slowly between her fingertips.

'Breakfast!' Etta steps on to the lawn.

'Careful!' yell Gene and Christina, and then Etta sees the clear fishing line strung from tree to tree like some elaborate game of cat's cradle. She ducks under it again and again until she reaches Gene and Christina.

'Breakfast,' she says.

'If you fell in there your flesh'd be boiled right off your bones,' says Gene.

Etta says, 'Don't scare them,' and she shivers, stepping back from the edge of the platform.

'Really?' says Christina, watching the steam swirl on the surface of the water. Through the clear patches she can see right down to the white floor. There are a few icecream wrappers and chip packets drifting along the bottom, their colour leached away by the boiling water. Christina holds the metal railing, and it is hot from the sun or the water, she doesn't know which, and she can feel the initials and obscenities and shaky hearts scratched into the paint beneath her palm.

'Dad,' says Bridget, 'can we have an icecream?'

On the bridge they look into the river for fish.

'There's one,' says Gene, pointing to a spot almost directly beneath them.

'He must be a grandad!' says Bridget.

Christina squints.

'See him? Down there, just moving in and out of those weeds.' Gene takes Christina's finger and points it towards the river. 'He's a rainbow. You can see his pink markings.'

Christina stares. 'Oh yes,' she says, but all she sees are the weeds moving with the current of the river.

Gene unlocks the door to pool number six. There is a sign nailed to it warning bathers not to put their heads under the water, and a picture of a bug. The bug is much larger than the writing. Christina tickles the back of her mother's knee with her beach towel and Etta jumps, letting out a small scream.

The pool is open to the sky and has wide concrete steps leading into it. Etta heads straight for the changing cubicle. The girls and Gene have their togs on underneath their clothes. They undress by the side of the pool, then ease themselves into the warm water.

'Mum, we're in,' they call. 'Mum! Are you coming?'

After a while Etta emerges wrapped in a towel, which she whisks off only at the very edge of the pool. She has a bathing suit on underneath; a thick, lined construction that feels rough to the touch when it is dry, and seems to be all points and edges: wide straps, thick seams, two floral cones jutting from her chest that can be dented with a finger. Around the hips is a stiff frill, a vestigial skirt that floats up in the water. She has a rubber bathing cap on her head – the floppy flowers move as she walks – and plastic sandals on her feet, which she leaves on as she inches her way down the steps. The girls giggle as the skirt rises and spreads in the water.

Bridget and Gene dog-paddle from one end to the other, racing one another. Etta sits on the second-to-last step, calling encouragement, her knees white islands above the water. Christina rests her elbows on the rim of the pool and moves her feet slowly, letting her body float. Above the walls the sky is a perfect square. Clouds end abruptly, tailored to the corners the Stiltons have rented for an afternoon.

'Best of five,' says Bridget, leaning on Gene's shoulder and jumping into the air. 'Go on.'

Christina observes her sister's thick body, her unformed waist, her convex stomach. Her flat chest.

'In a little while,' says Gene. 'I have to conserve my strength for tomorrow morning. So do you.'

'You're mad,' says Etta. 'There'll still be fish in the lake at a more civilised hour.'

'She doesn't get it,' says Gene, and Bridget says, 'She never gets it.'

'The early start's the whole point. The quiet, when no-one else is around. No screaming family groups scaring the trout away. The solitude. Man and fish.'

'Ah.'

'She still doesn't get it.'

'I'm not coming,' says Christina.

The other three turn to look at her. She kicks with her feet, keeping herself afloat.

'You always come.'

'I don't want to any more.'

'Well,' says Etta, 'maybe we can do something together instead. Go for a walk.'

'I'm going to sunbathe. And Mrs Styles said I could look at her new paintings.'

'Oh. Good, yes.'

'But you always come! Dad, she's not coming.'

'She doesn't have to if she doesn't want to,' says Gene. 'We are on holiday.'

Christina grips the edge of the pool with her elbows. She can feel the warm, rough concrete pressing against her skin, making craters. She watches Gene and Bridget moving around the pool, swimming, jumping, chasing one another, trying to run in water, and Etta, perched on the second-to-last step, checking her shoulders every so often for sunburn. Christina finds them ugly, her family, foreshortened by the water. They are whiter than ever. She observes her own tanned legs, her small ankles, her long arms. Gene, Bridget and Etta are white as pumice.

'Don't splash, don't splash!' Etta cries every so often.

Christina does not splash. She hardly moves at all.

Sydney is pretty exciting

On a Tuesday afternoon, in the middle of summer, the sky is blue and Christina goes back to the lake. She is surrounded by sun, clear water, even a wheat field. There is a perverse feeling of fertility in the air, as if you could fall pregnant just by stretching your limbs in the sun and breathing in.

She can't believe she's here again.

Things have changed, of course, shrunk to fit her adult perspective. The owners' house looks tiny to her now when she knocks at the front door, and when Mrs van der Wyst answers Christina finds herself staring down at an old woman who seems to be folding in on herself. That is a perfectly natural symptom of old age, Christina thinks. The cartilage between the vertebrae slowly degenerates and the spine shortens, causing the person to shrink. But she feels enormous beside this tiny woman, and she ducks her head as she steps inside.

'Now what was the name?' says Mrs van der Wyst.

'Oh. Stilton. Christina.'

'And it's just you, is it?'

'Just me.'

'Right, we'll pop you in Unit 5 then. Towels are over there already, and I bring fresh ones round every morning at nine.'

Christina wants to say, I know that. And I can ask you if I want extra ones, and the sheets are changed every third day at one o'clock. I can borrow an iron if I need one and the dairy down the road closes at seven.

'Thank you,' she says. 'I'll be staying until Saturday.'

Every time she comes back to New Zealand from Sydney something seems smaller. The railway station, Lambton Quay, the Hutt River. Her circle of friends. Etta always says, 'It must seem pretty slow to you now,' or, 'Wellington must be a bit sleepy for you now.' Christina knows Etta wants her to deny this, to reassure her that she will come back, that she will not be living overseas forever.

'Sydney is pretty exciting,' she tells her mother. 'I do enjoy the faster pace in Sydney,' or, 'There's so much going on in Sydney.'

Unit 5 has only one room; two single beds with brown candle-wick covers, a formica table and two chairs, a television. At one end there is a kitchenette with a squat fridge (no freezer compartment), a sink and two electric rings. There are thick white plates and cups in the cupboard and white lino tiles on the floor. They are speckled with gold. The bathroom is so small Christina has to squeeze against the toilet to get out. Of course, she reminds herself, this unit is designed for a couple at most, not a family of four. She pulls on her swimming togs – high-cut, to show off her legs. Thorsten chose them.

The sand dunes have eroded to gentle swells, and crossing them requires no particular effort. The tussock only reaches to her ankles. It brushes her bare skin, teasing her, trying to make her smile as she heads for the lake. That's still there – what was she expecting? – and is just as cold as she wades in. Her hair furls around her in the water like a slow secret. She lies on her back, only her face breaking the surface, moving her arms as if in flight. All she can hear is her own breathing, amplified to that level where you remember how easy it would be to stop. Or, another possibility: to just walk to that part of the lake where the velvet mud drops away – this is always closer than you imagine – and sink.

Eileen could appear at any moment.

She was there every year when the Stiltons came to the lake at Christmas. Bridget and Christina could see her house as their car, hot and smelling of strawberries and sun-softened vinyl, pulled into the motel driveway. There would be that familiar crunch of pumice gravel, that particular summer sound, slow and crackling like an unwrapping present. They would see her on the second or third day; as if by chance she would be walking in the evening about the same time they were. Then she would ask them did they want to come in for a piece of Christmas cake – at least one month of luck, at least – and they would ask how her painting was going. Don't traipse sand all through the place, their mother always warned at the door. Mrs Styles doesn't want sand all through the place.

Call me Eileen, she reminded the girls every year. Christina sometimes caught herself imagining she was her natural mother, whom she always pictured living by a lake or a mountain or in a lush valley, but this possibility was disproved whenever Christina compared Eileen's features with her own. Eileen was short, with wide hips and a fleshy nose, small eyes, plump hands.

Her hair was crinkly, sometimes frizzy, depending on the weather. Up close, tiny red lines scrawled their way across her face, making her cheeks look evenly rosy from a more polite distance. She could have been a Stilton. Say thank you to Mrs Styles for the cake, Etta told them each time they visited. Actually the girls hated almond icing and those chunks of bitter peel, but they thanked her anyway.

Christina has heard rumours over the last few days, since she has been back in New Zealand, that this summer will be disappointing. She can't be sure, though, if there really is a chill in the air, or just speculation clouding and spreading. At evening – or rather, that time just before, when you can no longer decently talk of afternoon – the oyster sky curves down around her and she thinks this weather will never stop.

✧

Etta's father wanted her to be called Eileen, but Etta's mother insisted on Henrietta as a first name all through the pregnancy, and during the child's dangerous unchristened days. Even on the way to the church, she argued with Owen. He was fond of the name Eileen – after a sister of his who died at birth.

'There has always been a Henry Moynihan,' Maggie stated. 'The tradition must be continued, even though she's a girl.'

As the priest held the silent child over the water, Maggie was still arguing. Henrietta prevailed, with Eileen as a second name.

Etta did not cry at her christening. It's good luck if a baby does, but Maggie was not superstitious. Owen was glad that his child had been baptised; that her soul was now safely recorded. He did call her Eileen at times, though, when Maggie wasn't around.

Christina is out quite far in the lake now; past the raft, even, that was always such a long way away. Etta never liked them swimming out to it, and warned of poisonous splinters, and probable head injuries if the water became rough. Christina laughs, and the sound seems to come from a great distance. And she floats on her back, catching accidental garlands in her hair, and watches the sky for changes.

Etta was always cautioning the girls to be careful in the lake. They think she was afraid of it; she is afraid of water in general. This extends to shower cubicles – she hates all that water around her face, she says, and the walls so close. She always has baths at home – shallow ones – but at the lake motel there was only a cramped shower. Mouldy, unhygienic things, she said, help me take down the curtain. She never came swimming with them, although there is a photo of her standing knee-high in the lake, her modestly frilled swimsuit awkwardly dry. She is clutching Bridget's chubby three-year-old fists while Christina creeps up, ready to splash. Even at the hot pools, they had to coax her in by insisting it was just like a big bath. She could just tolerate sitting in the private, cubicled ones specially built for holiday-makers, as long as the girls didn't splash, but she went nowhere near the outdoor pools. Splashing here was also prohibited; everyone knew that invisible bugs could crawl up your nose and make your brain explode. Etta would sit on a deck chair at the edge and call warnings.

Eileen Styles snorted at this. She went under all the time, she told them, it was marvellous, and Christina should try – Quick, girls, interrupted Etta, we have to get some eggs before the shop closes.

It is possible that Etta's water phobia dates back to her early childhood. There is a rumour, some murky story about the stream on their farm, and Etta, aged about three, escaping from Maggie and wandering down to look at the wild swans. Christina imagines her reaching out to pluck a black quill, then suddenly finding herself under water. She does not imagine the actual falling or sinking, just her hair, tangling in the reeds and holding her under.

She had it cut soon after she and Gene adopted Christina, and Bridget was born. It was too much work, with two children under three. The last evidence of it appears in the first photo of Bridget. Etta's exhausted face is turned towards a bluish bundle in an incubator beside her bed, and her hair is spread out around her as if the strands are reaching for the child in her glass box. (There are more photos of Christina than there are of Bridget – she was the first child, after all – but there are none of her this young. She was already two weeks old when Gene and Etta collected her from the Home of Compassion.)

As girls, Bridget and Christina were never allowed long hair. Too much work. It is a new feeling now, Christina's hair fanning around her in the lake, writing messages just to the side of her field of vision. She had short hair then, and a flat body. Now she displaces the water in a much more complicated way; hollows and swells surprise her, as if they have appeared overnight.

She tested the ground before she came back to New Zealand. Not with her mother; she would have had to explain too much. Instead, she rang Bridget in Germany. It was simpler.

'That woman who was there every year when we went to the lake, the one who painted.'

There was a pause, longer than the time lapse between Sydney and Berlin.

'Eileen was her name. A Mrs Styles.'

'Eileen?' Bridget couldn't remember any Eileen. 'A painter? What did she paint?'

'Landscapes, the lake . . . I think she did some horses –'

'Were there horses up there?'

'I know she did watercolours of some of the baches.'

'Sorry,' said Bridget. 'Hey, I hear Dad's taken over the garage with his fly-tying stuff. Mum can hardly squeeze her car in.'

'Yes, she told me in her last letter,' said Christina, suddenly aware of her own voice, the way the words snagged. Lately she'd found herself making many such comments; casual challenges. It was as if now, in their mid-twenties and living in different countries, there was space enough for Christina to spread out their rivalry, to unroll it between Bridget and herself like a blanket on a beach. And then the jostling, the prodding would begin, because one of them could lie on it but not both, never both. If Bridget had received a postcard from Etta, Christina had been sent a fat letter. If Bridget mentioned a letter, Christina mentioned a phone call. And there was nothing Bridget could say about the family, no piece of information she could reveal, that Christina did not already know.

'Don't let him near you with those hobby scissors of his,' Bridget was saying. 'Before I left he was after me to give him some of my hair for a trout fly. Actually,' she said, lowering her voice, 'I didn't come over here to study German at all.'

'No?'

'No. I came over,' she dropped to a whisper, as if Gene and Etta could hear her, 'to escape from *them*.'

'Ah.'

'Nobody else's parents are that old.'

'No.'

'And Dad will simply not admit he needs a hearing aid. Can't even hear the phone ringing in the next room.'

'Yes, Mum said last time she rang,' said Christina. Another snagging in her throat. But she is sure she receives more calls than Bridget; she has not run off to the other side of the world. She is much closer. 'I'm leaving Thorsten with the parents while I go up to the lake. For a few days.' Another prod.

'Is he aware of this,' said Bridget, 'or is it a Christmas surprise?'

'He knows. He's fine about it.'

'Dump him. He's obviously peculiar.'

'Mum'll love it. You know how she is with guests.'

Bridget paused. 'You know the only thing she never wanted

me to do?' she said. 'Have an abortion. She didn't care what I
did, I'd always be welcome at home. She didn't care if I came
home and announced I was a lesbian, but she never wanted me
to have an abortion.'

'She said exactly the same thing to me,' said Christina.

✧

Christina wonders what her parents do all day. If they enjoy
pottering around the place, choosing curtain material for their
new low-maintenance townhouse, paying some enterprising
schoolboy to clean the cars, which are all of a sudden too big to
look after. When she gets letters from her mother, Christina
would like to know if Etta misses the house where she grew up;
if she has bad dreams; if she ever wishes she had sons. Perhaps
she really is writing these things; her writing is so poor Christina
often has to fill the gaps in herself. She could make it up, she
supposes, pad out the bones with muscles and tissue and blood
and fat. But then it would be her story. Sometimes she can't
untangle the two, anyway; sometimes she thinks it is herself
caught in the reeds and drowning; that she had all those
unspoken miscarriages; that she was forced to become right-
handed. She cannot add flesh, however much she would like
to. She can only expose bone.

Etta must have begun school on her fifth birthday. Christina
imagines she would not have cried when she was parted from
Maggie, her mother, who had dressed her in gumboots because
the unsealed road was muddy.

'But remember to take them off at the door, my girl,' Maggie
would have said. 'We don't want you traipsing mud all through
the place. We don't want to have to get the strap out again.'

The nuns called her Ettie, and sometimes, on more formal
occasions such as the calling of the roll, Henrietta. (But never
Eileen.) They had white-framed faces and plain, sensible hands.
Each wore a dull silver ring that married her to God, that old

polygamist, and each had an oversized set of rosary beads at her waist. These were the only source of sound when a nun walked. Or floated; it was never proved. Nuns had no footsteps. They were, in fact, mostly robes. Black and floor-length, these both concealed and created mysteries, such as whether nuns had any legs at all. These women seemed to glide like the black swans on the stream. Etta was afraid of the swans.

The nuns had an astonishing range of powers vested in them. The wooden pointer, in particular, was a versatile tool. It could be vaguely swept over the map of the world, indicating the desert homelands of starving children. It could be used to single out the disobedient, and pointed like a dried bone at the trouble-maker. It could be rapped across insolent buttocks or visited upon lazy, scale-fumbling fingers. It could be slipped through the elbows of a sloucher, enforcing good posture, and it could be pointed like a wand at the alphabet that uncurled across the top of the blackboard, inciting the class to chant.

Ettie would have had no problems learning her alphabet; it was a nursery rhyme, a game. The nuns noticed nothing wrong with her. A little shy, a little pale, perhaps, and she seemed to bruise easily, but nothing troublesome. Nothing that deserved a dose of the pointer, certainly. Children like Ettie never needed physical punishment.

A flaw must have been discovered, however, when the class moved on to writing. Ettie would have gripped the pencil in her left hand, ready to express her five-year-old self. This was not a good sign. Sister Ignatius prised it from Ettie's fingers and inserted it into Etta's clumsy right fist.

Christina wonders if this moment was all-deciding. Etta might have become an actor, a dancer, a painter, had she been allowed to describe her world back-to-front. She might have become Eileen. But habits, once acquired, are hard to break. Each night when she goes to sleep, Etta still crosses her arms over her heart as the nuns instructed her. In case she dies in the night. Christina has observed her mother's body feigning death when she has caught her sleeping.

There is a swishing in the tussock, a soft shattering of pumice stones. It is a woman, a little stooped, leathered arms bare in a brown swimsuit. An Indian print skirt flaps around her ankles, and the flesh on her back has been scalloped by gravity. Long, smoky strands of hair trail behind her. She shades her eyes and looks out across the lake.

'Hello,' she calls out to Christina's bobbing, watching head. 'Lovely day, isn't it?' Her old voice shivers across the water. 'Don't stay out too long, the sun's pretty fierce.'

Exactly the sort of thing a mother – Christina's mother – would say. She crunches away again, pausing at the peninsula to skip a pumice stone across the lake. It looks as if it will reach right to the other side. Christina doesn't see where it stops, and when she turns back the woman is gone.

When she returns home for Christmas, Christina plans to try and write in her diary with her left hand. With the creative side; the female side. The awkward side. She imagines her hand shivering across the page, mapping out vibrations and fissures, jerking out jagged points like a seismograph. She sees days, stories lying parallel to one another, converging somewhere in the distance, at infinity.

Some time during her last week at the hospital, before she caught the plane to Wellington, Christina insisted on taking Andrew Martin out for a drink. To thank him for making her feel so welcome in Sydney, she said.

At the bar she leaned into him like a gossip. 'Andrew,' she said, 'what do you know about mesothelioma?'

''Tis the season to be jolly, eh?' He took tiny sips of margarita, trying to avoid the salted rim of the glass. 'Nasty business, actually. Cancer between the lungs and the chest wall. Always terminal.'

'Yes,' said Christina.

'Lies dormant for about thirty years and then up it pops. Usually from asbestos exposure years before. A lot of old electricians, plumbers, builders starting to drop like flies now.' He licked grains of salt from his lips, screwing up his nose. 'Costing the industry huge amounts in claims. Not that compensation helps the poor buggers much. Once it gets going they give you about ten months.'

'Have you seen anyone with it?'

'A couple. Like I say, they're only just starting to pop up now.' He lowered his voice. 'Lot of cases misdiagnosed as lung cancer, in my view.'

'Is it . . . painful?'

'Like any cancer. You can choose between extreme pain and being lucid, or a lesser amount of pain and being incoherent on morphine and whatnot. There's a guy down in Ward 9 if you're interested. Go have a prod, he won't mind. Won't even know.'

'Esther. I've been meaning to tell you, I can't come to the wedding. You mustn't hold it against Mum, it's not her fault, you know how she is.' The man clawed at Christina's sleeve.

'That's all right, it's okay,' said Christina.

'Poor Esther, her special day, her day . . .'

'Yes.'

The man squeezed Christina's fingers. 'You will tell her, you'll tell her, won't you?'

'Yes, it's all right, try and rest.' Christina summoned a nurse. 'He's quite agitated,' she whispered. 'Can you give him something?'

'Are you all right?' The nurse was looking at Christina, not at the old man. 'Do you know him?'

'Me, no I'm fine, goodness me.' Christina took one of the

man's tissues – soft apricot ones in a floral box, not hospital white – and rushed off, looking at her watch. She found a spare seat in a corridor and sank into it, giving the bored people leafing through magazines something else to look at while they waited.

✧

One year, they found Eileen Styles with her arm in plaster. She'd fallen off a horse.

'I should know better than to go riding horses at my age,' she said.

Christina asked her how she would be able to paint with the cast on, and Eileen picked up a pencil in her right hand and wrote 'E M Styles' on a ten-dollar note, right over the Queen's face. Then she gave it to Christina, despite Etta's protests, and said she'd simply taught herself to use her right hand instead. For the whole holiday, Eileen's arm was cocooned and turning surprising shades of brown and purple, which you could see when you peered down the cast. But it didn't hurt a bit. She showed Christina a painting she was doing of the lake; she didn't normally let anyone see her work before it was finished, but just this once. It was a slightly different lake from her left-handed ones. Christina could take it home with her, if it was finished in time. It was a slow business, becoming ambidextrous, but well worth it. Christina should try it.

On the way home in the car, she held the lake on her knees. By the time they were back, she couldn't remember the word Eileen had told her, the one for people who can use both hands equally well. Every time she tried to recall it, all she came up with was amphibian.

It's getting colder in the water, but Christina doesn't want to get out just yet. Her hair will probably be a mess of knots, she knows, but she didn't want to plait it. It would have felt short. Thorsten tells her she has mermaid hair. He held it over her face once, and kissed her through it, and she felt like she was drowning. He doesn't know what she looked like with short hair. Sometimes she threatens to have it cut, but she never would. She just enjoys hearing his protests.

He wanted to come with her. A few days at your famous lake would be great, he said. But she made excuses, slipped away, alone. Her parents were keen to show him round Wellington, she told him, take him Christmas shopping, make him feel welcome. They'd keep him busy. He couldn't refuse; they'd be offended.

'I think I do remember her,' Bridget said just before she hung up. 'She did pottery.'

'That's her,' said Christina.

'I think she had a crush on Mum. She was always patting her on the hand and giving her little winks when she thought we weren't looking.'

'I don't remember that.'

Bridget laughs, confident of her own knowledge. 'Have you seen the photos of what they used to wear? Not an elegant decade for swimwear, the seventies.'

Christina doesn't know what she was expecting. Eileen would be elderly now, if she were even still alive. It's hardly likely she would just come walking past, recognise Christina Stilton floating in the water and invite her home for a cup of tea.

Christina closes her eyes and summons Eileen's face. Fleshy nose, she thinks. Rosy cheeks. Small eyes. It's no use. Eileen becomes more and more transparent. She dissolves. Christina should get out now, she should go. There's a chill in the air, and she's wrinkling.

'We used to come here all the time,' she says. 'Every Christmas.'

Mrs van der Wyst opens a drawer and rummages about. 'You'd be amazed how many we lose. People just take them with them when they leave. I'm sure they don't mean to, but it's such a bother. Here we are.' She hands Christina a pen.

'We were always in Unit 2. Dad used to store his trout in your freezer.' Christina signs the cheque with her physician's scribble, one wavy line except for the capital S.

'A doctor,' says Mrs van der Wyst, reading the typed version of Christina's name above the signature. 'We didn't know we had a doctor staying with us.'

Christina places the pen on the table and loops her bag over her shoulder. She closes her hand round her car keys, the metal ring heavy in her palm and warm from the sun.

'You're not Gene and Etta's wee girl are you?' says Mrs van der Wyst, suddenly making herself bigger with interest.

'No,' says Christina. 'You must have me confused with someone else.' She walks to the door and steps out into the warm morning.

'Because we used to have some Stiltons here, every summer.' Mrs van der Wyst is following her down the steps, growing taller by the minute.

'I've left the dirty towels in the shower,' says Christina. 'Thank you. Goodbye.'

'Yes,' calls Mrs van der Wyst. 'Merry Christmas!'

Christina starts her car. She doesn't bother to turn it around in a careful three-point turn like Gene always did. Instead, she eases down the drive in reverse. She can watch the lake the whole way. In the foreground is Mrs van der Wyst, waving madly. She's still waving when Christina reaches the road.

❖

She's watching for the statue. Every year it had signalled to her that the car trip was nearly over, that she could undo her safety belt and get out, away from her parents and Bridget, and find her things exactly as she had left them. The statue meant there was only half an hour to go. Twenty minutes, with Christina driving. Another shrinkage.

On the passenger seat Christina has placed a cardboard box

filled with strawberries. She can take or leave strawberries, but she knows Etta and Gene will be expecting them. She stopped at one of the market gardens just out of Levin that had huge berry and vegetable placards swinging from stands at the side of the road. A carrot as tall as Christina, an apple the size of her car. She parked in the shade of a giant loganberry.

'So cheap,' Etta will say. 'You'd be a fool to pass up such a bargain.'

Christina got two kilos of strawberries for $5. As an afterthought she bought some nectarines ($1.50 a kilo), some sweetcorn (twelve for $2) and some green beans ($1 a kilo). She drew the line at watermelon.

The sun's shining right on the strawberries now, making the car smell like freshly made jam. Christina's tried putting the visor down but it's no use; it's coming through the side window. As she rounds a bend a few of the berries topple from the box. She can see them rolling around on the floor each time she turns the wheel.

And then the hillside appears, and in the middle of the rich green she can see a figure, tall, straight, completely white. It gleams in the afternoon sun. It seems to float. Christina keeps glancing at it and then back to the road. Statue, road, statue. Statue. Statue.

She hasn't gone to church for years, not since she left school. Unless you count Midnight Mass, which she still manages to attend for Etta's sake. She and Bridget sit at the back and snigger about the experimental choir pieces, the men who can't stay awake, the woman who has supported the same bouffant hairdo for the last twenty years. Christina's certainly never had a religious phase, like Bridget did. In fact, she likes to take credit for pulling her sister out of her churchy period by introducing her to pink Chardon – $4.95 a bottle and it tasted like fizzy Ribena, she told Bridget. So she cannot explain why she is now almost veering into oncoming traffic to see a statue of the Virgin Mary. She pulls over to the side of the road and eats a strawberry, flicking the star-shaped base out the window.

'There's Our Lady,' Etta would say, turning round in her seat to the girls. 'We're nearly home now.'

Christina puts the box of strawberries in the shade on the floor and winds the windows up.

At the bottom of the track there is a cluster of pine trees. Someone has wound red plastic tape around them, looping from trunk to trunk, enclosing a small area as if for private use. *Keep out danger keep out danger* says the tape.

The walk is steeper than Christina expected, and she is panting by the time the trees start to thin out and the sky reappears. She watches the ground as she walks, watches her feet moving, listens to her breaths. One, two, three, four . . . Bridget had missed seeing the statue on the way home one year. She'd been asleep. There'd been a piercing tantrum on the Haywards Hill when she woke up, and Gene had finally turned the car round and they'd driven back. Bridget always got her own way.

When Christina emerges from the mouth of the track there is a sweep of grass sloping up from the edge of the hill. At the top is the statue.

She looks different up close. Cruder. It's like seeing a famous person at a restaurant or in a shop, a person who was previously familiar to you only through photographs or film, and you realise he or she is fatter than you thought, or has bad skin, or thin hair, or is short. And you can't help staring and feeling somehow betrayed; lied to.

Christina takes in the thick cables mooring the statue to the hillside, the crazed paint, the lightbulb halo. She follows her gaze out to sea. An empty horizon.

'They had to turn her halo off during the war,' Gene told them one year.

'Really?' said Bridget.

'But we were never bombed,' Christina pointed out.

'Preventive measures.'

'Actually,' said Etta, 'it wasn't erected until well after the war.'

Bridget and Christina were silent in the back seat then, both refusing to believe their mother. Christina remembers rolling her eyes at Bridget, and Bridget laughing and copying the gesture. Their mother had placed her head back on her pillow, trying to out-sleep motion sickness, too weary to argue her point.

Christina sits down. She leans her back against the base of the statue, against the word *conception*. There are a few empty beer cans scattered around, and some cigarette butts, and there are floodlights positioned in the trees like Christmas decorations. It would be a great view from up here at night. Christina thinks of the statue during the war – she has decided that it must have been there then – camouflaged, stalwart on the dark hillside, her stone eyes scanning the horizon for threat. Or she might have sung to approaching men, drawing them to her, telling them lies, her white carved hair unadorned by electricity, her voice like the sea.

Christina closes her eyes. There is plenty of time. She is in no hurry to get home.

The front door is flung open and Etta runs down the drive to Christina's car.

'Thank goodness, thank goodness,' she says, over and over.

'Hi Mum.'

'Where have you been?'

Christina frowns at her. 'The lake,' she says slowly, as if to a small child, and hands her mother the bag of vegetables and the strawberries.

'You said you'd be back for a late lunch. We were expecting you hours ago.'

Christina lifts her bag from the boot and walks up the neat drive. It's still strange coming home to this small townhouse.

She feels she should be dumping her holiday toys, sandy jandals, giraffe beach towel in the room she shared with Bridget and running out to the big garden to see if the plums are ripe, if the grass has grown knee-high.

'We rang the motel and they said you'd checked out at ten,' says Etta.

Christina deposits her bag in the compact guest room, with its twin beds made up for her and Thorsten, and in a few steps she is in the living room.

'Hi Dad, hi Thorsten.'

'Your mother's been frantic. The quiche is *ruined*,' says Gene cheerfully.

'Now, then. I was wondering about lunch, that's all.'

'I stopped off for a while on the way home,' says Christina.

'Ah,' says Gene. 'The Army Museum.'

'Christina's brought us some strawberries, isn't that nice? And some corn and things. I'll bet you got a bargain.'

'Did you pick them yourself?' says Gene. 'That's what she's been doing, she's been out picking strawberries.'

'We can have them for tea. You are here for tea, aren't you?'

'Yes, Mum.'

'We put the tree up, do you mind? Thorsten helped me decorate it.'

'It's very nice.'

'Thorsten did the lights and the miniature apples. He's been telling us about his operations. Imagine, two emergency appendectomies in one day!'

'Why don't you sit down, Mum, and we'll get some coffee.'

'No, I'll get it, you've had a long drive.'

'A very long drive.'

'Gene. She's here now.' Etta heads for the kitchen. 'How about a sandwich? Does anyone want a sandwich? The bread was still warm when I bought it.'

'Mum, sit down, we'll –'

'I think Christina would like to *get the coffee*,' says Gene.

'With her *boyfriend*.'

'Oh,' says Etta. 'Yes. Actually, I'd rather have a cup of tea.'

'So has Dad been keeping you supplied with beer?'

'Beer, whisky, port . . . I can hardly remember Tuesday. I think we went on the cable car.'

'Probably just as well then.'

'They took me to the zoo yesterday. They thought I might like to see a kiwi.'

'God, I am sorry. I had no idea.'

'Couldn't see a thing. By the time my eyes had adjusted to the dark the place was full of German backpackers.'

'Nightmare.'

'Your Dad kept trying to point out kiwis to me. All I could see were pieces of bark, or bits of neon clothing. And your Mum didn't come in with us. She went and queued for icecreams.'

'She's not fond of small dark spaces. Except confessionals.'

'She got me a double cone of hokey pokey. Chocolate dipped.'

'She likes you.'

'I thought as much.'

'We took Thorsten to the zoo yesterday,' says Etta.

'Yes, he was just saying.'

'He saw his first kiwi.'

'Really? That must have been exciting for you, Thorsten.'

'Oh yes. Such mysterious creatures. Very good at hiding.'

'Thorsten? Are you asleep?'

'Mmm.'

'Is that a yes or a no?'

Thorsten opens his eyes. 'Where have you been?'

'Watching TV. *General Hospital* was on.'

'Do you ever sleep?'

'It was a double episode. They had a heart transplant from

a baboon. Ethical challenges, pleading families, animal rights activists. Except you could tell it was meant to be shown in two parts, because after the first hour it said to be continued, and then there was an ad for The Amazing Abdominator, and then it did. Continue.'

'You're a robot, aren't you?'

'Yes.'

'Can I go to sleep now?'

'No.' Christina pulls back the blankets on Thorsten's bed. 'Isn't that cute, all tucked up with his jim-jams on.'

'Your mother's taken to bringing me breakfast in bed. I can hardly sit up and take the grapefruit and scrambled eggs and toast strips – what do you call them? – with nothing on.'

'Soldiers. You never know, she might be hoping to catch a glimpse of your taut young European body and that's why she's bringing you food, did you ever think of that?'

'I'd prefer not to. Can you pull the blankets up, it's cold.'

Christina slides in beside him. 'It's the middle of summer.'

'It is in Sydney. This is not the tropical paradise they tell you about in Austria, you know.'

He pushes half the pillow over to Christina. She curls into his back, and breathes in the fresh laundry smell of his pyjamas. They smell familiar. They smell like the washing powder Etta has always used.

Snow

comes

inside

Before Bridget Stilton went to Germany to study, she made tapes of herself. She recorded words in English, with a pause between each one so she could say the German equivalent back to her own voice. She realised they would sound strange to anyone who came across them, but at that stage her main concern was to be able to understand, and make herself understood. She'd forgotten all her German from school.

'Mother,' her voice said, 'Father. Toilet. House. To be.'

Etta worried about her going.

'For God's sake try not to look foreign,' she said. She gave her objects which Bridget felt obliged to take with her. A sewing kit in a gold cardboard purse, an inflatable neck pillow, a My Trip notebook, a Saint Christopher medal. Etta had never been overseas.

There were tears at the airport; even Gene cried.

'I'm not dying you know,' said Bridget. 'I just want to learn a foreign language. I am coming back.'

Which made Etta cry even more.

'Ring us as soon as you get there,' said Gene. 'Don't worry what time it is.'

Etta writes every week. Their new townhouse is wonderful, best move they ever made, Christina is coming home for Christmas with an Austrian boy, isn't that a coincidence, it's really quite hot now for November, Jimmy – no, I mean Jim – won a prize for a deer he shot, Colin and Janet had a boy and they want to call him Clifford, I mean I know it's a family name but really. She hopes Bridget is making lots of new friends at university, and that her German's improving, and that she's not too cold.

Gene sometimes adds a note at the bottom.

When Bridget writes home, she is careful. She is not losing her English, exactly, but some of the words feel strange in her mouth. Sometimes she's not sure if she's said things quite right. She doesn't want to make any mistakes.

Her room in the hostel is quite small, she writes, but it's clean, the other students are friendly, there is one Indonesian woman who eats only in her room. The campus is huge, the European Languages department alone covers several kilometres, the students never call the lecturers by their first name. Here is a photo of the Wall, they left a bit of it intact as a reminder. That's her on the left. Here is a key-ring for their new townhouse. It has a piece of Wall in it. She has a feather duvet which is very warm. There are huge black birds everywhere in the city, she thinks they might be crows, they have beautiful feathers. She would send one, a feather she means, but she thinks it would be illegal. She'd like to be able to bring some back with her. Remember when she used to collect feathers? She is very happy here.

Bridget used to collect feathers; Etta called them letters from birds. Sometimes she found pieces of curved blue eggshell, and she saved these too. She cupped them in her palms and carried them home as souvenirs of outside; pieces of sky. She laid them on clouds of cotton wool. Gene gave her swan and goose and mallard feathers after he'd been shooting. You could write a letter with those if you wanted to, he told her.

'I have never been so cold,' says Bridget. 'How cold is it? No, don't tell me.' She stretches a cable-knit jersey over layers of shirts and sweatshirts.

Gülten cringes. 'You're not wearing *that* clubbing.'

'Mum knitted it. She made me bring it. It's her fault.' Bridget pulls on her thickest jacket and tries to zip it up. 'Damn!' She pulls a tuft of jersey from the zip. 'Why do they make jackets so small, when they know you'll be wearing ten layers underneath?'

Gülten smiles. 'I told you to get the XL,' she says. 'But no, Bridget's not an XL, she's not even an L, she takes after her grandmother, she's at most an M. At *most*.'

'Shut up, Gülten.'

'Why are you going out today, anyway?'

'I told you.'

'Yeah, but why today? It's on for another three weeks.'

'I want to avoid the weekend crowds.'

'You'll get the school groups instead.'

Bridget pulls on her striped woollen hat. 'How do I look?'

'Like a giant mutant bee.'

'Perfect.'

❖

She has to wait in line to get into the exhibition. There are copies of the catalogue on sale, but she decides she'll buy one afterwards. She is learning how to be sensible in this cold. Browsing through the catalogue in advance, she says to herself, is like having the answers to a test before you enter the classroom.

Gülten was right about the children. There appear to be several separate groups, but it's hard to tell how many schools they represent as none of them are in uniform. There are copies of *The Very Hungry Caterpillar* on sale, in German. Bridget recognises the cover.

She moves past fibreglass insects as big as cars and with moving parts: a dragonfly whirrs its clear wings, broad as a hang-glider; a dung beetle manipulates colossal pincers; a family of grasshoppers, hugely green, sinks down on spindly haunches and rises up again in unison. Squat and up and squat and up; a strangely gymnastic demonstration.

Bridget settles into a curved wooden seat and pulls on a headset. A female voice tells her to sit right back into the chair, placing her arms on the rests. Bridget does so, peripherally aware of other people next to her, in other chairs, doing the same thing. The voice begins to talk about the Hawaiian wood cicada, and how the male attracts a mate by humming a low, searching song, and how the female replies with a higher-pitched, faster tune. Then recordings of both songs are played, the voice assuring the listeners that they will experience the songs from the perspective of a cicada. The panels in the back of the chair and in the armrests begin to quiver. Several people have stopped and are watching Bridget and the others in the chairs as if they are part of the exhibition. The Hawaiian wood cicadas sing and sing. Bridget feels as if she's eavesdropping and, what's worse, being watched while eavesdropping. She removes her headset and vacates the seat, which is promptly taken by a schoolgirl.

'This is the rude stuff Konrad was telling us about,' the girl calls to a friend, who is examining a glass-sided ant farm.

In the next room there is a full-scale model of a Victorian

study. Behind thick silky ropes which indicate that, unlike the other exhibits, nothing here is to be touched, pieces of sullen furniture cluster. There is a desk covered with bound notebooks, dark bottles of ink, a brass microscope. Seated at it, on a chair with a wicker back and twisting legs like the cables on Bridget's jersey, is an old man. Or rather, a mannequin, dressed up like a Victorian gentleman. He is sleeping. Persian carpets, probably silk, overlap on the floor. A potted aspidistra perches on an oak stand. There is a cabinet with very shallow drawers; one of them is open to display various insect specimens, mounted and named. Clifford had a similar cabinet, Bridget recalls, which he kept polished stones in. He'd salvaged it from a printer's; he told Bridget they used to keep rows of letters in there, entire ordered alphabets, commas, question marks, full stops. The pale interior wood – pine? ash? – had been stained with dots of ink.

'Hello, children,' says an old voice in German, and Bridget jumps. The mannequin has started to talk, blinking its eyes and stretching. 'I didn't notice you standing there. My name is Charles Robert Darwin. When I was young I liked to collect beetles. You might already have seen some of the beetles displayed here today.'

Children swarm towards the Darwin corner, pushing in front of one another, jostling at the silken ropes. Bridget extricates herself, hurrying away from the awoken mannequin, but she can still hear its voice following her, listing various insect delights.

At the back of the room several people are making their way through a doorway hung with strips of cloth. It reminds Bridget of the ribboned curtain Etta used to have on the kitchen door in their old house, to keep flies out. When the door was left open in summer, the bright plastic ribbons would sometimes rise and fall in the breeze like party decorations, or, other times, like streamers cast towards departing ships.

Bridget follows an elderly couple through the doorway; the man holds the strips back for her like a tramper holding back a resilient fern. Bush etiquette, Gene calls it. Bridget smiles at the man. One of the strips escapes his hand and brushes her cheek as they move through, and Bridget realises the fabric is very soft, like the skin of a peach, not plastic at all. Beyond the first curtain is a second one, which the man also holds back. Bridget feels as if she's in *The Lion, the Witch and the Wardrobe*, navigating her way through layers of hanging coats to Narnia, but when she has passed through a third curtain of ribbons it's not an endless winter she finds herself in, but summer. The air is heavy and still and warm, and she is surrounded by trees and tropical flowers. There's even a small pond, dotted with water lilies. A path arcs through the green, and here and there along its edges are tree stumps patterned with sliced fruit. Someone has taken a lot of care in laying out the slices, ensuring there is a combination of colours and shapes, different on every stump, like stills from a turned kaleidoscope. There are banana flowers with apple-wedge leaves, fanned orange segments, discs of kiwifruit circled by grapes, fingers of mango and pineapple. Generous offerings, for such a winter. In front of Bridget, the elderly couple pauses. The man points towards one of the tree stumps, and the woman nods, smiles, bends to look. A luminous blue butterfly settles on it and feeds on a strawberry. And then a red butterfly joins it, and a velvety black one lands on the man's pointing finger. And Bridget realises that the enclosure is filled with butterflies; that they are on the flowers and the trees and the fruit, and fluttering all around her as she walks through this small, manufactured summer.

She's left her jacket at the coat check, but she's still far too hot in all her wrappings. She wishes she could stop and rest by the lily pond, take off some of her layers, maybe cool her feet in the water. But already she's at the end of the path, where there is another doorway leading out, and the elderly man is once more holding back the curtain for her, having ushered his wife back into winter, so there is nothing Bridget can do but follow.

❖

'You should have come. They had a butterfly house.'

'You're a sick person, Bridget.'

'I went through it three times.'

Gülten sighs. 'You need to do some real sightseeing. You haven't even been along Unter den Linden yet, have you?'

'No.'

'Prenzlauerberg?'

'Ah, no.'

'Alexanderplatz? Potsdamer Platz?'

In the Former East – although it is still in the east – the sky is dark with cranes. Everything is being renovated; it's costing billions. Some of Berlin's most beautiful buildings ended up in the East, and were never maintained. A cathedral which was bombed during the war stood open to the sky for fifty years. Birds have damaged the interior.

All the old apartment blocks are having their asbestos removed. It is carcinogenic. And cheap, and fireproof, that's why they used it. The Wall had asbestos in it, says Gülten. Before it was demolished and disposed of, people chipped chunks off it as souvenirs. They keep these safely tucked away, in cotton wool.

Bridget has a friend, she writes. She has the room next to Bridget's in the hostel, and her name is Gülten. She is Turkish, but she grew up in Berlin.

Etta and Gene have met some of their new neighbours, who seem very nice. They have joined their street's Neighbourhood Watch; you can't be too careful these days. Some of their neighbours have had burglar alarms installed, but they seem to be nothing but trouble. Etta and Gene are getting quite cunning in their old age – instead of having a whole alarm system put in and having the thing going off all the time, they've just had an empty alarm box fitted to the outside of the house. As a deterrent.

Much cheaper, too. Does Bridget think she'll be having a white Christmas?

Gülten combs her eyelashes with a tiny brush, not blinking once. Bridget draws on some lipstick and studies her own reflection. So this is how she looks on the other side of the world. She likes the glint of silver at her throat (Gülten's choker) and the scent of her hair (Gülten's shampoo). You look great, Gülten tells her, the men won't be able to stay away.

They are going drinking. They have discovered a bar with old aeroplane seats round the tables and fur on the walls. A CD of nature sounds plays in the toilets.

'You order,' says Gülten. 'Do it in English. We might get free drinks.'

At the best clubs, she says, you can jump the whole queue if you speak English or know one of the DJs. Gülten is going to lose her virginity to a DJ. She's not exactly sure which one yet.

'That guy by the door,' says Bridget. 'He's staring at you.'

'At my tits you mean,' says Gülten. 'He's Turkish. Turkish men treat women like dirt.'

The bartender pours two glasses of red wine for them. Then he offers them a joint. A transvestite in a slinky gown begins singing and sliding a balding feather boa across the tables. Bridget and Gülten sink into the furry walls. They leave an impression when they go.

Germans have the strangest ideas, Bridget writes to Christina. Whenever I say I'm a New Zealander the first thing they say is oh, I've heard you can't go outside there in summer, otherwise you get skin cancer. And those are the ones who know a bit about New Zealand. The others think it's in Australia.

✧

Christina plans to come home to New Zealand soon, maybe for Christmas, with her Austrian boyfriend. Thorsten is a doctor too.

Christina's letters are always more personal than Bridget expects. She tells her about a pregnant woman she was treating. Everything seemed to be going perfectly, then right before the birth she had to tell the woman and her partner that the baby was dead. Christina held her hand right through the delivery. She's never having children, she says. All that pain for a dead baby.

Bridget finds an old medical textbook in an antique shop. She sends it to Christina for Christmas. Christina probably can't remember much German from school, but maybe Thorsten can translate. It's mostly pictures, anyway, labelled in spidery old text. There are whole bodies with lines all over them, like the animals in Etta's old cookbooks showing cuts of meat. There are parts of bodies, too, in cross-section. Bridget can read the names of these; she learnt them early on. The eye; the hand; the brain; the heart.

Bridget and Gülten are on their way home from the bar. They keep tripping over. Gülten catches her toes on the curb and falls. She just lies on the road, laughing. Bridget lies down and laughs too. Gülten lapses into Turkish.

'Hey,' says Bridget, 'I can't speak Turkish.'

'Was I speaking Turkish?'

'I don't know, I can't speak it.'

Gülten laughs even harder. 'Sorry,' she says, and then she's off in Turkish again.

'I can't understand you,' says Bridget, but Gülten doesn't seem to have heard, and Bridget suddenly cannot find the words to explain herself. All she seems able to remember are the most basic terms.

'Drink,' she says. 'Book. Friend. Street.'

But Gülten isn't listening, so Bridget pulls her up off the road and they start walking again. Bridget talks back to her in English, just to have something to say. She tells her about the time she burst into the laundry to change out of her togs and found her father standing at the tub in his shooting clothes, his sleeves rolled up to the elbows. His arms were bloody, and he was holding a half-feathered bird by the neck. The laundry smelled of sweat, and rain on wool, and gun oil. Gülten doesn't understand a word she says.

When they come to a Turkish takeaway, Gülten drags Bridget inside. She buys a Käsetasche and starts eating it, and it must have been low blood sugar or something, because she's back to normal after a few bites.

'My mother makes the best Käsetaschen,' she says. Her chin glistens with oil.

She is not dieting any more, ever again. She started a diet a few months ago and ate nothing for twelve days. For the first four, she was hungry, and her mother cooked all sorts of special food to tempt her. All the family favourites. Gülten did not eat. By the fifth day, she wasn't really hungry any more. Which was good, because she had other things to think about. She had blackouts if she stood up too fast, and sometimes she felt giddy for no reason at all. By the twelfth day, her old jeans fitted her again. Gülten was happy. Gülten's mother cooked. Gülten collapsed at university and had to be carried out of the lecture theatre. When she came to she began to eat. And eat.

They sit on the sticky concrete outside the takeaway while Gülten finishes her Käsetasche. This is a bad neighbourhood, she says, we're right in the middle of Kreuzberg, last month there were nine murders here in a week. Some schoolboys found a woman's head on a park bench; an elderly man was robbed and pushed under a train; a baby was thrown out an eighth-storey window. There are a lot of Turkish men in this neighbour-hood. If they speak to you or even look at you, you must ignore

thcm. Do not answer back, or gesture. Do not assert yourself.
In their minds, this is a sign of interest.

On the phone, Etta asks Bridget if she's met anyone nice.

Yes, says Bridget, she's met lots of nice people.

But no-one special?

No. Well. She's getting on really well with that Turkish girl
she wrote to them about. They go out together a lot.

Gene is on the other phone. He wants to know what the
food is like.

It's all right, says Bridget, if you like pork.

Etta says she's heard the bread is excellent, hundreds of
varieties.

Bridget says yes, there are, it's very confusing.

Christina's coming in a few days, says Gene. She's bringing
Thorsten with her. They'll all ring Bridget on Christmas Day.

Bridget says she'll look forward to that.

Etta thinks it's nice that Bridget has made a friend, and
that they live in the same hostel. That way Bridget doesn't have
to travel home by herself at night. She hopes she is being careful.

Oh yes, says Bridget, it's really very safe, in fact she sometimes feels safer here than she does at home.

Gülten wishes she could stay in Berlin with Bridget for
Christmas. Her family doesn't celebrate it, they're strict Muslims.
In the holidays they go to stay with relatives in Istanbul, and
Gülten hates it. She saw her father slaughter a lamb in the garden
last year. If my mother knew what I get up to here, she says.

Gülten's mother has had cancer ever since they came to Germany.
Her stomach has been removed, mostly. She can't eat much,
and has lost a lot of weight. Gülten tries not to be jealous of
this. Gülten's mother cooks. She wants her daughter to move
back to Turkey with them, where they have bought a beautiful
new house in their old neighbourhood. She worries about her

daughter living in Berlin alone; there have been a lot of attacks lately. She wants her to marry a nice Turkish boy.

No wonder I'm still a virgin, says Gülten. They make you so afraid of it.

When she reached puberty her mother removed all tempting objects from her room. Candles, deodorant bottles, tall vases, everything. Gülten is not allowed to use tampons.

Bridget's duvet is leaking feathers. Every day she finds more strewn on the carpet, around her bed, under it, drifting like snow when she opens the door. They gleam in the dark; cold crescent moons. She knows they must be coming from somewhere. At night, when she pulls the covers around her, she can feel the spines of the feathers inside bend and snap like tiny bones. It is getting colder.

There have been bush fires, writes Christina. They are still burning in some parts. She knows Bridget must have seen about it on TV. Her apartment is not dangerously close to the flames. She has had a few burn victims to deal with; some of them have died. It is very hot because of the fires, as well as the usual Australian summer. She wears SPF45 the whole time. She misses Bridget.

She took Thorsten home with her at Christmas to meet the parents, as Bridget was no doubt informed. Christina is glad Etta and Gene shifted to their townhouse when they did. If they'd left it any longer they would have been too old to move. The new place is reasonably spacious inside – they've even got a room for Christina and a room for Bridget – but there's only a strip of garden. Which is good. Gene was finding it difficult maintaining the old one. Actually he didn't seem quite himself. He made an embarrassing scene at the table one night, throwing salt around the place and stuff, and then afterwards he insisted on showing Thorsten his German pistol. God, can you imagine. I've got something you might be interested in, Thorsten, he says. And Mum just freezes, you know how nervy she's always been about having it in the house. So he makes a big thing about getting it down from the roof, and claps Thorsten on the shoulder and says he knows he can trust him not to mention anything about it. And then he unlocks the box, and unwraps the thing and holds it like it's the hand of John the Baptist or something. And poor old Mum stands there squirming and finally manages to ask if anybody would like a Milo, but Dad just starts telling Thorsten about how his best friend's father took the pistol from a dead German in the war, and how when the friend had children his wife didn't want it in the house any more so he gave it to Dad. Mum mutters that they had children too, and Thorsten doesn't know what to say, so he says well they turned out all right didn't they? And then next door's alarm goes off, and one across the street, and one somewhere else down the road. Really weird. So that breaks the moment, thank God, and Dad says they sound just like a whole gaggle of crows screeching don't they, horrible birds, crows. And Thorsten actually corrects him! He says I think you mean a murder of crows, Mr Stilton, we learnt generic terms in English class, strange what you remember isn't it?

Actually, though, the letter continues, their father has been having some chest pains. Christina doesn't want Bridget to worry, but she didn't think he looked well at all. She did listen to his heart, though, and it was fine.

In fact, Bridget has not heard about the bushfires in Australia. She has not heard about the earthquake in Los Angeles, either, or the toxic spill in the North Sea. She has avoided disaster. She has been very busy. There are so many museums, exhibitions, churches, concerts, bars. She tries to write as often as she can. There was a big parade when the American troops left Berlin, which she missed. She can't be everywhere at once.

✧

The bartender at the bar with the furry walls knows Bridget and Gülten by name now. He gives them free drinks tonight. Gülten thinks he's gorgeous. So does Bridget, but she seems to forget all her German in that place.

Ask him out, she says, but Gülten says no, he'd get the wrong idea, and anyway he's not a DJ.

They get home at nine in the morning. Neither bothers to take off her makeup. Bridget has just got into bed when her phone rings.

Etta is fine; she hopes she's not ringing too early but she thought Bridget would be off to lectures soon.

Yes, soon, says Bridget.

There is a bad time lag on the line, which makes it sound like Etta is pausing before she speaks.

'Actually,' Etta says, 'I was ringing about your Dad.'

It's six in the evening when Bridget wakes up. She feels as if her whole body has been poisoned. She's not sure if her mother really rang or not. But there's a note by the phone, scribbled in her writing: Biopsy. Asbestos. Two weeks. Lufthansa?

It is in her writing, but it's in German.

Gülten bounds into her room and flings open the curtains. 'I've made breakfast,' she announces. 'Turkish style. Cucumber and cheese and tomato and lettuce on rolls. You'll need some vitamins for the party.' She throws Bridget's duvet off. 'You look like shit,' she says.

Bridget and Gülten have been invited to a private party at the furry bar, invitation only. The bartender asked them to come. This is our big chance says Gülten, all the club crowd will be there, we might be able to get our names on the permanent guest lists.

She is hoping there will be lots of DJs to meet. Bridget will have to speak English.

She grabs a top out of Bridget's wardrobe. Can I borrow this, she says, thanks.

❖

It's already dark when they set off, and it's starting to snow. Bridget stops to put on her hat. She heard about a man who went cycling without a hat on and one of his ears dropped off.

There are even more cranes against the sky. The whole city is a construction site. It's hard to tell if some places are being renovated or demolished. It's costing billions, says Gülten, but it's a great chance to make your fortune if you're enterprising enough. She's heard that one guy plunders old bits of concrete from the apartment blocks in the East, breaks them into chips and sells them as pieces of the Wall. They're the same material. Nobody can tell the difference.

Bridget wants to know how safe this is, but Gülten is already talking about something else.

The gorgeous bartender kisses them both on the cheek and leads them to a table. Gülten flits about the place, chatting to acquaintances, getting free drinks. She returns to Bridget, flushed.

'Don't turn around,' she says, 'but that guy by the speaker is the DJ from Globus. He just bought me a drink.' She grabs Bridget's arm. 'Come over.'

Bridget says she might later. She is feeling tired, she just needs a bit of a rest.

She leans into the soft wall and wonders what she is going to tell Gülten. If she even knows the right words. Gülten, she wants to say, listen. She thinks about what the correct expressions might be. She thinks about it the whole evening.

Further emergencies

During her first few weeks at the Queen Victoria Memorial Hospital, Christina greets everyone whose name she can remember. It projects friendliness, she decides, calling people by their names. Sydney is a big place. She watches out for the Austrian man from the barbecue, but he's nowhere to be seen.

'Good morning, Andrew.'

'Christina.'

'Hi, Alicia.'

'Hi . . . Claire.'

'Evening, Pam.'

A nod.

Most of them just keep walking down the lino corridors, following the blue line that leads to Cardiology, or the yellow to Radiology, or the green to Oncology. Christina soon learns by heart the meandering route of the red Maternity line. The department's official title is Obstetrics and Gynaecology, but nobody calls it that. The gynaecology component is negligible anyway, Andrew Martin tells her; it is a wealthy suburb, and most women see private specialists. The ones who do come to the hospital, he says, are mainly the over-sixties.

He's right. During her first two days Christina sees a dozen retired women; they lean into her face with their worried questions and their breath like tea. They remind her of Etta. Christina wonders when she'll see anyone of childbearing age, let alone pregnant. HRT, advises Andrew Martin. Hormone Replacement Therapy. It is a modern miracle. Slap an oestrogen patch on their bums and they'll be happy. Attention. That's all they're after. Christina will be assigned some of the pregnant patients when she's been there a little longer; when she's settled.

'Hello, Claudia.'

'No, stupid,' the woman says, stopping. 'Not Claudia as in "Melbourne is Cloudier than Sydney". *Clau*dia. As in *claw*.' And she walks off to Radiology, the yellow band glowing in her wake.

Christina makes a point of saying her name properly from then on. Or at least, she says it the way Claudia does. She'd been taught the other pronunciation, the *Cloudier* one, and it is a shame she can't use it, she feels, because it is one of the few things she remembers from third-form German.

'Ich heiße Claudia. Wie heißt du?'
'Ich heiße Peter (Pay-ter). *Ich bin 13 Jahre alt. Wie alt bist du?'*
'Ich bin 14 Jahre alt. Ich wohne in München. Wo wohnst du?'
And so on.

❖

Christina wakes herself with her own crying. She doesn't remember the dream, but throughout the day small details return to catch her off guard. At the letterbox, fields of broken glass. Cooking lunch, a man calling for help. In the shower, flames. Shift work has thrown her sleep pattern, and she's given up on trying to get a regular eight hours. She sleeps whenever she can.

'Just prescribe yourself something, stupid,' says Claudia. 'It's the only way you'll be able to cope.'

They're in the hospital staff room, Christina slouched over an instant coffee that is having little effect.

'Claudia,' she says, 'I don't want to tell you to shut up, but shut up.' And she lays her head on her arm.

'You ask anyone here. Nurses, doctors – especially doctors – orderlies, reception. Andrew Martin. They're all on something.'

Christina grunts.

When she finishes work in the morning, she writes a prescription for herself and gets it filled on the way back to her flat. Then she takes a pill, climbs into bed and has the best sleep she's had for a month. No nightmares, not even any dreams. Which may or may not be a good sign, but it is one she is prepared to ignore.

When she wakes up, it is the weekend. She takes a letter out of the back of her diary and looks at the address again, although she knows it off by heart. Joanne Fairfield, 43 Simmond Avenue. It's not that far away. It is possible that Christina has already seen her crossing the street, or on a bus, or at the supermarket. Or that Joanne has seen Christina. Recognised some likeness and wondered.

It would be silly not to go, she decides; everyone has said so. Even Etta.

She isn't what Christina was expecting. Mothers do not wear red nail polish, they are not blonde.

'Christina? You don't look like your photo.'

'Neither do you.'

Joanne invites her into a house that smells very new. At the windows are curtains hanging all the way to the floor. They are hooked back with puffed bows, and above them, along the tops, ample swathes of fabric have been draped. Around the walls, slightly higher than eye level, are floral borders. Arched doors lead from one room to another and grooved columns, which Christina doubts are structurally necessary, have been painted to look like marble.

'We haven't been here long,' says Joanne. 'We were searching for ages to find the right carpet.'

Christina notices the red and gold medallioned pile. She says nothing.

Joanne is wearing heavy makeup. Her eyelids have been shaded purple to match her suit, and the too-red lipstick emphasises the narrowness of her lips, the tiny lines around them. Blusher sweeps over her cheekbones, as high as her temples, and Christina finds herself rubbing distractedly at her own cheeks, although she has only applied lipstick and mascara. She watches Joanne put on a CD, adjust tasselled cushions on the couch. There is nothing in the house that corresponds to Christina's taste, but as she observes Joanne she notices something about her face, hands, certain gestures, that is familiar. The line of the nose. The tapering of the fingers.

'Would you like something to drink? Tea, coffee? A glass of wine?'

'Wine sounds great.'

'I like to indulge myself when it's so hot here,' says Joanne. 'Not that I'm an alcoholic or anything. Although there is a family history of sorts, I suppose you'll want to know about that kind of thing . . . not that there's anything wrong with being an alcoholic. Well, healthwise there is, but –' She stops, wineglasses clinking between her fingers.

'I talk a lot when I'm nervous too,' says Christina. 'Dad says I should have gone into sales, not medicine.'

'He's an . . . architect?'

'Not exactly. He's a manager for a construction company. Was. He's retired now.'

'Ah.'

'He started out as a builder. He did a lot of the old State houses.'

'They're very fashionable now. My sister's bought one and stripped all the floors back. Solid rimu.'

'Mum and Dad have just shifted, too, into a smaller place.'

'They must be in their sixties now?'

'Dad's sixty-three, Mum's sixty-one.'

'Yes, they told me – Social Welfare – that they were an older couple. I didn't mind, I thought it would be better to have someone more mature looking after you.' Joanne eases the cork from a bottle of wine and the glasses ring as she pours it.

'So you never married?' says Christina.

'God no, I don't believe in it. I've been with Dominic for fifteen years now though, we might as well be married. We act like we are.'

'Did you ever think about marrying my father?'

Joanne snorts. 'I hope you won't take this the wrong way, but I can hardly remember what he looked like, let alone his name.'

'Oh.' Christina takes another sip of wine. On the rim of Joanne's glass there is a print of red lipstick; half a smile.

'It was a one-night stand at a party, when we were students. In the bathroom actually. We were both so drunk I'm still amazed we managed it at all.'

'They told Mum and Dad you were university lecturers. Catholics.'

'Ha!' Joanne swallows some more wine and refills the glasses. 'They told me your dad was an architect.'

'You were engaged to be married.'

'Your mum was infertile.'

They stare at one another for a moment, then Joanne bursts

out laughing. 'I'm sorry, it's not funny –'

'In the bathroom, really?' says Christina.

'In the bath!' Joanne laughs even harder. 'People were knocking at the door wanting to go to the loo. One guy tried to climb through the window!'

Christina drains her glass. 'Where's the bathroom here, by the way?'

Joanne shrieks. 'You want to know where the bathroom is!'

Christina places her glass on the coffee table and stands up.

'The bathroom. Sure. Down the hall, third door on the left.' Joanne wipes the wet mascara from under her eyes.

Christina thinks of excuses. She has an assignment due tomorrow, she's on nights at the moment so she's really tired, she's parked the car illegally. In the mirror she watches herself drying her hands. Some people react badly under pressure. They make bad jokes about the mother of the bride, they drive on the wrong side of the road, they talk too much, they laugh when nobody else does. They have pink toilets installed. She splashes her face with water and presses it dry with the embroidered hand towel.

'Well, I should be getting back,' she says. 'The cat will be wanting its dinner.'

'Oh,' says Joanne. 'All right.' She holds out her hand and Christina offers hers and they shake on it as if to agree that Christina is leaving.

'It's been lovely meeting you. I hope we can get together again.'

'Me too,' says Christina. 'Well –'

'Why don't you leave me your number? You can come round for a meal some time, and meet Dominic.'

'Yes, okay,' says Christina, and scribbles on the piece of paper Joanne provides.

'Maybe you could find some photos to bring. Of when you were little.'

'I'll try.'
'I've only got the one of you.'
'I'll see if I can dig some up.'

Christina doesn't feel like going straight home. She wants to be around other people, in a crowd. She discovers an open-air art market just five minutes' walk from her flat, and wonders why she's never seen it before.

She lingers over glazed bowls, silk scarves that feel like skin, hand-made paper. She runs a finger over a row of coppery hair clips hanging from a ribbon. The stall owner approaches, and asks if Christina needs any help.

'We make them all ourselves,' says the woman. 'My brother and myself. All original designs.'

Christina nods and turns to look at the slide combs with their spiked metal teeth. She notices the mirror in front of her, and sees herself in it, and the woman behind her, watching.

'You're welcome to try some. Although I'd go for one of the wider ones if I were you. You have such lovely thick hair.' And she comes over, and Christina has to slide the comb into her hair. She feels the cold teeth scrape her scalp, and is afraid she will push too hard, and draw blood.

'Here, let me show you. It's a bit tricky getting the knack.' The woman takes the comb and secures a swathe of hair to the side of Christina's head. 'It suits you.'

'Could I try one of the round clasps?'

The woman stands behind Christina and her cold painted fingers twist her hair into a coil. She holds a clasp to Christina's head and slides the pin through. Both ends of it are visible, but not the middle, like one of those trick arrows children fix around their necks to frighten and deceive. The woman gives Christina a hand mirror, and holds another behind her head so she can see better. A few people have stopped and are watching. Christina hopes she won't see anyone she knows, although this is very unlikely. The woman is waiting for an answer, but Christina's mouth is empty. Leaves are falling on to the tables and she hears every one as it lands like a dry breath. One falls into her lap.

'Perhaps you'd like to try a different one?' The woman slides out the pin and Christina's hair uncoils and writhes against her cold neck.

The second clasp drags at the roots of her hair, giving her a look of taut surprise. She shakes her head and they try a third one, more intricate than the others and also more expensive.

'These ones take a lot of work to produce,' the woman explains as her hands wind through hair.

Christina sits there until they have tried every single clasp. There is something reassuring about the woman's fingers working her hair into elaborate knots, and every so often brushing the back of Christina's neck or the side of her face. As if this is their natural routine. A man stops to look, and smiles at Christina as her hair is transformed with a few expert twists. When the woman says there are no more to try, panic begins to seep up through the autumn ground and the soles of Christina's feet. She has no idea which to choose, and holds the mirror up again to have a look at the last one, hoping it is right. All she can see is the woman's ringed hand on her hip, expectant fingers spread, and her own eyes. She looks at the row of clasps on the table, trying to remember which one she liked, which one the woman liked, but the leaves are still falling and it seems they will cover the whole table with their whispers. Christina clears her throat.

'They're all so beautiful . . . which one do you think suited me?'

The man who was watching walks past again. 'That one with the flower design, the big round one,' he says, pointing. His hand is almost transparent, and shakes. Every vein is visible.

The woman smiles and picks up the clasp he is pointing to. 'Yes, that would be my first choice as well. Shall I wrap it up for you, or do you want to wear it now?'

The man walks off, picking his way through the crowd with ease.

Christina realises that she hasn't eaten all day, and makes her way to one of the takeaway stands. She passes through rows of stalls selling antiques and second-hand clothes. Incomplete sets of etched glasses, rich velvet coats with only one or two buttons missing, jointed teddy bears loved smooth, manicure sets monogrammed with someone else's initials.

A young man in a leather jacket stops to look at the glass cases of jewellery. Christina can tell by the way he scans each one that he is looking for something special. She forgets that she is hungry and she follows him from stall to stall, picking up glass beads, books with inscriptions in them, a silver shoe horn shaped to a Victorian heel. He asks to see a few pieces: a marcasite watch, a cameo brooch, some heavy lockets. He has good taste, and politely refuses to be shown junk. Christina reaches past him for a brass-bound Victorian photo album, and asks the stall keeper if there is a key for it.

'No, unfortunately. But any locksmith could open it for you, and probably find you a key that fitted. It's on special today.'

By the time Christina has insisted she doesn't need a locked photo album, the man in the leather jacket has disappeared.

She buys some chips and stabs them with a flimsy plastic fork. She hears male gulps of laughter behind her, and when she turns around she sees the man who chose her clasp and the young man in the leather jacket stopping and climbing into an expensive car together. They have bought some flowers, which they place on the back seat, and the young man slips a small package wrapped in lilac tissue paper into his jacket pocket. Then they drive off, the engine so smooth it is almost silent.

✧

Christina is glad to be away from the market, and kicks up clouds of leaves when nobody is watching. She still has some time before she can go home and make dinner for herself. She could keep walking until her cheeks are red and her nose is running. She could go and feed the ducks. She could gather some wild mushrooms. She's seen people doing this, young couples, mainly, and has always meant to try it herself.

She finds a bench and sits down. Through the clearing, the presence of water is indicated by the shimmering of trees. After a while a woman comes and sits on a bench nearby, but she doesn't stay long.

Tonight Christina will go out. She will get dressed up, put on makeup, twist her hair into an elaborate coil. She will go to a bar and secure a high stool for herself, one that shows off her outfit to its best advantage. She will sip stingy glasses of champagne. Men will come and talk to her, and some of them she will answer. She will let them buy her drinks and offer her cigarettes. They will fumble for their lighters and lean forward, illuminating her careful makeup for a second. Her fingers will be spread, elegantly, framing her cigarette with nails filed to safe curves. She will collect several phone numbers. She will not make the mistake of giving hers. She may allow herself to be persuaded into another bar when that one closes, but only if it is within strolling distance or if they go in a taxi, which he will pay for. She may decide to take someone home with her; she will not, of course, agree to go to his place. Her apartment will have been tidied in advance; interesting books will have been placed open and there will be wine cooled. In the morning, or perhaps the afternoon, she may decide she has a pressing engagement, and will promise to phone that week.

'Well?' says Claudia.

'Hmm?'

'What was she like?'

Christina opens her locker, runs a comb through her hair. 'These mirrors are pathetically small. How you're supposed to see more than a nostril –'

Claudia takes the comb and places it back in the locker. 'Don't you dare go all evasive and kiwi on me. I've seen *The Piano*, I know your little foibles.'

'Are you all this nosy?'

'Come on, it's not every day you get to meet your mother. Your real mother. You know what I mean.'

'She was –' says Christina to her reflection. 'She was –'

'A man? A nun? Fat?'

'Rich.' Christina pushes her locker shut.

'Ah. Rich.' Claudia considers this for a moment. 'Is that bad?'

'They won Lotto. They actually *won*, millions of dollars. I mean, how many people do you know, personally, who've actually won?'

'People win?' says Claudia.

✧

Christina keeps waiting for winter to arrive properly.

'Remember to keep warm,' she says to her pregnant patients by way of ending a consultation. Most of them simply stare at her then, bare arms extending from sleeveless maternity dresses. 'Warm, yes,' they say, frowning, and then they leave the air-conditioned hospital and step into warm August weather.

I don't miss the cold, Christina writes to her parents. I don't miss the wind. The pay is much better here, although the shifts are demanding. At the moment I am treating a premature baby which weighed less than one kilo when it was born. We do not expect it to survive. Mum, I wonder whether you have heard much about HRT. It really is a miracle drug, I've seen quite remarkable results in the patients I've prescribed it to. It would probably stop you from shrinking any more. I feel like such a giant next to you now. You should talk to your GP about it. Hope Dad is well.

Christina never knows how to finish letters. She stares at

her pen. Rulide, it reads. Three hundred milligrams once-a-day.

Winter does not arrive. There are some rainy days, a couple of thunder storms. She wears her long coat twice. She uses the heater in her apartment maybe four times. And then the weather starts getting warmer again, and daffodils and freesias are all over the place, stuffed into vases on the café tables, overpowering the eggs benedict brunches, and then in what seems like a few weeks it is thirty degrees every day. Christina receives a letter from her sister, who has arrived in Germany at the start of a raw European winter. Bridget misses the Wellington winters terribly.

Claudia insists on regular picnics. The one at the beach is the usual sort of affair: sandwiches, bacon and egg pie, powdery summer apples. Thorsten has brought some Austrian wine.

'It's made in Neusiedler See,' he says. 'We used to go there for holidays. I found it at Message in a Bottle.'

Sand has worked its way into everything; it even circles the rim of the wine bottle, and floats in the glasses. Christina wipes her tongue with a tissue.

'He should,' says Claudia, watching a sunburnt man in Speedos. 'She should. He definitely should.'

She's playing a game of her own devising. She calls it Melanopoly. She passes judgement on the surrounding sun-bathers, announcing which of them should have particular moles checked. A freckled red-head picks his way across the hot sand to the water.

'I give him two years.'

'You're a morbid cow, aren't you,' says Max. Max is Claudia's new boyfriend.

'One does what one can.' She smiles demurely. 'He should. He should. Both of them should. Oh! Oh, how sweet! An entire high-risk family!'

Mother, father and three pink children walk past with dripping icecream cones.

'Hello!' calls Claudia. 'How are we all today?'

The mother stops, peering towards Claudia, trying to recognise her. 'Fine thanks,' she says, smiling, nodding. Strawberry ripple drips over her hand. The children stare at Claudia.

'Come on, back to the car,' mutters the father, taking his wife's elbow and guiding her away, flicking up sand with his quick steps.

'Who's that, Mum?' says the girl, looking back.

'See you!' Claudia waves at the receding family. 'Fairly soon, no doubt.'

Thorsten opens a second bottle of wine, a red, and balances it on the sand. 'Got to let it breathe.'

'Robust, fruity and full-bodied,' reads Claudia from the label. 'Enjoy at room temperature. Typical of your region, would you say, Thorsten?' She feels his biceps.

'This one's French, actually.'

'Hey!' says Max. 'Christina, did you see that?'

Claudia takes a swig from the bottle and swallows. 'Any more breathing and it'll be singing Happy Birthday Mr President.' She spits. 'Bloody sand.'

Christina inspects the view across the water, shielding her eyes against the glare. Everything is too bright here.

Thorsten places his sunglasses on her nose. 'At least you can't see the Opera House from here,' he says.

'That,' says Claudia, 'reminds one of bathroom fixtures.'

'I quite like it,' says Christina. 'It's what people think of when they think of Sydney. It reminds me I'm really here.'

'The Opera House. Surfers Paradise. Ayers Rock,' says Claudia. 'There's more to us than landmarks, you know. We are a complex, misunderstood, highly sensitive people.'

'Yep. Chuck us another tinnie, would you love?' says Max.

❖

Claudia and Max have monopolised the rug. Thorsten and Christina sit on a pair of sheepskin carseat covers plundered from Thorsten's car.

'Were they a present from Christina?' asks Claudia. 'Traditional first anniversary gift, I understand.' She and Max roll themselves in tartan.

The sun has gone down, and the beach is almost empty. They have finished the wine, thrown away the leftovers made stale by the sun. They have slapped at twilight mosquitoes, put on extra garments, moved back and back from the incoming tide. When the beach is too small for them, they leave.

'Shit.' Thorsten grabs a slip of paper from the windshield. 'Fifty bloody dollars.'

'It's so *cute* when he swears,' says Claudia.

Christina takes the ticket and reads it, as if to check its authenticity. 'We'll all chip in, darling.'

'Bollocks we will.' Claudia grabs the ticket. 'I'll do you a letter.'

'Sorry?'

'Dear Officer –' she scans the ticket, 'Menzies. On Saturday November 18 at 1.45 p.m. I parked my maroon BMW – registration blah blah – on the corner of Hillcrest Avenue and High Street in order to call at the nearby home of Mr and Mrs Braithwaite. Upon my arrival at their place of residence I found Mr Braithwaite to be suffering a cardiac arrest and, as my Hippocratic Oath demands, I treated him. I then accompanied him and his distraught wife in an ambulance to the Queen Victoria Memorial Hospital, where I am employed as a Trauma Surgeon. I am delighted to say Mr Braithwaite has made good progress and, thanks to my timely intervention, his chances of a full recovery are high. Unfortunately, when I returned much later in the day to collect my car, I discovered that I had been issued with a parking ticket. I appreciate that you were simply performing the proud duty demanded by your Traffic Officers'

Oath, and that you were unaware of the emergency situation that demanded my infringing the parking limit by several hours. However, I am sure you will understand *my* obligation to fulfil the demands of my own oath. I therefore respectfully request to be excused from the payment of this fine. Yours sincerely, Doctor Thorsten Schildling.'

'I can't do that.'

'I do.'

'But I've never treated a Mr Braithwaite. He doesn't even exist, does he?'

'They never check.'

'I don't know,' says Christina, taking back the ticket. 'He could get deported for that.'

'Nonsense.' Claudia pokes Thorsten in the stomach. '*You* should make yourself a sign. For the next time.'

'A sign.'

'Claudia keeps it in the glovebox,' says Max. '*Medical emergency. My name is Dr Claudia Foster and I may be contacted at the Queen Victoria Memorial Hospital.* It's kind of scrawly, like it's been written in a hurry. Never fails.'

Claudia traces circles on the footpath with her toe. 'You're making me blush.'

It is past midnight when Christina remembers. The carseat covers, they'd left them on the beach. She sits up in bed, groans above Thorsten's snores, thinks about getting up. Then she lies back down and pulls the sheet up to her chin.

She can see the covers, soft on the flat sand. Or floating, white in moonlight. She can smell the wet wool. Sodden, perhaps. Or sunken, fleecing the ocean floor. She thinks, salt water is a preservative. A brine. Thorsten will say it doesn't matter, it doesn't matter. He will tell her she worries too much, she is too mindful of trivialities. He will bring up the inordinate amount of time she spends making the bed, straightening curtains, arranging coffee-table books. He's not sure he could live with her. He will probably mention the care she takes in packing a suitcase; how she found, just last week, a glove coiled in the tip of a seldom-worn shoe. When she tells him how she remembered the covers in the middle of the night, he will laugh. He will say, in his precise English, that he did not know kiwis were so attached to their sheep.

Christina rolls on to her side. She regards the smooth, boy's body beside her, the fine wrists, the narrow shoulders. You belong to me, she repeats to herself as he sleeps, his lips apart, a long hand resting on a hairless chest. We look alike, she thinks, we could be brother and sister. She expects other people – Gene, Etta, Bridget perhaps, when she returns from Germany – will comment on the likeness. She hopes they will.

'That's the patches, isn't it,' says Etta on the phone. 'Shirley tried them for a while.'

'Right,' says Christina. 'They look like sticking plasters, or those ones you can wear to wean yourself off cigarettes.'

'But I don't smoke. I've never smoked.'

'She hasn't,' says Gene. He's on the other phone.

'No, Mum,' says Christina. 'They're nothing to do with smoking, they just look like those other patches you can get.'

'Shirley says you wear them on your bottom.'

'On the buttocks, yes.'

'Would they do to fix my waders?' says Gene. 'There's a hole in the left thigh needs repairing.'

'Shirley says they made her feel sick.'

'Some people do experience slight nausea for the first few days.'

'Shirley used to be a nurse.' Etta is beginning to sound quite agitated. 'And I don't need repairing. I am not punctured.' The words rush out of her.

Christina sighs. 'It's up to you, Mum. I just thought you might be interested. Have you heard from Bridget yet?'

Native Birds
of
New Zealand

'Do you like your new room?' says Etta. 'Dad spent so long making those shelves I thought I'd go mad.'

'It's very nice,' says Bridget. 'All my old things there –'

'It was so lucky we shifted when we did, you know. We couldn't have stayed in the old house the way he is now.'

'No.'

'I just couldn't have looked after him there. All the bedrooms right at the end of the hall, and that big cold lounge.'

'Yes.'

'It was fine when you girls were little, of course –'

'Yes,' says Bridget, thinking of the deep wardrobes, the fig tree, the many places to hide. The brass doorhandles that smelled like money.

'We've still got the three bedrooms, though. Too cramped otherwise. We had Colin and Jim to stay a little while ago, I think I wrote to you, and Aunty Beryl came up the week we heard about Dad. You will say thank you for the shelves, won't you love?'

'Mum,' Bridget says, slower than is necessary, 'I will say thank you for the shelves.'

She doesn't like her new room. In fact, she hates the whole house. She is profoundly irritated by the flat formica kitchen, the carpeted bathrooms. The lightweight toilet seats. Although Gene and Etta have been able to keep most of their old furniture, none of it seems to fit in this neat little townhouse. The heavy oak lounge suite, with its fat flowers and honeycomb cane, has squashed itself in front of the gas fire. And as if the stairs weren't cramped enough already, a motorised chair has been fitted to the banister so Gene can go up and down.

The noise of it is enough to wake Bridget up. On her first night home – in this new house – she was shaken from a German dream by what sounded like a concrete mixer.

'At least we can hear him coming,' said Etta when Bridget remarked on the noise. 'In case I'm on the phone to the hospice, or something.'

Bridget is not convinced that this is an advantage; the new house is small, and her father has developed the habit of announcing his every move.

'I'm just off to the toilet,' he'll say, and then, a little while later, 'Just back from the toilet.' Or, 'I think I'll go and sit in the sunroom for lunch.' Or, 'Might turn the radio on now.'

'Do we have to know that?' Bridget hissed once, after Gene had finished explaining his walk from the lounge to the kitchen via the dining room.

Gene looked at her for a moment and then said, 'Well, I

might just pop into my electric chair now and go upstairs for a rest.'

He seems to enjoy referring to the stair chair in this way, and Bridget is never sure if he is being deliberately morbid.

'You must see my electric chair,' he says to everyone who visits, and he wriggles into it and gives a quick demonstration. 'It's just wonderful,' he says. 'I'd only have the run of half the house without it.'

Spent the day at Bullens Rock, Goose Bay. Had New Years Eve on the beach cooked about 40 Crayfish on a fire. Around Midnight I played the part of a ghost with a white sheet around me & I danced on the road as the cars came along. Colin & Jim behaved very well.

'I didn't know you played the flute,' says Antony, clapping.

Bridget spins around. 'How long have you been listening?'

'Only a couple of minutes. I was coming up to tell you I'm off home now. I have to drop the car back to Dad.'

Bridget puts her flute down on the dressing table and goes to the bed. She leans across it, straightening the blankets, smoothing the sheet.

'Naughty Antony,' she says to Gene. 'He crept up to the door while I was playing. Isn't he sneaky?'

Gene's head lolls back on the pillows, his mouth slackening in an unformed reply.

'Night night then,' says Bridget, kissing his forehead.

In the hall Antony puts his arms around her and tries to hold her in a tight hug. She wriggles free and gives him a quick peck on the cheek and says, 'You'd better get the car back.'

She decides to stay home on Saturday night.

'I thought we were going to Rachel's party,' Antony says when he phones.

'You go,' says Bridget. 'I should really spend some time with Dad. Watch a war movie or something.'

Antony can hardly argue. 'Okay. But it would be good to see you some time this week.'

Etta looks at her watch. 'Time for your eight o'clocks,' she says to Gene, and leaves him sitting with Bridget while she goes to get his medication ready. The only place for it all in their compact new kitchen is by the window, so she keeps the bottles and boxes hidden under a teatowel saying Native Birds of New Zealand.

'No I don't think it's being silly,' she told Bridget. 'There have been cases of homes being broken into, the hospice said. So if anyone asks, Dad is just on medication.'

Outside, the neighbours' pohutukawa is still flowering. It attracts a lot of birds in summer; sometimes they get a few tuis. Any Etta doesn't recognise she compares with the teatowel, but she has had no successful identifications as yet. She thinks it might have been washed a few times too many to be an accurate index; most of the birds on it have faded to light blue or grey. Gene knows his birds. He can even do convincing birdcalls. Etta remembers when he used to come back from hunting trips and tell her about the birds he'd seen, or sometimes just heard. The tiny fantails were his favourite, he told her; if you made a sound like a kiss they would come and flutter around you, making the same sound back. Sometimes they would even settle on Gene's shoulders or hat, or on the cool rifle barrels.

Etta busies herself measuring syrup and counting pills. She ticks these off as she goes, on the little chart from the hospice. Amitryptilene 25mg, tick; Lorazepam 10mg, tick; Diazepam 5mg, tick; MST elixir 20ml, tick; right down to Melleril 10mg. Tick. She had been worried that she would accidentally give Gene the wrong dose, or a lethal combination. She knew what sort of drugs she was dealing with, and what their potential effects were; she'd asked the hospice doctor to explain everything to her when Gene was out of the room, and to draw up the medication chart. The doctor said that the relatives of home-care patients often asked her for charts. Etta is grateful for Gene's one, which makes it all so simple; the days are divided into squares and columns, and all she has to do is count and tick, as regular as a clock, or the beating of a heart.

She places the tray of medication on Gene's side table and hands him a glass of water.

'Why don't we have two-dollar notes any more?' she says. 'I used to like the twos. All these coins weigh you down.'

Bridget inserts the first video – she has rented four – into the machine. 'Do you know what two dollars buys you these days, Mum?'

'They had fantails on them, didn't they. A beautiful dark purple.'

'The ones had the fantails. And they were brown.'

'Really? The ones, not the twos?' She looks at Gene, pats his hand. 'Obviously I never saw enough of either of them, did I, love. What did the twos have on them, then?'

Bridget sighs. 'Wood pigeons I think. Something fat. Can I watch my video now?' She has fast forwarded to the end of the copyright information and paused it. The room is filled with a flickering warning.

'Aunt Ursula,' says Gene, 'died of a swollen finger.'

Bridget sighs again and puts down the remote control. 'Dad,' she says, 'you sound tired. Why don't you go up to bed now?'

'No, he's right, Bridget,' says Etta. 'Her finger did swell up.'

Gene looks at Bridget. 'We're not doddering wrecks yet.'

'She was my mother's sister,' Etta continues. 'She was living on the farm with us for a while, when my mother – wasn't well. Yellow one first?' She feeds Gene a capsule. 'She went out to get some kindling from the orange crates, and when she came back in she said her finger hurt. Then it started swelling and turning black.'

'Oh, gross.'

Etta holds Gene's arm steady as he takes a sip of water, then she pushes another capsule between his lips. 'It travelled right up her arm, and within half an hour she was dead. They thought she must have been bitten by a spider.'

'It was Maggie,' says Gene behind his hand, and laughs. Etta takes the glass of water from him just before it tilts over. The video flicks off pause, and an ad for fly spray blares from the television.

'Poison in a can,' says Etta. Since Gene has been sick she has been suspicious of a number of products.

'Couldn't they have taken her to hospital?'

'Out where they lived? The nearest doctor was over an hour away, and they only had a horse and trap. Let's have a look.' Etta pokes her finger in Gene's mouth. 'You naughty thing! It's still on your tongue.' She holds the water up to his lips. 'One of my uncles died out there of an asthma attack, and there was nothing anybody could do.'

'Uncle Henry?'

'Big gulp now. Good. No, no this was my mother's brother Bernard. It happened before I was born. No, Henry died over in Ireland, not long after he went back.'

'He was the one who played the violin?'

Etta shakes a tiny white tablet into her palm and passes it to Gene. 'That's right. I can't really remember that, though. He lost three fingers and the thumb off his left hand when I was about seven.'

'What, did he get bitten as well?'

Etta peers into Gene's mouth again and places another white oval on his tongue. 'He had bad arthritis, and then he got a splinter in his hand which became infected, so he had to have them removed.'

Gene makes a gurgling sound and his mouth drops open. He stares at a point above Bridget's head, water trickling down his chin.

'Oh God.' Bridget jumps from her chair.

'Swallow,' says Etta. 'Swallow . . . that's it.' She holds Gene's hand, looking over at Bridget. 'We just forgot to swallow, that's all.' She plucks some tissues from a packet and wipes his chin.

Bridget puffs out her cheeks and exhales slowly.

'He should never have gone back to Ireland,' says Etta. 'He was a lovely man. Very much missed at the farm. It was like having a second parent.'

'Is that why he left the farm to your father?'

Etta is silent for a moment. 'He never married. We used to look after him, tie his shoes and button his braces and cut up his meat. Then when we got a letter from him, after he went back, he sounded so sad to be home.' She holds a measure of syrup up to Gene's mouth, but Gene grasps the tiny plastic cup, pulls it away from her. The two of them sit there staring at one another. Finally Gene says, 'I'll hold it myself,' and Etta notices how white his knuckles are.

'He said his nieces there didn't know him,' she says, 'and didn't understand about braces and shoes and cutting up meat.'

'Are there any photos of him? Or Bernard?'

Etta strokes Gene's hair. 'My mother never kept things like that.' She takes the newspaper from Gene's lap and folds it. He is still on page one; he doesn't seem to make it past the tragedies these days. 'The rifleman, that was the two-dollar bird,' she says. 'On the count of three then,' and she takes his hands and hauls him to his feet.

As Etta leads him to the hall she can hear Bridget sigh with relief, settle into Gene's armchair and click the remote control.

I have been trying to polish the opals but they are giving me a lot of bother   I cannot find anything that will stand up to them as they tumble. The container must keep a very smooth surface & glass is the only thing suitable but it breaks. I have broken all the ½ gallon jars about the place but when I get a good run for 24 hours I get results.

'That's it, love. It's right behind you.'

Gene lowers himself into the stair chair. 'An ingenious bit of engineering, this,' he says. 'Bridget should see it in action.' And, before Etta can stop him, he calls, 'Hey, Bridget! Come and have a look at this!'

'Custom built,' he says when Bridget has appeared, the remote control cradled in her hand. 'The track curves right round the landing. Ingenious.'

'Shall I push the button or can you manage?' says Etta, hovering at the bottom of the stairs, making sure Gene is holding on to the arm rests and that there are no sections of dressing gown dangling near the track.

'I'm fine,' says Gene. 'Don't fuss.' And he presses his finger on the end of the arm rest and begins to move up the stairs. 'Chocks away!' he calls.

Bridget and Etta watch as he rounds the corner. As the chair turns him to face them they wave, as if he is on a fairground ride.

Gene waves back. 'Hey Bridget,' he shouts over the noise, 'do you ever hear this from your room?'

'Oh no, not at all. It's fine.'

'Good,' yells Gene. 'I wouldn't want to disturb you. A girl needs her beauty sleep.'

'Really, it's fine, Dad,' says Bridget, and she and Etta wait until he has disappeared behind the wallpapered corner and is gone.

Etta tidies up the bench, screwing the lids on bottles of pills and wiping down Gene's table. Some of the medication has leaked on to the embroidered tray cloth, so she puts it out to be washed and unfolds a fresh one. They are not necessary, of course, but she likes to keep things looking nice.

'I'm not going to let things get on top of me just because Dad's sick,' she tells Bridget. She replaces Native Birds of New Zealand and says, 'Right then. I'll just go up and get him settled.'

*I got caught in my own trap today my cardigan the one that Mum
knitted got pulled into the belt drive on the rumbler   believe me
it threw me a beaut but only a few bruises
Marsha 6.30 p.m.*

She lifts Gene's legs into bed and pulls up the blankets.

'The thing is,' he says, 'how do you tell a healthy possum
from a sick one?'

'Do you want that many pillows?' asks Etta. 'Let's get rid of
this one, shall we?'

'I'll tell you what I'm not doing any more,' says Gene,
leaning forward while she arranges the pillows. 'I'm not
balancing any more bloody teacups for any more lions, and
that's that.'

'All right,' says Etta.

She creeps back down the stairs to the living room, being
careful not to catch her foot on the chair track.

Bridget is pouring herself a brandy.

'That was nice of you, what you said about the noise,' says
Etta. 'I know you were lying, it's like a pneumatic drill.' She
tries to squeeze her daughter's hand, but Bridget plops herself
down in Gene's armchair again and stares at the television. 'It's
just he worries, I think,' Etta goes on. 'About being a nuisance.'

'Mmm,' says Bridget.

'He made me move into the guest room, because he was
worried I wasn't getting enough sleep.'

'You probably weren't,' says Bridget, thinking of her
mother's soft nocturnal footsteps.

'He's slipped such a lot lately. Even he admits it.'

Bridget aims the remote at the television and switches it
off. 'Sit down, Mum. I'll make you a drink.' She pours a second
glass of brandy. 'Might as well use the good stuff.'

'You know, they've increased his morphine again,' says Etta.
'It's quite interesting, the hospice nurse was round this morning

and she said he's not addicted to it, even though he's taking so much. She said the pain absorbs it, and it's only if you take it when you're not in pain that you get addicted.'

Bridget nods, swallowing slightly too much at once.

'These were my mother's,' says Etta, holding her glass up to the lamp and watching the brandy tremble behind the crystal. 'I don't know what happened to the rest of the set. She wasn't very careful with breakable things.'

The fridge shudders and falls silent. Bridget munches on an ice cube, sucking in her cheeks.

'On his last x-ray,' says Etta after a while, 'three of his ribs had been eaten away. Imagine that, bones, just gone.'

✧

The Stiltons have become very popular. Every Sunday afternoon a party of visitors descends, and Bridget greets them and ushers them into the lounge.

'Look, Dad, Mrs Kerr's come to see you,' she says. 'Mr Crandell's just popped in for a visit.' 'Look who's here, it's Mrs Fitzroy.' 'What a nice surprise, Mrs Davis.'

'Isn't he good?' they say, looking Gene up and down, sounding surprised and, Bridget suspects, a little disappointed. She excuses herself and goes to the kitchen, where she counts teacups and saucers and arranges biscuits, and listens to the visitors tell Etta and each other how good Gene is.

'Here we are then,' Bridget says, pushing the lounge door open with her foot. As she distributes afternoon tea, manoeuvring around the enormous handbags the women have brought and placed at their feet like obedient dogs, the visitors comment on her own goodness.

'Aren't you lucky to have her?' they say. 'Isn't she marvellous?'

'How are you doing with your tea?' asks Bridget, offering Gene a scone. 'Or would you rather a cool drink?'

'Actually, that would be just the thing,' says Gene, so Bridget goes out to the kitchen and pours 20ml of morphine syrup into a glass of orange juice. She came up with this code herself, and Gene says he wishes they'd thought of it years ago, particularly for Shirley Davis' visits.

Had 12 members of the Ladies Guild round in the afternoon to see the stones.

'There you go, Dad,' Bridget says now, the ice cubes clinking like distant bells. 'Your favourite.'

'Ooh, that looks lovely,' says Shirley. 'I couldn't have one of those too, could I Bridget?'

And Mrs Fitzroy says, 'Orange juice! What a good idea, yes, I'll have an orange juice, if it's not too much trouble.'

'No trouble at all,' says Bridget, smiling.

'You are lucky, Etta,' they murmur. 'Isn't she good?'

'Look what Shirley gave me,' says Etta after they have all left. 'Well, lent me.' She pulls a plastic supermarket bag away from two small speakers. 'It's a baby monitor. Jodie and her husband bought it after they lost their first child.'

'Is her hair still thinning?'

'Bridget!'

'Sorry. Is it?'

'They said we can use it for as long as we need.'

Bridget sets it up beside Gene's bed, with the receiver in the living room.

'Now you won't have to shout when you want something,' says Etta.

Unfortunately, it only works one way.

Gene jolts awake at the sound of the phone and looks around the room, blinking.

Carnelian busy with last-minute packing. The family were round in the afternoon for tea (except Gene) I took photos with a coloured film. We took Carnelian to the airport & when the time came to go she did just what the Queen does she walked out smartly, mounted the steps turned & waved & was gone. We followed the next four hours very closely.

Pulse 94

'I'll get it,' says Bridget. He hasn't seemed to realise what the noise is. She reaches across him.

'How's it going?' says Christina's voice.

'Hey! How are you?'

'Great, really good. How's home?'

'Oh, you know,' says Bridget, glancing at Gene, who has resumed watching *Dad's Army*.

'Stupid boy!' says Captain Mainwaring.

'Don't panic!' says Private Jones.

Gene smiles.

'It's great to be back,' says Bridget. 'The house is really nice.'

Christina cackles. 'They're there, aren't they? For Christ's sake, swap phones. I think I can afford the extra thirty seconds while you run upstairs. Or glide in motorised comfort at the touch of a button.'

'Mum?' calls Bridget. 'Could you hang up for me?'

Up in Gene's room she shouts, 'Got it!' and waits for the click.

'So,' says Christina, 'is that Antony boy still hanging round?'

'They are driving me in*sane*,' Bridget says through gritted teeth.

'I did warn you.'

'If I have to see the stair chair in action one more time I swear I will tie myself to the track and press go.'

'Come over for a holiday, then.'

'No,' says Bridget. 'I'd feel bad, you know, if something happened.'

'Thorsten wants to meet you. He likes nice strapping kiwi girls.'

'I am big-boned,' says Bridget. 'No, I can't afford it, anyway.' She groans. 'Mum's so jumpy, you only have to *glance* in the direction of a curtain and it's pulled, and if you actually *ask* for something you can't see her for dust.'

'You could slip her some Diazepam.'

'And Dad's pretty glazed, most of the time. It's like she's making up for it by doing twice as much.'

'He's as bad as Grandad used to be.'

And then Christina begins telling Bridget about what a wonderful time she's having in Sydney with Thorsten, and how they went to a gay dance party a couple of weekends ago – with her friend Mike, the gay lawyer, who goes out with Andrew Martin, the Medical Superintendent – and they took a trip, and she just loved everyone and everyone loved her. She wore this ob*scene* PVC miniskirt and a matching bra top, and Thorsten proved to be a very popular boy indeed.

Bridget says, 'Aha,' and, 'I see,' and, 'Right,' every so often and just lets her sister chatter on, because all of a sudden she has no idea what to say to her. She wonders if, in Sydney, Christina even realises that Gene's bones are dissolving, that his lungs are turning to stone.

'So do you think I should come over for a visit?' says Christina.

'Sure. They'd love to see you.'

'Yeah, but do you think I *should* come? I mean, do I *need* to come?'

'He has good days and bad days. You're the doctor. You should know how it advances.'

Bridget hears Etta climb the stairs and turn on the bath. Then she comes into the bedroom.

'I might come next weekend then,' says Christina. 'No, wait, that's the Globe party. I promised Claudia –'

'Won't be a minute,' whispers Etta. 'I'll just get some clothes.'

'The club scene here is really amazing,' Christina is saying.

'So how's Thorsten?' Bridget cuts in, watching Etta select a singlet and a pair of underpants. 'Are you improving your German?'

Etta looks up.

'I know lots of new words now,' says Christina.

'Is that Christina?' says Etta, rushing over. 'Why didn't you tell us? I'll say a quick hello.'

The *Dad's Army* credits are sliding across the screen, and soldiers run towards Gene, bombs exploding behind them.

At 1.15 p.m. an announcement came over the air from the police that a tidal wave was approaching the East Coast at the speed of 500 miles per hour and was expected to arrive at 1.30 p.m. We shut the shop (Rob didn't see the need to but I insisted) and hurried home the police don't put things like that over the air unless they have good reasons. It did not arrive but the sea is still acting very strange and yesterday they had more earthquakes in Chile. There will be no stones gathered this weekend. Bowels Poor.
Pulse 95

'Dad,' says Bridget. 'Can I switch this off now?'

'Mmm,' he says, staring at the television.

'I'll put some music on. Do you want anything to drink?'

'Mmm.'

She flicks through the CDs, but there is nothing she feels like listening to. In the end she plays the one that is already in the stereo.

'Mozart's flute concerto,' she says. 'You like this one.'

She wishes she was accomplished enough to play it herself; she is sure the neighbours are tired of her meagre repertoire, to say nothing of Christmas carols in May.

'You play,' says Gene now, sitting up and looking more alert. 'Go on, you play me a few tunes.'

'If you think you're up to it,' says Bridget, and she takes her flute from its blue velvet case and fits it together, lining up the mouthpiece with the row of silver keys. She remembers something her first flute teacher, an elderly English man, told her: if you let someone play your flute it is like letting them kiss you. She'd gone to his funeral a few years ago. During communion, while walking past the coffin, his wife had bent and kissed him. Bridget had been disgusted.

'I wish I'd learned to play an instrument,' says Gene. 'My mother always said I had the hands of a violinist, but that was as far as it went. Boys don't play the violin.'

Bridget begins an unsteady rendition of 'Greensleeves', and Gene leans back in his chair and closes his eyes.

'I like this one,' he murmurs.

Just as Bridget is starting the third verse, there is a cry from upstairs.

'The bath!' shouts Etta.

Bridget rushes up the stairs two at a time and finds her mother leaning over the bath, turning the taps off.

'I think I got it in time,' she says. 'It was just overflowing when I came in.'

'Shit,' says Bridget, grabbing some towels from the cupboard and throwing them on the floor. 'Are you sure? I can feel it squelching underneath the carpet over here.'

'Oh dear,' says Etta, all of a sudden sounding on the verge of tears. 'I was talking to Christina and I just forgot about it. Oh dear.'

Bridget pushes up her sleeve and reaches into the warm water to pull out the plug. 'Come on, come downstairs and have a cup of tea, and I'll take care of this.'

The carpet on the stairs is wet too, and as they walk past the lounge door Bridget hears a trickling sound. She switches on the light and she and Etta both gasp at once. Water is streaming down the walls, and out of the light fitting on the ceiling. The torrent is gold in the electric glow, and for a moment both of them stand there open-mouthed. Then Bridget snatches at the light switch again, and the room is dark. All they can hear is running water and, above their heads, the strangulations of the draining bath. Etta bursts into tears.

'Our house,' she sobs, 'our beautiful house, I've ruined it.'

Gene appears at the door. 'What's going on?' he says. 'What happened to my concert?'

'Mum, Dad,' says Bridget sharply, 'go and sit down in the

living room. I'll take care of this.'

When they do not move, she takes them both by the wrist and leads them away from the dripping lounge. Then she puts the Mozart CD on again, and pours them both a sherry. Etta is still crying.

'I've ruined everything,' she whispers, 'it's all my fault.'

'You have not ruined anything, Mum,' says Bridget, trying not to shout. 'You're just over-tired. Now, drink this, and I'll be back soon.'

She grabs as many towels as she can carry from the linen cupboard and dumps them in the dark lounge. The ceiling lamp is still gushing, so she positions a bucket on the coffee table underneath it. Water drums against the plastic. Bridget can hear her mother sobbing above the flute music.

In the cupboard under the stairs Bridget takes the fluorescent storm lantern from its labelled hook and switches it on. Straight away she sees that the cupboard walls are also drenched, and the uncarpeted floor is wet.

'Oh shit.' She crawls into the very back of the cupboard, where the back-to-front stairs meet the floor, and she drags out Clifford's diaries, boxes of Gene's old work notes, plans of various buildings, and bundles of family photos which have never been put in an album.

'Shit, shit, shit.'

A lot of the plans are soaking; they bend and wilt in Bridget's hands, and she lays them as carefully as she can on the garage floor. The photos seem unharmed – they were in plastic bags – but the diaries have suffered. Bridget opens one and can hardly make out the entry on that page. Spots of ink spread on the wet paper like opening flowers; words melt into arrangements of blue and black.

She removes load after load of stored boxes from under the stairs. She feels along the shelves at the very back, where it is darkest; she doesn't dare turn the overhead light on, and in the narrow corner her own body blocks the beam of the storm lantern. The floor is cool under her stockinged feet. She feels as if she is conducting an excavation in some dripping underground cave.

The insurance assessors inspect the scene the following morning. They stroll around with clipboards and step-ladders, prodding bubbled wallpaper and pressing their palms against the ceiling. It's not as bad as some they've seen, they say. Sometimes people actually leave for work with the bath still running, and when they come home at night they find their furniture floating round the place. This, they say, gesturing at the lounge, is a routine accident. There is no serious damage. They'll send the carpet men round and that should take care of it.

✧

Although it's the middle of May and there is frost on the ground in the mornings, most of the doors and windows in the Stilton household are open.

'I do apologise for the temperature in here,' Etta says to visitors, 'but it's what was recommended.'

She and Bridget have retreated upstairs to the warmth of Gene's room, where the gas heater offers its steady blue flame and the air does not catch in their throats. Downstairs, the wet carpet has been lifted and huge electric fans placed underneath. All day these whisper to themselves in the deserted lower half of the house, expelling air as if through softly held lips.

'It'll just take a couple of days for it all to dry out,' said the carpet men, flicking obedient cables behind them as they paced the lounge, the hallway, the living room in their workingmen's boots, levering unwilling nails from the wood and soft wool.

'Fools,' says Gene that evening, rumbling down the stairs on his motorised chair, surveying the damage from above. 'They have no idea about the flow of air. The behaviour of particle board when exposed to heat. Apprentices were they?' He gestures at a fan. 'That one at least should be shifted over here.' He places a slippered foot on the billowing carpet and begins making his way to the far corner of the lounge, where the squat fan is murmuring. The carpet rises and falls beneath him, and for a moment it seems he will be lifted away on a wave of soft beige. His dressing gown flaps at his ankles. When he reaches the corner he turns back the edge of the carpet and grasps the fan, curving his arms around it and hugging it to his chest. The noise is louder now.

Etta's voice rises. 'I don't think that's such a good idea, do you? Love?'

Gene's breathing becomes harder as he attempts to lift the fan.

Etta crosses the rippled carpet and places a hand on his shoulder. 'Sweetheart. The men put it there for good reason. They've done this hundreds of times before.'

'Just get off my back, would you?' snaps Gene, and Etta snatches her hand away. For a moment all that can be heard is the blowing of the fans and Gene's careful gasps.

Up 4 a.m. Cyril took his car & me to Barossa Station past Mount Somers (92 miles). We went up about 2000ft in search of Amethyst. I found a nice agate weight 36lbs & Cyril got a moss agate 38lbs and some nice pieces of crystal. I got a massive piece of Amethyst part of one I left there 30 years ago. We carried them out on an old army stretcher. When we arrived home Mum was showing some visitors the stones

When he rises to his feet again he runs a soft foot over the particle board floor and clicks his tongue. 'Look at this rubbish,' he says. 'All the leftovers glued together. On the old State houses the floors were heart rimu.' He laughs. 'State houses! Now they're ripping up the carpet in them and polishing the floors. Or recycling the timber. Making coffee tables out of it.'

'Come and sit down, love, please.'

'They won't be recycling this rubbish, will they?'

'Love,' says Etta, and she takes his loose hand and leads him back to his motorised chair, and he sways, as if the floor is shifting beneath him.

The troops require sustenance

Etta doesn't say much on the way home from the airport, and Christina keeps glancing at her as if her mother's white knuckles on the steering wheel and her tensed lips and her rigid eyes will reveal what is wrong. She decides not to mention meeting Joanne yet; she'll wait until Etta asks. Instead she says, 'You've lost weight.'

'A bit.'

Etta continues to stare ahead at the road. A little bell sounds whenever she exceeds a hundred kilometres; Christina's never heard it before.

'There's no hurry, Mum.'

'I don't like leaving him for too long.'

'Bridget's there.' Bridget's always there.

The bell sounds again. 'That is driving me mad,' says Etta. She glances at Christina. 'It's very expensive to get it disconnected, Shirley told me.'

Christina watches the sea. Even at low tide there is never much beach along this stretch; the waves seem to reach right up to the road, and it is possible to imagine she is in a boat. The motorway is all reclaimed land anyway, heaved up by the 1855 earthquake. She never feels entirely safe on it, and now, with Etta so distracted and with the jagged hills to her left and the harbour to her right, Christina can think only in single words: the sea, the green, the trees, the sea, the sea. The landscape is too extreme; it swallows her, occupies her.

She can remember quite a big earthquake one summer, at the lake. It was the middle of the night and the jolt woke her (but not Bridget), and she'd not been able to move she was so scared. She lay in her bed until Etta came running in, snatching at the lightswitch, and then Bridget had woken up too and they had both started crying. Gene told them the next morning that when he'd been out fishing at midnight, before the quake, he'd been amazed to find that the shallow water he was standing in, right near the shore, was thick with trout. He'd caught fish after fish. A local man, fishing alongside him, said they only came in that close when there was going to be an earthquake. And three hours later, just after Gene arrived back at the motel, it happened. This is a story Gene tells often. The biggest fish of my life, he says, and the best run. They were darting around my legs. Christina has always wondered why her father had not come straight home to warn his family, to save them from their nighttime alarm.

She is relieved when Etta turns off at the landscaped sign marking the end of the motorway: Petone, spelled out in flowers.

'I got you some Ribena,' says Etta.

'Thanks. You can get it in Sydney, though.'

'Oh.'

'But it doesn't taste the same. The water's different.'

'I hope you're being careful,' says Etta. 'Remember that time at Christmas?'

'Mum. I do know about these things, I am a doctor.'

Etta swings the car into their street. The trees have been pruned again, their tops flattened so they're not touching the power lines. They look like giant stalks of broccoli.

'You'll notice a big change in him.' Etta turns carefully into their narrow driveway. Leaflets pushed only halfway into the letterbox flutter in welcome, announcing power-tool sales and discounted baked beans. Etta presses a blue button hooked onto the dashboard, and the garage door lifts.

Just before they go inside she touches Christina's arm and says quietly, 'Don't talk to him about Joanne, will you? It'd be too upsetting at this stage.'

'How much longer do we have to listen to those bloody Christmas carols?' says Christina. 'It is nearly June, you know.'

'I guess that depends,' says Bridget. 'Dad likes them. And I wasn't here for Christmas.' She leaves the room.

'She's being a real little bitch,' says Christina. 'She acts like it's her house just because she's been living here since she came back from Germany. Rent free, mind you. And Mum still does her washing.'

'Maybe I could come over for a little while too,' says Thorsten on the other end of the phone. 'Take your mind off things a bit.'

Christina can't wait for him to arrive. It's not so much that she's missing him – and sex is the last thing on her mind, which she hopes won't be a problem when he does get there. What she needs him for is to remind her that she has an existence apart from this family; something she has created by herself, and something they play no part in. She watches Bridget feeding Gene his jelly and custard and tells herself, I have my own life, I have my own apartment. I have Thorsten. I can go home whenever I want.

The problem is, whenever she comes back to Wellington, and particularly this time, Sydney begins to seem more and more unreal. As if she has imagined some distant, ideal location where she would like to go for a holiday, if it really existed. She has lost the concrete details of it the way one loses the memory of a particular teacher's face, the voice of a discontinued television presenter. Certain components can be recalled, but there is no completion. She creates inventories for reassurance: a yellow and white duvet cover, striped; a claw-footed bath; six matching ivory towels; a set of copper-bottomed pots and pans. An Italian cafe in Glebe that serves almond cake; a giraffe at the Western Plains Zoo that licked her hand with its long blue tongue. A red vinyl armchair in the hospital staffroom; two cut crystal vases (twenty-first presents); another armchair, covered in green velvet. This does not help. I know I have a bike, she can say, and I know it is blue. That is all.

In Wellington it is other details that define her, items she would rather disown: the padded plush headboard on her parents' bed, Bridget's cheap stereo, the stuffed pheasant with the skewed neck (she can't remember how it happened), the stag's antlers in the garage. Sometimes she can't imagine how she developed the knack of choosing lampshades to go with couches, or duvets to harmonise with curtains, or makeup to match clothes. It's certainly not a talent she's inherited from Gene or Etta. Or Joanne, for that matter.

She stretches out in the bath and rests her head against the tiled wall. On her stomach she can see the sheen of her scars, three white triangles, stretched, a stylised ship in full sail. She fell on to a photographer's lights when she was two and she and Bridget were having a studio portrait taken. She sometimes jokes – to curious lovers, beach companions – that Bridget pushed

her. But she couldn't have, could she? they say. She only would
have been, what, ten months old? Christina used to think the
scars were a sign that she would become a sailor, and for a while
she collected objects connected with the sea: driftwood, shells
given to her by a delighted Clifford, a broken barometer, a ship
in a bottle. 'That's a cheat's one,' said Bridget, and pointed out
the ribbon glued around the base of the bottle, covering the
join where the glass had been cut and the ship inserted whole.
Christina did not like Bridget to tell her facts such as these:
Christina was the logical one, the one with common sense. I
will run away, I will go to sea, Christina thought then, and they
will be sorry. I will fill my school bag with bottles of Vitamin C
and I will cure the crew of scurvy.

'Christina!' Bridget knocks on the bathroom door. The
locked handle rattles. 'I need to do my makeup!'

'Dad, look who's here to see you.'

'Hello Gene,' says Thorsten. 'I brought you some fudge.
It's one of our favourites.'

*Wrote to Gene today & I am sending him 16 stones plus one
brooch for Etta & they are beautiful they will be very pleased with
them*
Dolly 6 p.m.

'I hear you're thinking about going fishing.'

Gene stares at him, unblinking. Thorsten unwraps a piece
of fudge and hands it to him. It rests in his palm like a pebble.

'He won't eat it,' says Christina.

'The trout won't know what's hit them, eh?'

*After tea Cyril & I went to Lyttelton & fished alongside the
German boat the Rhein from Hamburg   the Germans fished also
they had a powerful light playing on the water   we caught 50
little cod Cyril 1 Trevalli. The Barracuda gave us some fun but
didn't land any (neither did the Germans)*

'We got three Jerries,' says Gene. 'Straight through with
the bayonets, like *that*.'

'We've made up your bed for you in the guest room, Thorsten,' says Etta. 'Where you were before.'

'Mum's been relegated to the floor,' says Christina.

'Oh dear, I hope I –'

'Nonsense,' says Etta. 'She's exaggerating, I'm on a perfectly comfortable mattress in with Gene.'

'On the floor.'

'Christina, Thorsten is staying in the guest room with you and that's that,' says Etta. 'I've put an electric blanket on your bed,' she says to Thorsten. 'Christina said you were a bit cold last time.'

'Not enough body heat,' says Gene.

'Don't be naughty,' says Etta. 'You are a naughty thing.' She arranges the rug on his knees, folding back the fringed edge so it won't tickle his hands.

'Mum. He's not a child.'

'Your father is unwell,' hisses Etta. 'In case you hadn't noticed.' She opens the door to the hall and aims her voice up the stairs. 'Bridget! Come and say hello to Thorsten!'

✧

Bridget lies on her bed and wishes Christina would hurry up and go back to Sydney. Etta cannot seem to relax with her in the house; she's always leaping up to tend to Christina's every whim, and now that Thorsten is here she will be fussing even more. Of course, when Christina leaves, the guest room will be empty. Available for guests. Aunts Carnelian and Theresa have both been threatening to 'come and help your Mum out a bit'. More cups of tea, more smiles.

Bridget wonders what Gülten is doing. If she has managed to bed her DJ. She wonders if Gülten still thinks about her; she has received no letters, although they promised to write.

Antony is no help. Bridget tried to describe Gülten to him, and showed him photos, and all he said was, 'She looks like a *very* nice girl.' He emphasised the *very* in a way Bridget did not care for, and he asked if she had a boyfriend.

She writes Gülten another letter and posts it to the hostel in Berlin. She wishes she had thought to get her parents' address in Turkey off her; perhaps, she thinks, Gülten is lying in the sun in Istanbul, her hair pouring over the hot stone, thinking about Bridget. Perhaps she is taking a dark purple olive with her fingertips and saying to a trusted female cousin, or possibly a neighbour, yes, she and I were very close, closer than sisters.

She wishes Gülten were here to look after her now, and not Antony. She can't bear to be close to him any more; she shrinks from his walnut-shell hands. He'd been there at the airport when she arrived back from Germany; his had been the first face she'd recognised. Then when he stepped towards her, she'd seen Gene behind him, supported by Etta.

'You must realise,' Bridget said when they went out for a drink the next night, 'that I'm still very jetlagged, and things are pretty weird at home.'

He nodded, squeezing her hand.

'And I'm very drunk.'

He nodded again.

'But,' she said, looking at the hand gripping hers and noting the long milky nails and the spiderweb hair, 'I see no reason why not.'

They went back to his flat and had unsatisfactory sex, and then Bridget left to catch the last train home.

'You can sleep here,' mumbled Antony as she was leaving.

But by then Bridget felt wide awake – from the jetlag rather than the sex, she decided – and she shut the door softly behind her.

On the train, she sat behind an adolescent boy and a woman of about fifty. They didn't seem to know each other, but the woman talked the whole time.

'I went to the dentist today,' she said. 'I had to have a new tooth moulded. They put one in months ago, but it didn't take, and just the pin was left hanging there, but I was too scared to go back so I left it for a while and then it abscessed and I had to go back.'

'Ah,' said the boy.

'I can tell you, it was worse than having a baby. They kept telling you there was only half an hour to go and there was ages to go – I was in there for four hours and they wouldn't let me go to the toilet and I do have a weak bladder. Well anyone would need to go in that time wouldn't they?'

The boy smiled and gave a brief nod, then stared out the window.

'It's like a different world in town isn't it?' the woman went on. 'Too expensive to live there though. I'm way out in Upper Hutt, so I don't make it in that often. I'm in a Housing Corporation flat so I'm all right, only $33 a week. I love the harbour at night – I wonder what would my English penpal say if she could see that view. I wish she'd come and visit, but it's such a long way isn't it?'

'Mmm,' said the boy.

Bridget felt sorry for him; she had been trapped next to passengers before who insisted on making conversation. But now, Bridget found herself straining to catch every word over the noise of the train. She hardly dared breathe in case the woman realised someone was listening.

'I've got a T-shaped kitchen,' the woman was saying. 'There's room for a table in front of the stove, but I've got the cats' dishes there of course. I was given a cockatiel not long ago. It used to be called Fred but I changed it to Susan. My penpal's husband's called Fred. I never liked the name.'

'No,' said the boy.

'They all sit round the heater at night, the cats and Susan. The cats don't mind her. It's just like having kids.'

The woman was silent for a moment then. Through the gap in the seat, Bridget could see her running her finger along a back tooth and looking out the window.

'You know,' she said, turning back to the boy, 'the whole time my tooth was abscessed it only ached twice. In ten months. The dentist couldn't believe it, he said something's wrong and x-rayed it and it was abscessed.'

The train began pulling into Bridget's station. She walked to the doors as slowly as possible.

'My church does the laying on of hands,' the woman was saying as the train stopped. 'When it ached those two times I had the laying on of hands and it went away just like that. We've had people in with diabetes, and burns, and cancer. You just have to believe.'

As Bridget stepped off the train and into the warm air she heard the woman saying behind her, 'I kept the moulded tooth. It was a beautiful tooth, just like a real one.'

At home, Bridget found Gene rummaging through the freezer. He jumped when she snapped the light on.

'Foiled again,' he said.

'Dad, what are you doing? It's past midnight.'

'I wanted an icecream. But that woman's eaten them all.'

'Mum? She hardly ever eats it, you know that.'

'To identify the culprit on the street,' he said, 'you need to check whether the nose is wet or dry. Healthy possums have wet noses.'

'I see,' said Bridget. 'Look, why don't you go on up to bed, and I'll dish you out some icecream in a plate.'

'Do you know,' said Gene, holding on to the fridge, 'that Dad came into the office?'

'Did he,' said Bridget, taking Gene's arm. 'Raspberry ripple okay?'

'I didn't tell anyone. They'd have thought I was mad. He's never been to the North Island, you know.'

'No,' said Bridget.

'I told him, though. I said I'd ring the police. Stroppy old bugger, bothering me at work.'

'Yes,' said Bridget, 'that's nice.' She took Gene's arm and led him out to the stair chair. 'There we are. In you hop, and I'll buzz you up.'

'I don't know why I said that just now,' said Gene. 'Do you?'

Now 9.30 a.m. Mum goes on the Plane to Wellington at 2.10 p.m. Mum is now getting ready to take to the air her first flight & her first trip to the North Island. She has promised to bring me back the very first stone of any description she can pick up in Wellington. I will add it to my collection suitably inscribed.

'You mustn't take any notice of me,' Gene said the next morning. 'I say some very confused things. These days I seem to be making comments that are more and more irrelevant.'

'Oh,' said Bridget. 'Okay. Well. You will call out if you want anything, won't you?'

When Gülten writes, it is a one-page note to say that her mother has been admitted to hospital and is not expected to last more than a few weeks. Gülten has had to move home, to Istanbul that is, to look after her father and her brothers, for a while at least. She thinks of Bridget often, she says, and hopes things are not too hard. Her aunts and their daughters all disapprove of her and talk about her behind their hands, but loudly enough. Look at her tight jeans and her low tops, they say. Look at the way she paints her lips. Gülten doesn't give a shit about them, she says, they are just jealous they don't have the guts to dress how they want. The men look at her too.

By the way, she writes, squeezing these last words in around the hugs and kisses, I have married.

Bridget re-reads the letter several times, trying to make sense of it, wondering if Gülten is trying to tell her something her family wouldn't let her write. If she is really saying, save me.

Dear Gülten, she finally writes, I was very sorry to hear that your mother is now so ill. I realise things may have altered even by the time you get this. I do feel as if I know what you're going through; Dad's condition is also advancing faster than anyone can believe. We're nursing him at home, with the help of the hospice, but it's difficult to keep up with the changes we're seeing every day. I must admit, I don't know much about Turkish weddings – you'll have to tell me all about yours, and send some photos. I know you would have looked beautiful. What is your husband like? Is he a DJ?? If I were him I would be very happy. Love Bridget xxxxoooo.

Antony rings just as she is sealing the envelope.

'Hi, how are you?' she mumbles, running her tongue along the gummed flap.

'Not bad. What've you been up to lately? I haven't heard from you for days.'

'Oh, it's been all action here, believe me. We've only just got the carpets back down and the furniture in from the garage. Mum flooded the place.'

'I see,' says Antony. 'Were the phones cut off too?'

'And Christina's come over for a visit, and Thorsten. Look, I've been meaning to ring, but Dad takes up all my time these days.'

'Hmm.'

'Sorry.'

'I'm starting to wonder if you –'

The baby monitor crackles.

'Father to daughter, father to daughter, come in daughter,' says Gene's hugely amplified voice. 'The troops require sustenance. Cups of tea: one. Mallowpuffs: three. Over and out.'

'Antony,' says Bridget, 'can I ring you back?'

She creeps up the stairs and opens her father's bedroom door. He is sitting up on the edge of the bed, his pyjama trousers gaping open.

'Aha!' he says.

'Do you need syrup too?'

'No no, I just had some before.'

'Okay. Back soon.'

Bridget plugs in the electric jug and peeks under Native Birds of New Zealand while she waits for it to boil. All of Gene's medication is laid out in neat rows, the edges of the boxes parallel with the sides of the tray. The embroidered tray cloth, too, is dead straight. She tweaks a corner, pulling it just a fraction out of line. Then she replaces the teatowel.

'Here we are, Dad.'

'Thanks love. What would we do without you?' He bites into a Mallowpuff and lifts his cup of tea to Bridget. 'Cheers,' he says. 'We're not dead yet.'

Oh Hell I had a dreadful experience at Birdlings Flat today. Cyril had a bad turn like an Epileptic Fit I yelled & yelled for help but the noise of the sea stopped anyone hearing me. I'll swear that Cyril died I was desperate I gave him mouth to nose resuscitation he was frothing at the mouth. Len Booth reached us first & he helped me carry Cyril back from the edge of the sea then I sent Len for help. He told them there was no hurry as Cyril was dead. Anyway about ½ hr later Cyril came to & I couldn't hold him down he kept picking up stones. I am still suffering from shock.
Dolly 7 p.m.

Bridget has noticed how Gene uses 'we' more and more these days. 'I'll leave you to it then,' she says.

'Did you bring the syrup?'

Bridget frowns. 'Oh . . .' She straightens Gene's slipping bedspread. 'Sorry. I forgot. I'll get you some.'

When she comes back upstairs, Gene has disappeared. She hears a thud from her room, and finds him trying to move her dressing table.

'I thought we could put all the beds in here,' he says. 'Along this wall, because you've got those extra power points.'

✧

Thorsten hands Christina a mug of coffee. She grunts.

'I thought I'd take Gene for a walk in the wheelchair, if you want to come,' he says.

'Oh. I wanted to go to Eastbourne today, actually. If it stays fine we can catch the ferry back into town.'

Thorsten frowns. 'The fresh air would be good, but I don't think he's up to a boat ride, is he?'

'I meant just the two of us. No parents, no sister.'

Thorsten puts down his coffee. 'I think he'd really like it if you came.'

'Would he? You've discussed this with him, have you?'

'You can't expect him just to sit inside all day.'

'What did he say, "To catch sausages you have to attach a feather"?'

'I just thought you'd want to spend some time with him, that's all. He is your father.'

'I get to see enough sick people at work,' says Christina. Her voice is becoming louder and louder. 'And he's not technically my father.'

'Sick people. In Maternity?'

Christina ignores him. 'Sick people shouldn't be at home. I don't know why they're persisting with this bloody hospice home care performance. Home is the one place where you can get away from sick people.'

'I already asked him if he wants to go.' Thorsten studies his hands. 'Etta's just getting his shoes on him.'

'That'll take a while then.'

'Bridget's coming too.'

Christina stares at him. 'Bridget. I see. Look, here's an idea, why don't you all spend the day together, get icecreams, have a picnic, skip stones, whatever. And I'll go to Eastbourne by myself. Keep out of your way, how would that be? And I know, while you're at it, why don't you feed him and give him a bath, too?'

'Christina –'

'And no reason to stop there. Mum's been kind of tense lately, can't imagine why, why don't you sleep with her, cheer the old thing up a bit?'

Before Thorsten can answer, Gene's motorised chair begins to rumble down the stairs.

'Here we are,' says Etta. 'We'll just get our jackets on. Left arm, Gene.'

While the others are out Christina wanders around the house. In Bridget's room she finds a letter next to the messy bed. She can recognise that it's in German, but can't make out any of the words. At the bottom are rows of kisses and hugs, and a scrawled name Christina cannot read. Something like Sulter, Geller . . . Günter? Bridget never mentioned anything about a boyfriend over there. She wonders if Antony knows.

In her parents' room, the double bed and Etta's mattress on the floor have both been made with military precision, blankets tightly tucked and sheet corners like origami. On the bedside cabinet, bottles of pills and syrup have been lined up in rows. The morning paper has been folded and placed neatly on a chair. Christina picks up a hairbrush. There is not a hair in it.

There are four loaves of bread in the pantry, all white, sandwich-sliced. A fifth loaf has been half-gutted; only emptied crusts remain.

The washing machine is shuddering in the garage, working itself up to its morning finale. On the floor, spread out on newspaper, are books and papers and plans. Bridget retrieved them from the cupboard under the stairs when Etta flooded the bathroom. Christina's heard all about that. You mustn't think it's your fault, Etta told her. I just forgot about the bath when I was talking to you. It's nobody's fault. We're all under a fair bit of pressure at the moment, aren't we?

Christina nudges one of Clifford's diaries with her toe. A page falls out.

he was up on their roof doing some repairs & he fell off, missed the fence, grabbed a very small tree & finished up at the feet of his neighbour, flat on his back on the concrete path next door. No bones broken but the Doctor has ordered him to bed for a couple of days. Etta saw Gene's dark form flash past the window she was very upset & said how could he climb all that scaffolding at work & then fall off the roof at home. Next time take a ruddy parachute with you Gene. Health all right but this bloody indigestion keeps me awake.

Next to the diaries is a buckled plan of the house Gene built in Christchurch when he and Etta were first married, and some of Christina's lecture notes from her first year at med school. In the margins she can see where she was practising her signature: Dr C Stilton, Dr C Stilton. She does not remember doing this. The notes Gene started making for his survival guide are splayed in a fan shape, the edges curling upwards like dried leaves. There is a neat chart with the heading *Ground to Air Emergency Visual Signalling Code*, and a column of symbols. *Signals should be at least eight feet in length and the area chosen to display them should provide as much contrast as possible*, it says.

1	Require doctor serious injuries	**I**
2	Require medical supplies	**II**
3	Unable to proceed	**X**
4	Require food and water	**F**
5	Require firearms and ammunition	**⋙**
6	Require map and compass	**□**
7	Require	

Gene's lecture notes from his night classes are there too: *Technical Mastery. The Development of Leadership. Avoiding Playing the Game of Favourites. Delegation of Authority & Responsibility.*

Christina looks at the tools hanging on the wall, all outlined in black marker so they will be returned to the same hook each time. She is aware that behind each tool, written by Gene within each outline, there is a label. *Electric sander. Plane. Hammer. Hacksaw.* A precaution against chaos.

The washing machine beeps twelve, thirteen, fourteen times and falls silent. Christina gathers up her lecture notes, feeling them to make sure they are completely dry, and tidies them away into the cupboard under the stairs. When she reaches back a hand to turn the cupboard light off she flicks the switch connected to the motorised chair by mistake, and underneath the stairs there is a sound like thunder.

'What have you got planned for the rest of the day?' says Etta when they arrive back.

'Thorsten and I might go to the beach,' says Christina.

'Why don't you get out of the house for a while on your own?' says Thorsten. 'Go shopping, visit a friend. We'll stay with Gene, won't we, Christina?'

'Oh no, I couldn't,' says Etta. 'If something happened –'

'Etta, we are both doctors. Nothing will happen, I promise. You could do with a break.'

'Christina?'

'Sure, Mum, why not,' she says, looking at Thorsten.

'There goes Eastbourne,' says Christina when Etta has gone.

'Look, he's going to be in bed anyway, it's not like you have to *talk* to him the whole time. Haven't you noticed how haggard she looks?'

'It suits her.'

A distant rumble begins above their heads.

'He'll be in bed, you say?'

Thorsten sighs. 'Help me get him off the chair.'

'And how's work?' says Gene.

'It's fine.'

'Long hours?'

'Yep.'

'Can't make babies come when you want them to.'

'No.'

'Any named after you?'

'I don't think so. Thorsten, could you put some music on?'

'Now tell me about her,' says Gene.

'About who?'

'Jane.'

'I don't know any Janes,' says Christina.

'Ah . . . Joan? The birth mother person you met.'

'Joanne.'

'Joanne. You did meet her, didn't you.'

'*Best of Crowded House* all right?' says Thorsten.

'Have you got any photos?' says Gene.

'No. No photos. But we're going to stay in touch.'

'That's nice. Your mother's been terribly worried about it.'

'Why would she be worried?'

'She likes to worry,' says Gene, and then he blinks very slowly and watches the lights on the stereo. 'We got a twelve-pointer,' he says. 'Three shots.'

'Dad,' says Christina, 'Thorsten and I have to fly back to Sydney tomorrow. Got to get back to work.'

Gene continues to watch the stereo. His lips move slightly, but he makes no sound.

'Our flight's quite early,' she says, 'but I'll come and say – I'll come and see you in the morning before I go.' She touches his hand.

They tried to swim Cook Strait today. Bill Penny swam South to North & missed by about 1 hour. Barrie Davenport got to within

1 mile from the South Island after swimming from Wellington. Perhaps next year someone will do it but it won't be me, too far away.

◇

Gene is in his prime time now, the hospice doctor tells him when she calls by, and she asks him if he still wants to go to the lake. Gene thinks this is an extremely stupid question, but he decides to answer her in a friendly manner because, he reasons, she cannot help her stupidity. Indeed he does still want to go, he says, there are some bloody big fish out there whose time has come. And the doctor says very earnestly that while she can't make that sort of decision for him, she would be going now if she were him, as there is no telling how long his prime time will last. I see, says Gene, I see. Well.

Etta agrees with the hospice doctor. 'I think now's the time, Gene,' she says, so although she has been wrong about a few things recently – the day of the week, for example, or which visitor baked which fruitcake – he agrees.

And once he has given this approval, Bridget and Etta pack everything into the car immediately, ready to go the very next morning. It's not the best time of year for fishing, of course, and his favourite spot – the tail race – will be muddy from the recent storms, but Gene is not one to argue with a pair of women once they have set their mind to something. Etta could probably use a holiday; they haven't been away in so long.

'But I'll organise my fishing gear myself,' he says. 'I don't want you and Bridget mucking things up.'

Mr Drury whom I do the rods for called for me tonight I put on a show of crabs & stones for business friends of his. Holy cow they handed me a prayer book & sang 3 hymns & had prayers. Save my bloody soul.

He unpacks all his reels and lays them out on the workbench in the garage. Most of them have become tangled; one of them he doesn't remember having seen before. He turns it over and over in his hands, wondering how it came to be with his things. It is very new looking, and an expensive model.

'Etta,' he calls. 'Etta!'

She bursts through the door, as if she is in a hurry to get somewhere. 'What's wrong? What is it?' she says, grasping his arm.

'Where did this come from?' Gene holds the reel up for her inspection. 'It's not a hidden present, is it? Because it's a pretty stupid place to hide it.'

Etta takes the reel from him. 'That was your retirement present,' she says slowly. 'They gave it to you at your farewell function, remember?' She peers at it. 'Look, here's the inscription. *To Gene Stilton, for forty years of service to Conway's Construction Ltd. 16.11.91.'*

Gene takes the reel back and looks at it again.

'Shall I give you a hand?' says Etta. 'Where's your fly box?'

Without waiting for an answer she begins rummaging round in the cupboards. She is a very efficient woman when she wants to be, thinks Gene, but unfortunately she has no idea what she's doing. She sorts through containers of tiny fluorescent beads, she fingers a pair of iridescent starling wings. Gene watches her examine and reject old cigar tins rattling with lures, packets of metallic twine, samples of possum fur, rabbit fur, deer hide. He wonders why she should suddenly be taking an interest in his hobbies; she's always hated his fishing and hunting trips.

'Here it is!' she says, waving an aluminium case. It slips from her hand and bursts open on the garage floor, scattering trout flies everywhere. Some of them land in patches of oil the car has left behind.

Gene didn't mean to shout at Etta, but really, she was fussing around so much he doubted they'd ever get away. She didn't seem to appreciate the amount of time that had gone into making the flies, the hours he had spent tying minute knots, lacquering, snipping feathers, binding the bodies with coloured thread. The sheer detail involved. The whorls and ridges of his fingertips becoming maps behind the magnifying glass.

Mum did a lot of painting of rods & some welding for me she doesn't mind just sitting there doing a quiet little job although she is not keeping so well. I'm too busy with rods to do much with stones. I have one crab that's been sitting on my workbench since Xmas and he's still only half out. Of course the rods are profitable & stones aren't you can't eat stones. Doreen Booth (expecting) aged 16 was married this afternoon a very pretty bride Dolly 6 p.m.

'If you'd just get off my back and let me get on with it,' he snapped.

Because now that he has decided to go, everything seems much more urgent. He can't wait to be standing out there again, his waders made slick by water, the lake hugging his chest.

It's not the best time of year for a lot of things. As they drive up through Otaki, Levin, Foxton, there are none of the usual signs advertising summer fruit. It is a Stilton tradition to stop and pick strawberries on the way to the lake, and to eat them with the Christmas pavlova. Gene watches the farms slip by the passenger window – it is quite a relief, to be a passenger this time – and feels very sad that they will have no strawberries. *Potatoes, apples, swede*, the signs say. *Parsnip, pumpkin. Broccoli, cauliflower.*

'Etta,' he says, 'we can't make do with apples and cream, it won't be the same.'

But Etta is concentrating on her driving, and only smiles briefly at him, and pats him on the knee.

And he finds himself standing in a bed of straw, the sweet-smelling air soft around him, and rows of fat berries stretching away in all directions. Bridget is running towards him, laughing, calling look, Daddy, look at this one, and biting into a strawberry as big as her fist. Christina bends low over the bright leaves, checking underneath for the berries that have been missed, filling her cardboard punnet with only the most perfect specimens. And Etta? He thinks he can see Etta in the distance, a tiny figure in a sundress, waiting at the end of the vast berry bed, where the nectarine trees start.

'There's the Army Museum, Dad,' says Bridget. 'Remember how you always used to stop there and drag us round?'

Gene's chest is aching. He wants to ask Etta to pull over and pour him some syrup, but she says, 'We don't have time for that today, Bridget. We have to get through the Desert Road while it's clear.'

And they whistle past the angular concrete building where, Gene recalls, there are drawers and drawers of medals, and then they enter the icy Desert Road.

Drury the swine has backed out of his order again   my advice is never mess with church people   & he will be sorry he messed with Clifford Stilton
Pulse 98

'Put the blanket over his knees,' says Etta, and Bridget leans through the gap between the front seats and tucks a tartan rug around him.

'Make sure his breathing's okay.'

Bridget holds her face very close to Gene's, and touches his cheek with her hand. He watches Mount Tongariro, covered in snow now, as it moves from one side of the horizon to the other with the turning of the road. He imagines himself stepping into that whiteness, losing himself in white, and the more he thinks about this the less his chest aches.

The motel is not the old one they used to stay at in Turangi, right beside the lake.

'Let's have a bit of luxury this time,' Etta had said. 'We deserve it.' And she had booked a unit at the Angler's Lodge, one of the most expensive motels right in the middle of Taupo.

Ask about our paragliding package! says a notice at reception.

Etta unlocks their door with a key on a fish-shaped ring. She is brisk, efficient, inspecting the main room in a glance, placing bags and suitcases in sensible positions, identifying immediately the location of lightswitches, coat hooks.

'There's a spa bath!' calls Bridget.

Gene stands in the centre of the room, turning a complimentary chocolate over and over in his palm.

✧

'Morning morning!' chirps the fishing guide. He's young, about thirty, and is wearing a baseball cap saying *Angler Dan's*. There are a few colourful trout flies hooked on the side; feathers dyed fluorescent pink and orange. On his spotless jacket, underneath the matching *Angler Dan's* stitching, there is an embroidered trout in mid leap, spraying tiny cotton droplets across his chest. 'All righty!' he says, clapping his hands together. 'Are we all set?'

'The Guide,' says Gene.

'That's me all right.'

'I must finish it, one of these days.'

'Let's do you up,' says Bridget, fumbling with the zip on Gene's jacket. It's all back to front from this angle.

At 8 p.m. there was to be a big explosion in the Lyttelton tunnel I went out & listened but never heard it. The tunnel will be completely through in about three weeks. Also at 8 p.m. the Yanks were letting off a Nuclear bomb of about 1,000,000 tons in the Pacific. The last one was seen from NZ.

– Thursday: Lyttelton explosion was 7 p.m. Nuclear was a fizzer.

'He doesn't usually fish from a boat,' Etta whispers to the fishing guide. 'He's used to chest waders.'

'Right you are,' says the guide.

Etta presses a small plastic bag into his hand. 'Here's his medication. Give him 10ml of syrup whenever he needs it. And

Dan,' she says, reading the guide's chest, 'if he's too sore then bring him back. He won't like it, but just bring him back.'

'Not a problem,' says Dan. 'Oh and I'm not Dan, by the way, I'm Rick. If you want to tell your friends about us.'

'Rick,' says Etta. 'Right. Yes.'

'Actually,' says Rick, leaning in towards Etta, 'there is no Dan. Looks good on the brochures, you know? The Yanks love it, can't stop blabbing about Angler Dan the Fishing Man.'

'Okay,' says Bridget. 'Let's get you into the car.'

'Please don't bump him around too much,' says Etta. 'He's not up to anything rough.'

'No problem. Gidday there, Gene! How about we go hook a ten-pounder, eh mate?'

Drury has once more withdrawn his rod order & that's it as far as I'm concerned he can find some other mug to do his slave labour for him   see if he can get anyone as skilled   It's his wife I feel sorry for   from what I hear the bastard has boozed himself more mental than when he was born. I would thrill to read of his accidental discharge from this planet & would give my staff a months holiday on full pay

Gene stares at the guide. 'Who are you?' he says. 'Where's Dad?'

Bridget and Etta manoeuvre him into Rick's purple four-wheel-drive.

'Can't interest you ladies in a couple of casts, can we?' says Rick.

'Now remember to tell Rick if you want any syrup,' says Etta, straightening Gene's collar through the car window. 'We'll be waiting here for you when you get back.'

'Let's go get 'em then!' says Rick, and in a moment, faster than Bridget or Etta or even Gene can imagine, the purple vehicle has pulled away from their door and is gone.

The boat is steady enough, Rick decides. He has anchored it more or less where the old guy told him to, and now they are unpacking their gear.

Barrie Davenport swam Cook Strait the first ever to do so.
11 hrs 22 mins   too bloody far for me.
Pulse 93

The old guy is fumbling with boxes of flies. Rick has offered to help, three times, but the old guy has pretended not to hear. He's decided to leave the stroppy bugger to sort it out himself.

'You look like you're a bit of an old hand at this fishing business,' says Rick. 'You won't mind if I get myself set up too, will you?'

Len Booth of Sheffield died in St George's Hospital this morning (Heart). He was a good Chap, a keen fisherman, he caught 18 groper in one season off the beach at Chertsey with Rod & Line.

The old guy ignores him. Rick turns his back and starts casting, trying four, five times until he gets it right. Great morning for it. Not too many tourists, this time of year. 'You'll sing out if you need any syrup, right?' he says after a while.

And then it happens: the old guy begins reeling something in, and it's jumping and thrashing, a big one by the looks, maybe eight pounds, and he still doesn't say anything and is so absorbed in playing the damned fish in that Rick doesn't say anything either, and it's no sooner in the boat than the old guy's recasting, and he's no sooner recast than he's caught another one, just as big as the first, and that's the way it goes all morning until the old guy says he'd like to go back now, thank you.

By Mid-day we had 80 Swans. When we got a chance we would have a cup of Mum's hot soup or some tea & a bite to eat. The way the birds were coming in we could have had a table & chairs & kept the guns beside our plates. Luckily Gene had brought his trailer with him. When we got to 90 we decided we would stop at 100 as the wind was not letting up at times we could hardly stand & that's tough work. We were back at the car by 4 p.m. Goodness knows how many we would have got had we stayed but 100 had more

*than satisfied us & we could not carry any more on the trailer, as it
was we had ½ ton of Swans.*

Rick has caught nothing.

❖

'Aren't you a clever old thing?' says Etta, zipping away the
camera. Gene insisted on photographs with each fish; when
Etta snapped the last one the film started whirring back to its
own beginning.

'Thank you so much,' she says to Rick. 'You don't know
what this means to him.'

'You're not wrong there,' says Rick, pocketing his cheque.
'Man of few words. See you next time then.'

The drive home is spent in silence. Gene thinks about the trout
he has caught, which Etta has packed carefully in the boot of
the car, in blue chillybins, in ice. Etta slows down at each sign
saying *Rest Area*, in case he wants to stop. Bridget sleeps.

When they get home Bridget helps him inside while Etta
begins unpacking the car. Gene watches her bring in bags,
jackets, a thermos.

'The fish,' he says, 'they'll thaw, they'll go bad.'

'They're in the freezer already,' she says. 'I unpacked them
first.'

But Gene refuses to believe her, so she takes his right arm
and Bridget takes his left and they lead him to the freezer.

'Look,' says Etta, opening the bottom drawer. 'There they
are, right down where it's coldest, all labelled.'

Gene nods, and they start to direct him to his motorised
chair, but he shakes his head and says no, no, no. He wants to
be shown the rooms downstairs.

'But Dad, you're tired,' says Bridget. 'You've just had a long
drive, we should get you into bed.'

Gene does not want to go to bed. He wants to be shown
the rooms downstairs.

'All right,' says Etta, and gives Bridget a look, so she takes his left arm again and the three of them move from room to room.

'This is the living room,' says Etta. 'There's the TV, and our armchairs. There's the calendar you gave me for Christmas.'

Gene nods.

'Here's the kitchen. Mind the rubbish bin –'

Bridget kicks it out of the way.

'Through the dining room,' says Etta. 'There's the dresser where all the good china is.'

They creep along the re-laid carpet as if they do not want to make any noise; possibly wake someone who is asleep in the house.

'And here's the lounge,' says Etta. 'Here's the suite we bought in Christchurch.'

Gene leans more and more heavily on their arms as they move across the flowered rug that is almost as big as the lounge itself.

'Here we are in the hall,' says Etta, 'and there's your chair waiting at the bottom of the stairs.'

They propel Gene towards the chair, moving past the battle scene on the wall.

'There's your Chunuk Bair print.'

'No,' says Gene through barely opened lips as they position him in front of the motorised chair. 'No no no no –'

'What's the matter love, what is it?'

'Airroom,' he says, '*air*room.'

'I think he wants to see every room,' says Bridget quietly.

They pass Chunuk Bair again. Rifles aimed, bayonets raised.

'This is the downstairs toilet,' says Etta. 'There's the soapdish you attached to the wall and the mirror we bought last year.'

Past the print again. One hand lifted in surrender.

'And here's the garage.'

The car is cooling down after the five-hour drive. The

metallic ticking, growing slower and slower, sounds very loud against the concrete floor, the hard walls. From above the door the skew-necked pheasant regards Etta, Bridget and Gene with its glassy eye.

Gene nods and they return to the hall, and the waiting chair.

✧

It's terribly windy outside; at times it feels as if the windows will be blown in. Etta can't sleep. She switches on her light, flicks through a *Woman's Day*. A lot of the visitors bring her magazines, to take her mind off things they say. To help her relax a bit. Etta thanks them; they mean well. She is too polite to tell them she has no wish to make a Handy String Holder For The Kitchen, or to Crochet This Cheeky Hat, or to solve the Wonderword. She's made a stack of magazines by her bed; every week a new covergirl watches her dress and undress. Now, above the shuffle of glossy pages and the mounting wind outside, she can hear Gene's uneven breaths. She closes the article on My Miracle Baby.

In the dark hall she almost trips over the cardboard box of diaries. Bridget put them there; after the flood they lay drying on the garage floor for weeks, getting in Etta's way whenever she did the washing. She nagged Bridget to tidy them away, aware of the fact that she was nagging. Bridget put them in the upstairs hall. Etta said no more on the matter.

She pushes the box into Gene's room with her toes, step by step, feet bare on the rough carpet.

A shock for me   Mum was taken to hospital this morning with chest pains   eleven degrees of frost & no fire until I got one going I'm not used to that   she will stay in for a few days yet   I am frightened to think about it

The night-light is bright enough to read by. She takes the top diary, comforted by its weight, the absence of pictures, horoscopes, recipes. Some of it seems legible, despite the water damage. It's half past one in the morning. She's got hours and hours.

Gene's fingers flutter against the sheet now and then, but he's not awake. Etta turns the radio on, very softly. The announcer's voice is kind, lulling, providing her with soothing information such as the time, the day of the week, the fact that the following piece is one of his personal favourites. She listens and reads, or reads and listens, depending on which is the more distracting. And then a piece of music starts that she thinks she has heard before. Classical, flute and orchestra. Sustained, tranquil notes. Etta finds herself listening very closely, straining to catch them all as if each one were extremely important. She wishes she knew the name of the piece. She grows restless, digs her nails into her palms, wanting to absorb as much as she can of the music and at the same time wanting it to finish so she can hear the kind voice telling her the name. Gene's breaths are very shallow, out of time with the deep, slow music. His fingers knead the sheet.

Had a phone call from my best girl friend and made a date to pick her up at Princess Margaret Hospital at 2 p.m.

Etta takes his hand – full, swollen – and waits for the music to end.

For the first time in years that I have kept a diary I have gone wrong somewhere   no record of today

As the music finishes she leans in to the radio, turns up the volume, holds her breath. And another piece of music starts, something Etta does not care for, from some stage show or other, and she is surprised to hear herself moan, actually let out a cry, and then she feels justified in doing so, because she was waiting so carefully for the name of the music and it never came, and the kind voice has cheated her. She lets go of Gene's hand then and holds her own hands to her face, weeping for her nameless music, and she is sure she'll never hear it again, because that's just the way of things. She switches off the radio and there is only Gene's breathing, and the small movements of his hands.

Etta watches him plucking at the sheet, rubbing the fabric between his fingers as if assessing its quality. It's one of her mother's, and still like new. There are shelves and shelves of them; Etta has never had to buy any linen at all. She offered some of it to Christina, and to Bridget as well when she was flatting, but they were not interested. White is so boring, they said, and none of the sheets are fitted, and none of them are queen size. How, they said, did couples ever sleep in those narrow double beds?

Etta brought Mum some flowers she is down staying with her folks as her sister Bernadette is unwell. Mother Moynihan can't know she's been to see us and we're not to ring Etta at the farm. I don't understand it and Gene doesn't either but Etta never mentions her mother   so it's none of our business I suppose

The wind beats at the side of the house, causing the curtains to move ever so slightly. On the roof the thick black construction paper is buckling underneath tiles, shuddering like stage thunder.

✧

One night it was so windy that Etta only got as far as the Hoffmanns' house before she decided to turn back. It was just past ten, not very late at all – although, as usual, everyone in her household had retired to bed – but she realised she'd make little headway in such weather. And if there was a storm, she did not want to be outside to see the lightning. Above her the electricity lines whipped like skipping ropes snapped at girls' ankles. Etta hadn't been on one of her night-time walks for a long time, but on this occasion she couldn't stay in bed. She was thinking about the boy she'd met at the dance, when she was wearing Bernadette's blue dress and Theresa's blue shoes, and had her hair pinned in a French roll although little wisps kept escaping and tickling the nape of her neck.

The boy's father was a butcher who was famous for his

rock and fossil collection, and he himself was an apprentice with Conway's, although he was also looking into journalism. When they were waltzing, and he placed his hand on Etta's shoulder, and his fingers couldn't help but extend beyond the narrow tulle strap, she noticed how soft his skin was. And she told him so. What soft hands you have, she said, not like a builder's at all, and then wished she hadn't. But they had circled around and around the hall, over the creaking floorboards, and then they'd had supper, and he pretended not to notice when she dropped a slice of cucumber from her tiny crustless sandwich.

The wind snatched at her hair, lifting it around her head as if she were under water. Above the noise of it Etta could make out piano music. It was seeping through the cracks around the Hoffmanns' drawn curtains; trickling through the velvety gaps. (Velvet drapes, said Maggie for years after her first visit to the Hoffmanns. Velvet, if you please, and the war barely over.) Etta left the piano music behind, let it be flung without an audience to the dark macrocarpas. She picked her way across the cattle stop. Her feet crunched on the gravel drive and grit blew into her face. She wasn't in the least bit tired. She was too distracted to read. She would run herself a bath.

Even the most ingrained habits can fade if they are not practised for a time. Etta turned on the bath, then went upstairs to get her nightdress, which she had left crumpled and tugged-at in her room. And she placed her right foot on the first stair and began to climb. And the ninth stair creaked.

Etta froze. She waited on the dark staircase, listening for a door to open, footsteps to approach. There was nothing but the wind.

She stepped into the green china bath and kept the water running until it was almost overflowing. Until it came up to her neck, and if she moved too much, if she splashed her legs or arms, the water would slosh on to the floor. She sighed. The green was the same colour as the boy's soft knitted tie. The wind tapped at the window, thrum, thrum, like Maggie's fingers on the arm of a chair when she was angry. The water lapped at the green china edges. It came up to Etta's neck.

The strange thing is, she did not hear the footsteps on the stairs, the bathroom doorhandle turning. Perhaps her head was full of the music that was played at the dance, or perhaps the wind was too loud. At any rate, she jumped when Maggie spoke, and water overflowed from the bath and dripped down its dark green sides.

Where have you been? Who has a bath so late at night? (Who, who? said the wind.)

Nowhere. Really, nowhere.

Mrs Morton tells us you met a young man the other night. No-one she knew from church.

No, no honestly. (You, you, said the wind.)

Sweet brandy breath gushed at Etta. A hand was placed on her wet shoulder.

You're lying. Wicked hurtful lies.

The wind pushed and pushed. Gusts of brandy. Another hand, beautiful, pale, was placed on Etta's head.

Then she was under the water, and the green was in her eyes and her nose and her throat and her ears, and it was all she could see, this soft green, until she caught glimpses of busy white fingers. And she opened her mouth and closed her throat to stop the green from swallowing her, and then she bit.

Etta spent as much time as possible with the green-tied boy. He came to her house on occasion, for Sunday afternoon teas during which Maggie summarised the morning's sermon for him, and cake forks scraped bone china for traces of cream, and fingers tapped the arms of chairs, thrum, thrum. More often, though, Etta went to his house, where she was shown polished shells and semiprecious pebbles and tiny petrified creatures, and even the head of a giant fish that had turned to stone. And eventually she left behind the green Royal Doulton bath, and the house around it. She could not bear to stay there any longer, not with the taste of blood in her mouth.

✧

The wind has died down now, and Gene's fingers have stopped worrying the sheet so much. His breathing is slight, hardly stirring the air in the quiet bedroom. Etta sits for an hour, listening to it change. Then she rings Christina and tells her to come.

This evening Cyril called with Herb Knight both took up valuable time   these days I don't get time to shit   Mum complaining of more chest pains   I hope she won't have to go to Princess Margaret again I am lost without her   I have never been so short of time

The
rainbow
catcher

She has gin on the plane. One whole bottle, in miniature. Things are becoming smaller and she's hardly left Sydney.

'I feel like Alice in Wonderland,' she says to the man sitting next to her, and he gives a short, tight smile and unfolds his complimentary *New Zealand Herald*.

'Are you sure you don't want me to come?' Thorsten said when he dropped her off at the airport in Sydney. 'I can come if you want me to, you only have to say.'

Christina did want him to come then. She wanted someone to attach herself to, who belonged only to her. 'I'm all right,' she said.

At Wellington airport, Bridget picks her up in Etta's car. The speed bell rings almost all the way home.

Over the next few days there are various groupings of people in Gene's room; slow shifting constellations. After that, however, visitors are kept to a minimum. Christina is surprised to see Etta handle them on the phone, at the front door, with increasing disregard for manners.

'He's slipping a lot. Just a couple of minutes, if you don't mind.'

'He's very weak. I can't let you see him for long.'

'He's not up to visitors. He won't know who you are.'

'We've decided he's to have no more visitors.'

Bridget says she's going to have dinner at Antony's. She won't be gone long, just a couple of hours. His number's by the phone. Of course, says Etta, of course.

'Can I get you a bit of tea, Mum?' says Christina. 'Something light, a salad maybe? A sandwich?'

But Etta says she's fine, really, she just needs a bit of a rest. She didn't get much sleep the night before.

'Okay then. I'll be up with Dad, if you need anything.'

It's just the two of them in the room. She's monitored his pulse, checked his oxygen tube, his drug pump, his catheter. Apart from these things, these practised, professional actions, there is nothing else to do. His breaths become tiny gasps, small private surprises. Christina's heard this before, once or twice – enough to know what it means – but she doesn't know what to do now. She could call down the stairs to Etta, she could telephone Bridget. Her mother, her sister, she could. But Gene frowns, and there seems so little time, and so she touches the back of her hand to his cheek, to her father's cheek, and then she leans towards him as if to kiss him, but instead holds her face against his, cheek to cheek now, a father and a daughter, waltzing, sort of, inexpert and unrehearsed at a debutante ball, a twenty-first birthday, a wedding. And there is no time.

She turns off the drug pump, silences the discreet, intravenous fizz. She removes the safety pin securing it to her father's pyjama pocket. She combs his soft hair. Safety pin, striped flannelette, green plastic comb.

At the top of the stairs she squeezes past the mechanised chair – the seat has been left down – and then she's at the bottom of the stairs and going through the door to the lounge and she realises she's still holding the green plastic comb and it's left a row of dots on her palm as if someone should place their signature there and she says, 'Mum.'

✧

On the way home in the car neither of them says much. Bridget sobs to herself and Antony drives one-handed, resting the other on Bridget's knee. She wishes that he would move the hand. Then she could fling herself around the inside of his car, hitting the curved interior, ricocheting off the walls like a gas trying to fill a space. She remembers being told this in fifth-form science.

'Will he still be there?' she says, ashamed at her own ignorance.

Antony glances across at her, smiling. 'Of *course*,' he says, striking her thigh for emphasis.

She wishes he would drive faster, but cannot bring herself to suggest this. It's not as if it will make any difference, she knows, but she cannot bear the thought of Gene's skin growing cold while they are skimming along the motorway, his blood pooling in strange locations.

'I want to be home,' she says. 'Now.'

'Welcome to National Radio, Linda speaking, how can I help you?'

'I wish to know the name of a piece of music that was played at 3.15 a.m. the morning before last.'

'Putting you through.'

'National Radio programming, Mandy speaking, how can I help you?'

'I wish to know the name of a piece of music that was played at 3.15 a.m. the morning before last.'

'You're sure about the time, madam?'

'Yes.'

'Can you describe the piece?'

'Classical. Flute and orchestra.'

'Will you hold for a moment, please?'

. . . sure to wear, some flowers in your hair, if you're going, to San Francisco, summer time, will be a love . . .

'The piece was Fauré's *Pavane*. Would you like the details of that particular recording?'

'Yes. Thank you. Yes.'

'Hi Mum, it's me. Just ringing to see how you and Bridget are doing. Give us a ring if you like. I'm on nights at the moment so early afternoon our time would be best. Thorsten says hi too.'

'Hello Etta, it's Shirley here. Not sure if you got my message on Tuesday, just thought I'd see how you were getting on. I didn't get a chance at the funeral to tell you how well you coped. I'm sure the Lord was a comfort. I hope you're enjoying the shortbread. I just thought I'd pop it at the door, don't know if you were home or not. I did think I saw a light on, but perhaps you don't want to be answering the door after dark now. Give me a ring, won't you?'

'Hi Mum. I'm catching the 7.05 home so can you save me some dinner? . . . *Tranz Metro service to Upper Hutt, stopping . . .* Antony's coming too. Okay. Bye . . . *will depart from . . .*'

'Etta, this is Beryl. Colin thinks he may have left his scarf at your place. He and Janet are away at the moment, so I said I'd ring for him. Could you just pop it in the post if you find it? No hurry. We're all well. Jim's thrilled with the rifle, says he'll get lots of use out of it. Bye.'

'Good morning, Mrs Stilton! This is Shana from Halliwell's Real Estate. We have a number of clients interested in purchasing homes in your area, and we're keen to get new properties on our books. If you and your husband are interested in selling, you can contact me on 567 6055. Looking forward to your call!'

'Etta. Theresa. I'm not sure if this is right. Can you hear this? I . . .'

'Etta, Shirley here. Not sure if you got my message the other day. I popped around this morning but you must have been out again. Good you're keeping busy. I was just wondering whether you'd finished with Jodie's baby monitor, sorry to bother you about it, I know how busy you are, it's just a friend of hers has had a wee boy and they'd like to borrow it. So if you could just drop it round some time on your way out. I'll call in soon. Bye now.'

❖

'Mum's never home. I either get Bridget or the machine.'

Claudia yawns. 'Maybe she's just leaving it on all the time.'

'Possible. No.'

'Max wants me to go to Melbourne with him next month. It's his Dad's seventieth.'

'You can see what you'll be waking up next to in forty years.'

'I've got him a waffle iron. I don't know what came over me.'

'Thorsten wants me to spend Christmas with his family. In Austria.'

'And?'

'I said no. I'm inviting Mum and Bridget over to stay. Joanne wants to meet them, show them round.'

'Christ.'

'What?'

'Christ. Collective manicures and lash tinting, I imagine. Could be worse.'

The train pulls away from Petone station and begins its arc around the harbour. The water is so smooth it could be a lake.

'He wanted to spare you that final sadness, Bridget,' was what the hospice nurses said. 'He knew you weren't home, somehow, and he chose that time to slip away.'

Bridget nodded, was generous with her gratitude.

'Thank you for everything,' she said. But she knew it wasn't Gene, the unconscious father, choosing his moment. The choice to go had been hers. It was her own living, breathing need to get out of the house, to escape the spotless room, the under-standing, efficient hospice staff, her mother's fussing housework, her sister's quietness.

She wonders, though, whether there was a sound, a movement, a rippling of the eyelids, something – all she knows is that Christina was sitting with him, and that Etta was downstairs, and that there was no time to call out. Bridget wants to ask Christina what happened; how the seconds uncoiled. Such details cannot be a mystery for her sister, who must have seen many deaths. But Christina has not offered the information, seems hesitant to relinquish it. So Bridget will not ask. Instead, on the train into Wellington, she watches the smooth harbour slide past the window and thinks of a lake.

The girls have risen early, coaxed from sleep by their father leaning over them in his lumpy jersey. It's still dark as they pull on layers of clothes. The lake can be cold, even after sunrise.

Their mother is asleep in the candlewick motel bed, her

arms crossed over her heart. The girls prepare a breakfast tray for her, trying not to make too much noise in the tiny kitchenette where everything clatters and is hard: concrete floor covered with lino, thick china, formica table, steel bench.

When they get to the lake their father wades into the water and starts casting, flicking the line back and forth in long arcs. All they can hear is the water lapping at the sand and the swish of the line through the air. You have to be very quiet, their father tells them, otherwise you'll scare the fish away. You have to trick them into thinking there's nobody there.

They hunt for sticks and jab them into the sand by the lupin bushes. They drape beach towels and blankets over the top and build houses.

Their father calls; he's dangling a trout from a line that's too far away for them to see. The fish seems to jump and dance in mid-air. It flashes rainbows at them.

Don't kill it, don't kill it, they cry, hiding in the lupin bushes, under the leaves shaped like running tears. The poor fish, Dad, let him go.

So he does.